★ Marion Duclos ★

# VICTOR & CLINT

**HUMANOIDSKIDS**

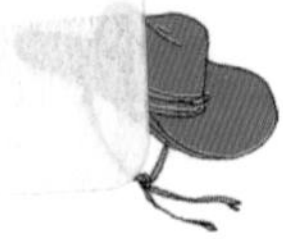

**MARION DUCLOS**
Story & Art

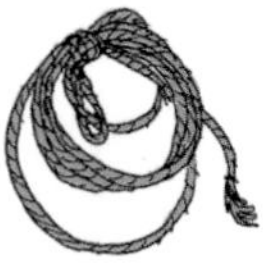

**MARK BENCE**
Translator

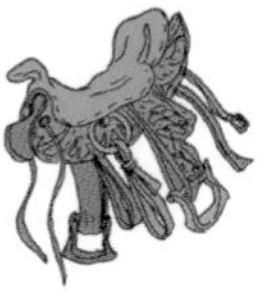

**FABRICE SAPOLSKY**
**& ALEX DONOGHUE**
U.S. Edition Editors

**VINCENT HENRY**
Original Edition Editor

**JERRY FRISSEN**
Senior Art Director

**FABRICE GIGER**
Publisher

Rights & Licensing - licensing@humanoids.com
Press and Social Media - pr@humanoids.com

VICTOR & CLINT
This title is a publication of Humanoids, Inc. 8033 Sunset Blvd. #628, Los Angeles, CA 90046.


HumanoidsKids is an imprint of Humanoids, Inc.

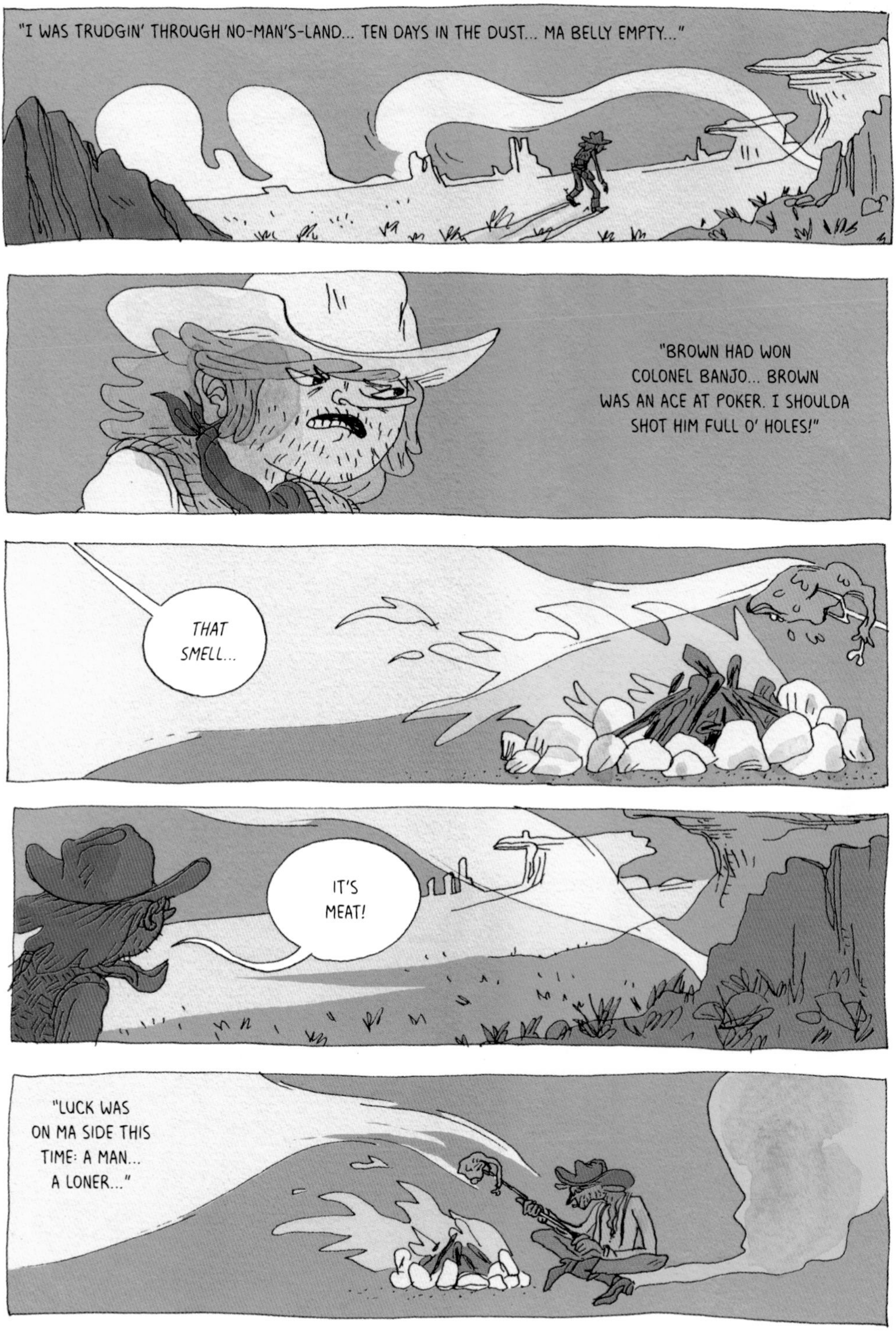
"I WAS TRUDGIN' THROUGH NO-MAN'S-LAND... TEN DAYS IN THE DUST... MA BELLY EMPTY..."
"BROWN HAD WON COLONEL BANJO... BROWN WAS AN ACE AT POKER. I SHOULDA SHOT HIM FULL O' HOLES!"
THAT SMELL...
IT'S MEAT!
"LUCK WAS ON MA SIDE THIS TIME: A MAN... A LONER..."

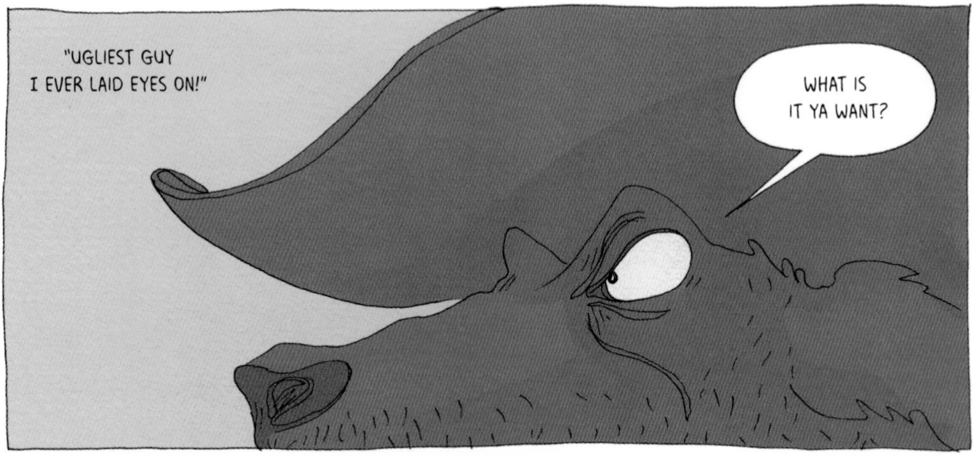
"UGLIEST GUY
I EVER LAID EYES ON!"
WHAT IS IT YA WANT?

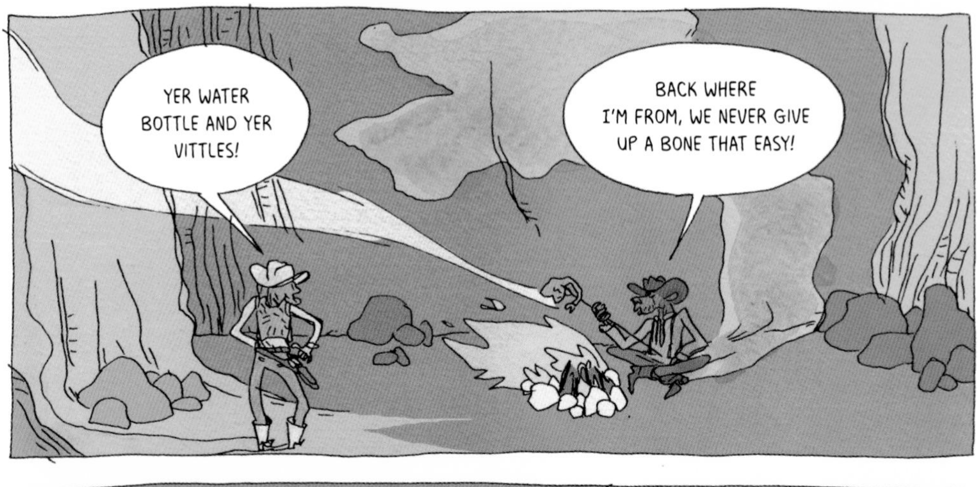
YER WATER BOTTLE AND YER VITTLES!
BACK WHERE I'M FROM, WE NEVER GIVE UP A BONE THAT EASY!

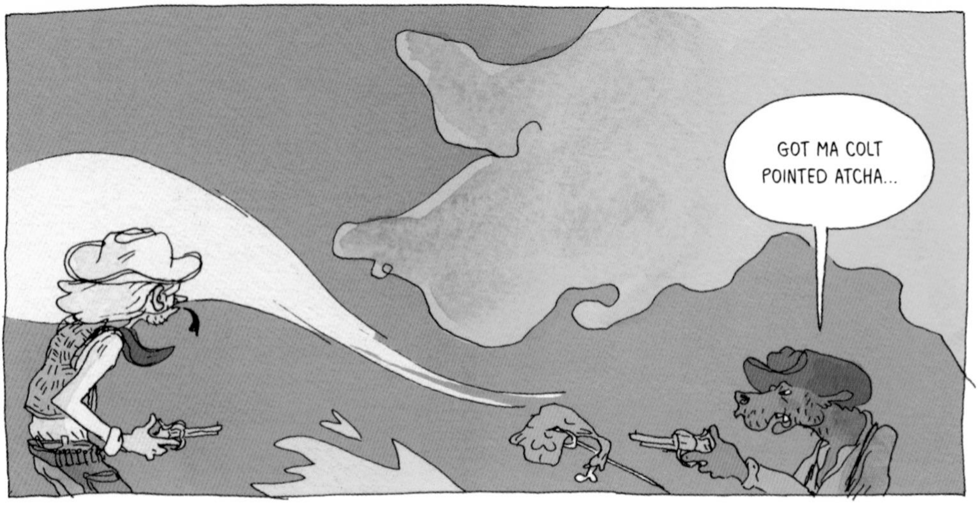
GOT MA COLT POINTED ATCHA...

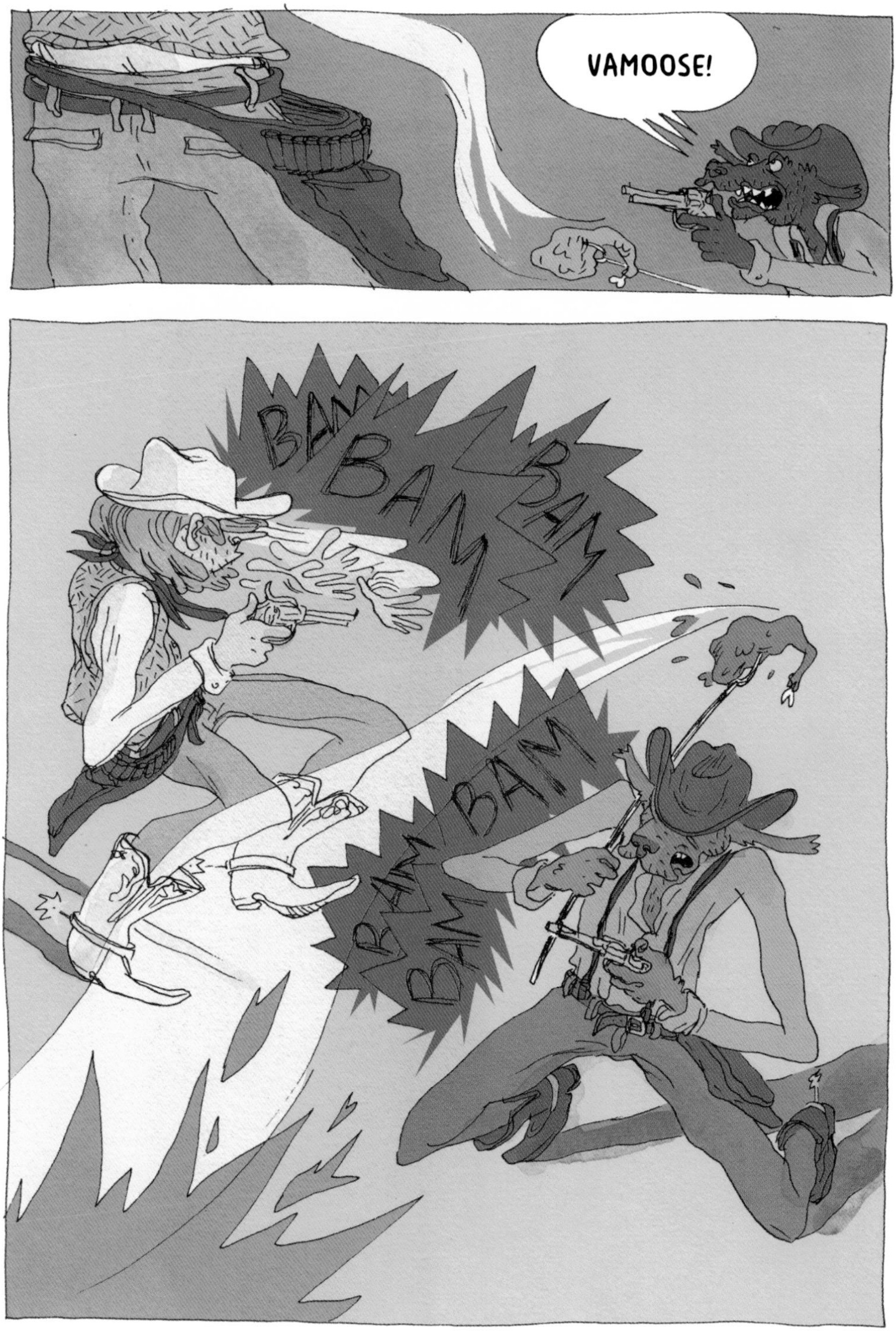
VAMOOSE!
BAM
BAM
BAM
BAM
BAM
BAM
BAM

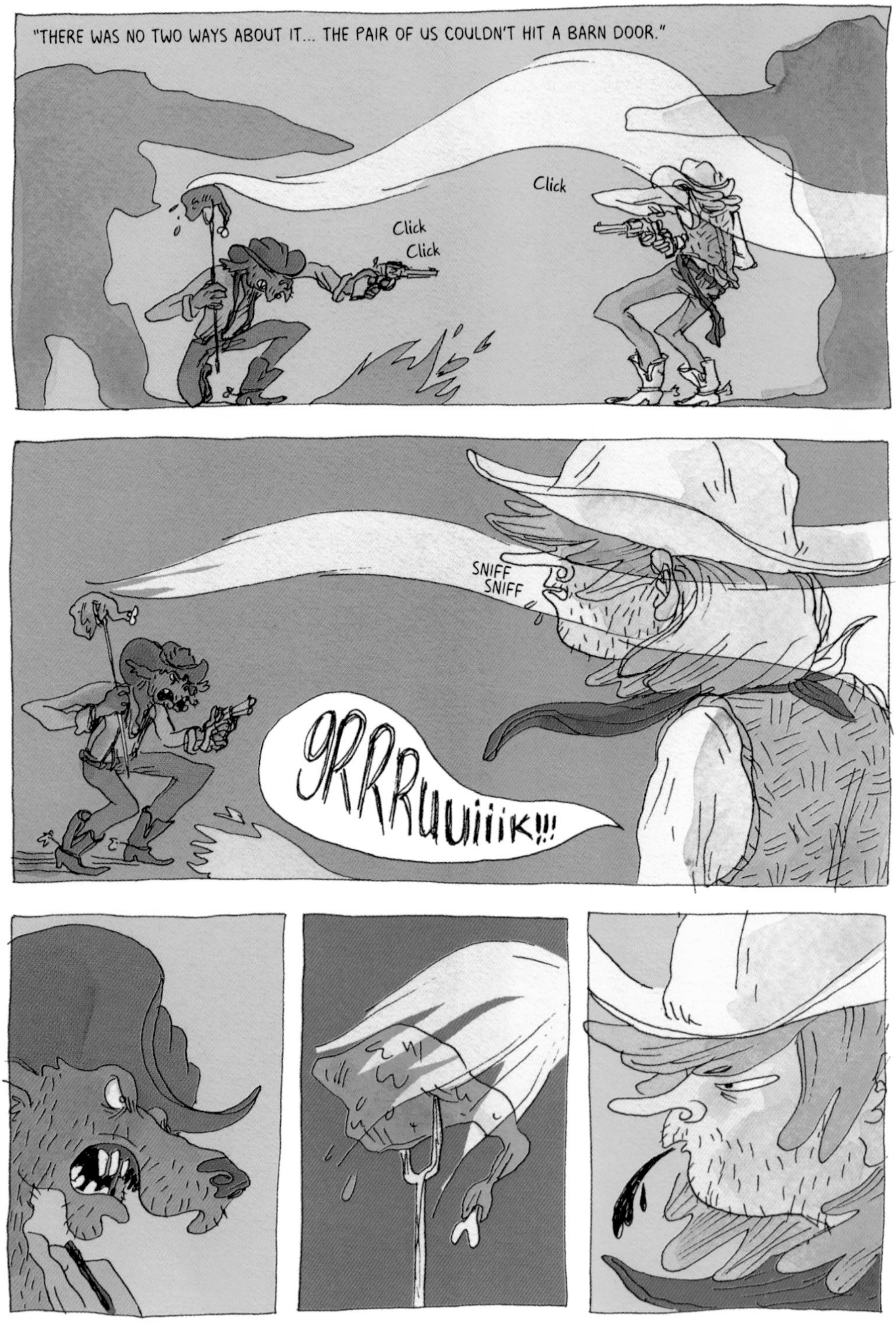
"THERE WAS NO TWO WAYS ABOUT IT... THE PAIR OF US COULDN'T HIT A BARN DOOR."
Click
Click
Click
SNIFF
SNIFF
gRRRUUiiiiK!!!

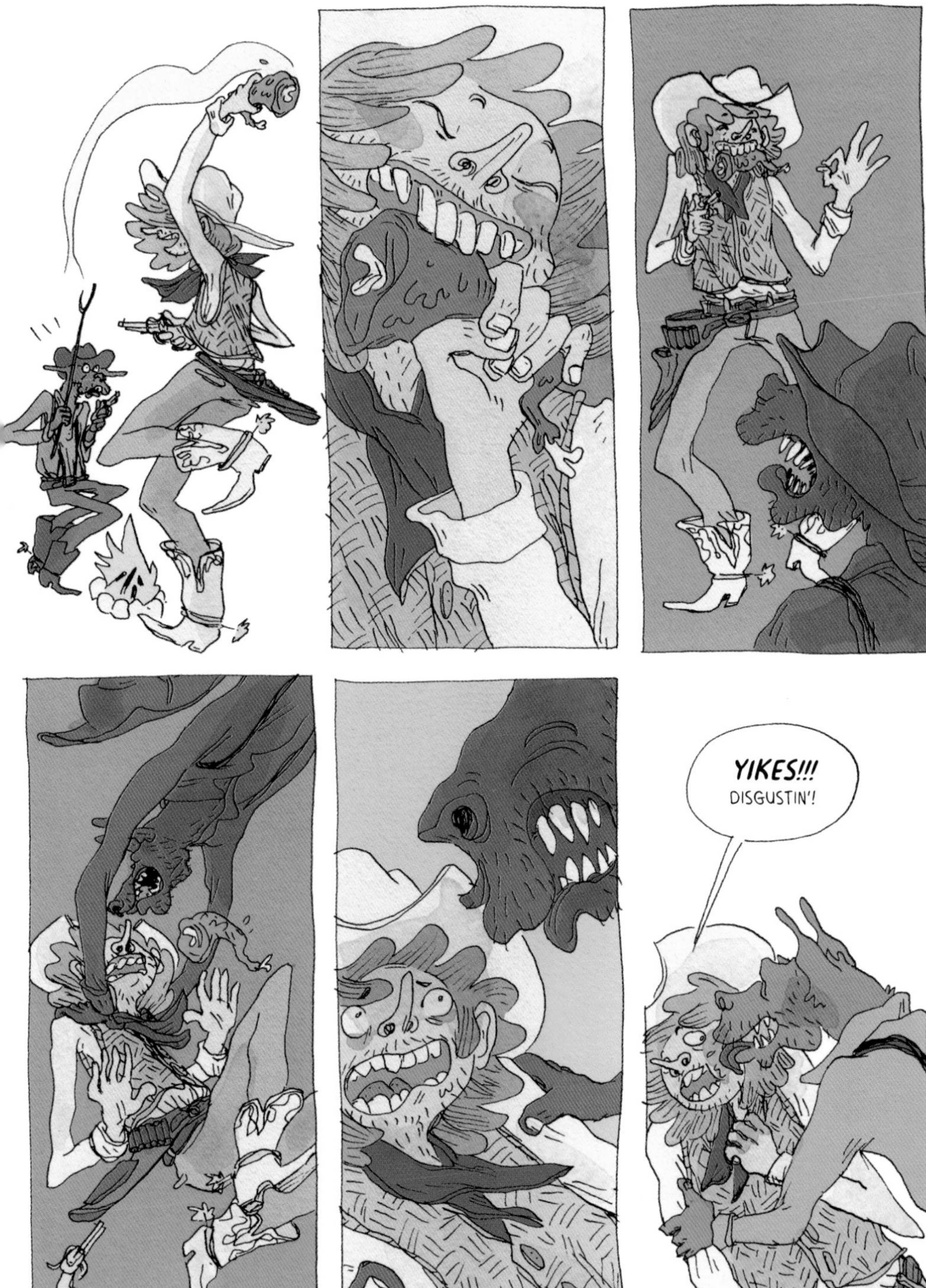
YIKES!!!
DISGUSTIN'!

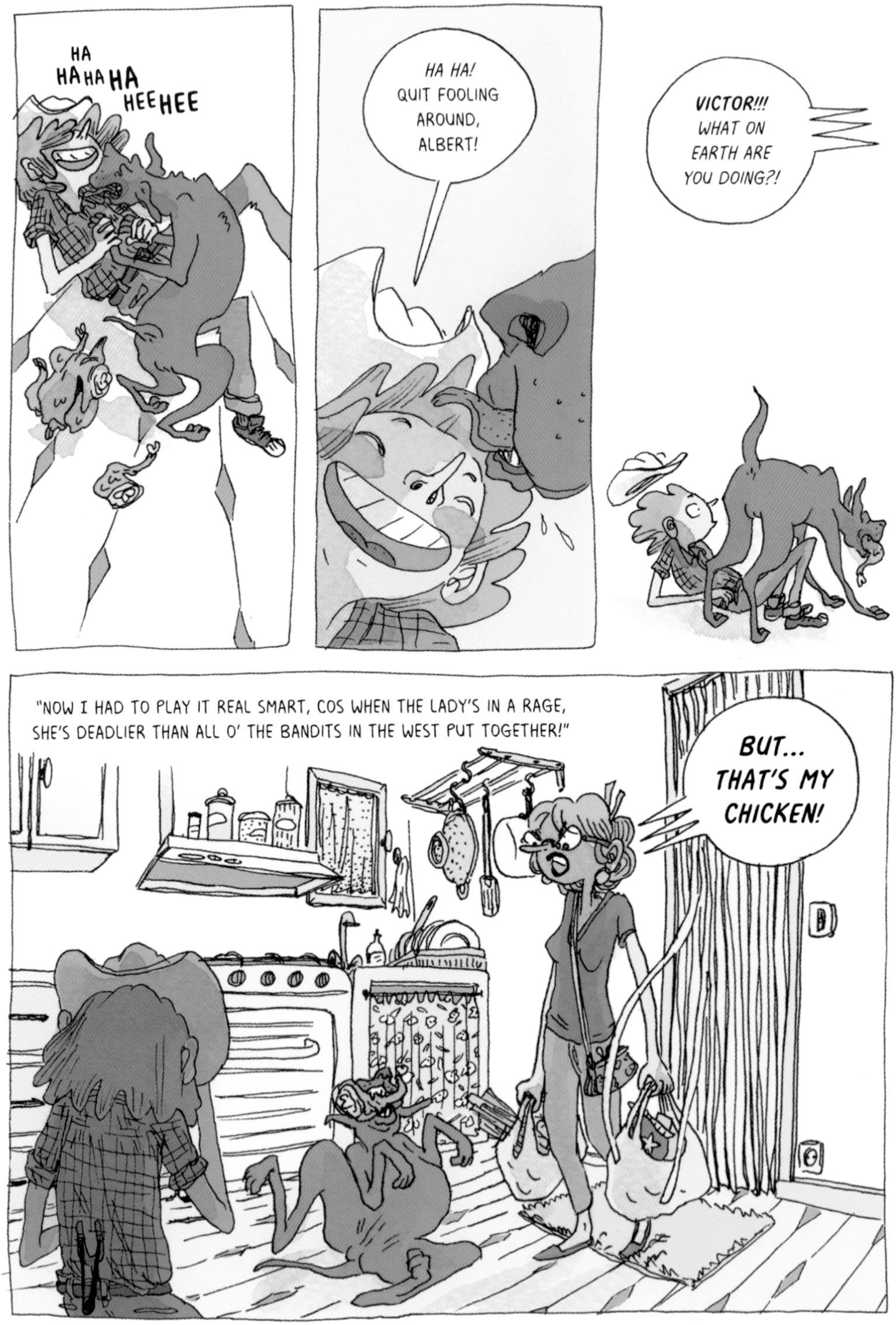
HA HA HA HA HEE HEE
HA HA! QUIT FOOLING AROUND, ALBERT!
VICTOR!!! WHAT ON EARTH ARE YOU DOING?!
"NOW I HAD TO PLAY IT REAL SMART, COS WHEN THE LADY'S IN A RAGE, SHE'S DEADLIER THAN ALL O' THE BANDITS IN THE WEST PUT TOGETHER!"
BUT... THAT'S MY CHICKEN!

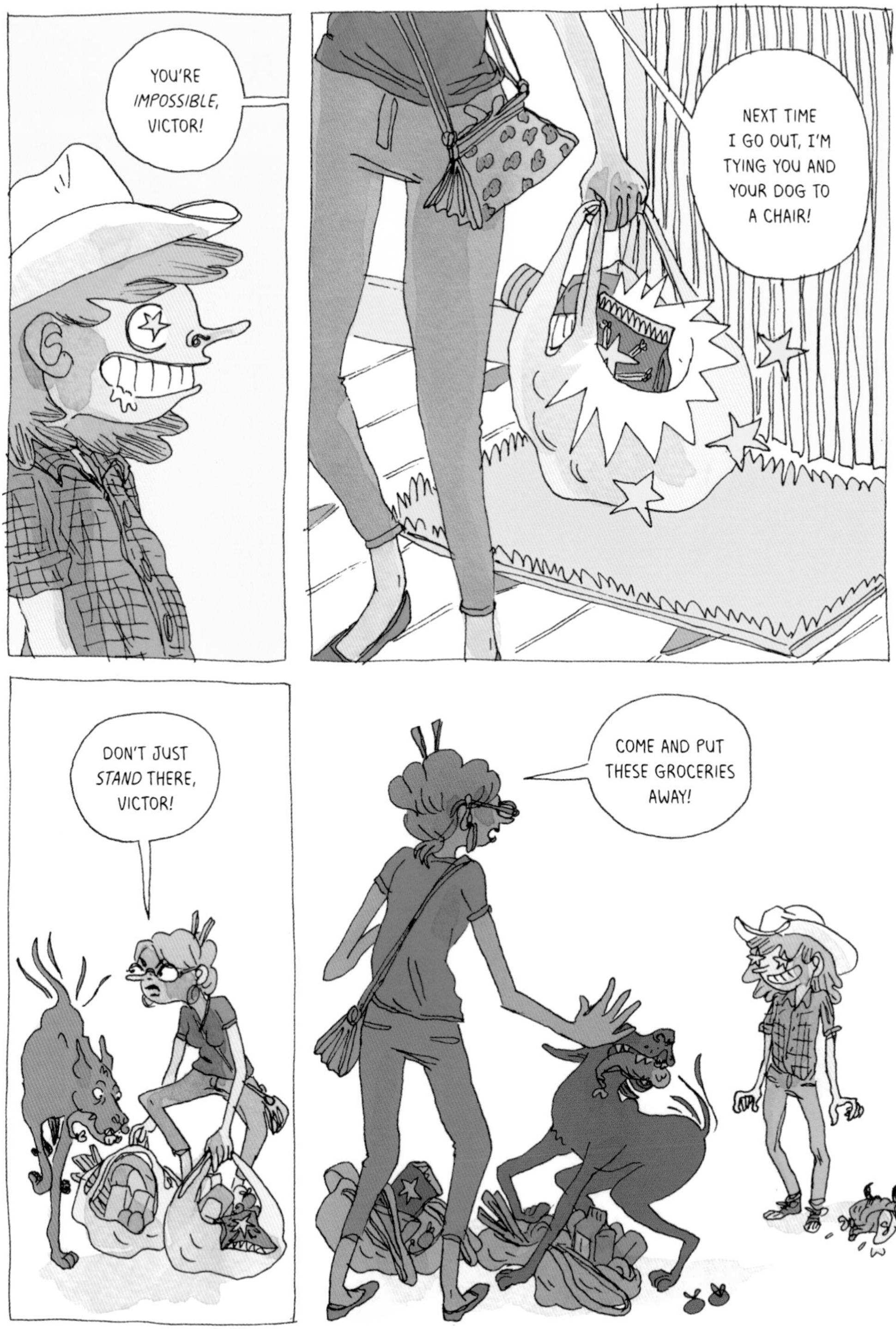
YOU'RE *IMPOSSIBLE*, VICTOR!
NEXT TIME I GO OUT, I'M TYING YOU AND YOUR DOG TO A CHAIR!
DON'T JUST *STAND* THERE, VICTOR!
COME AND PUT THESE GROCERIES AWAY!

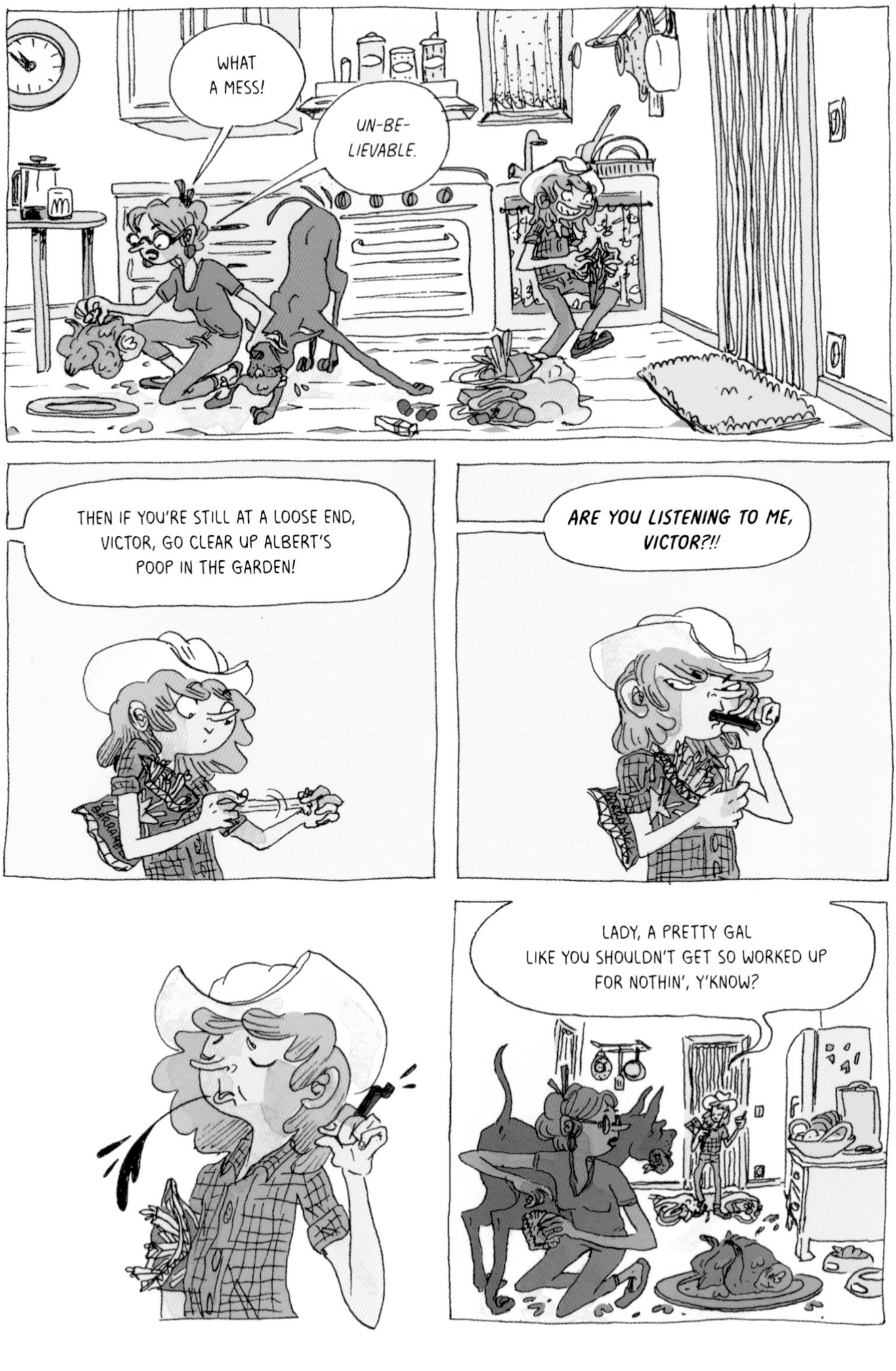
WHAT A MESS!
UN-BE-LIEVABLE.
THEN IF YOU'RE STILL AT A LOOSE END, VICTOR, GO CLEAR UP ALBERT'S POOP IN THE GARDEN!
ARE YOU LISTENING TO ME, VICTOR?!!
LADY, A PRETTY GAL LIKE YOU SHOULDN'T GET SO WORKED UP FOR NOTHIN', Y'KNOW?

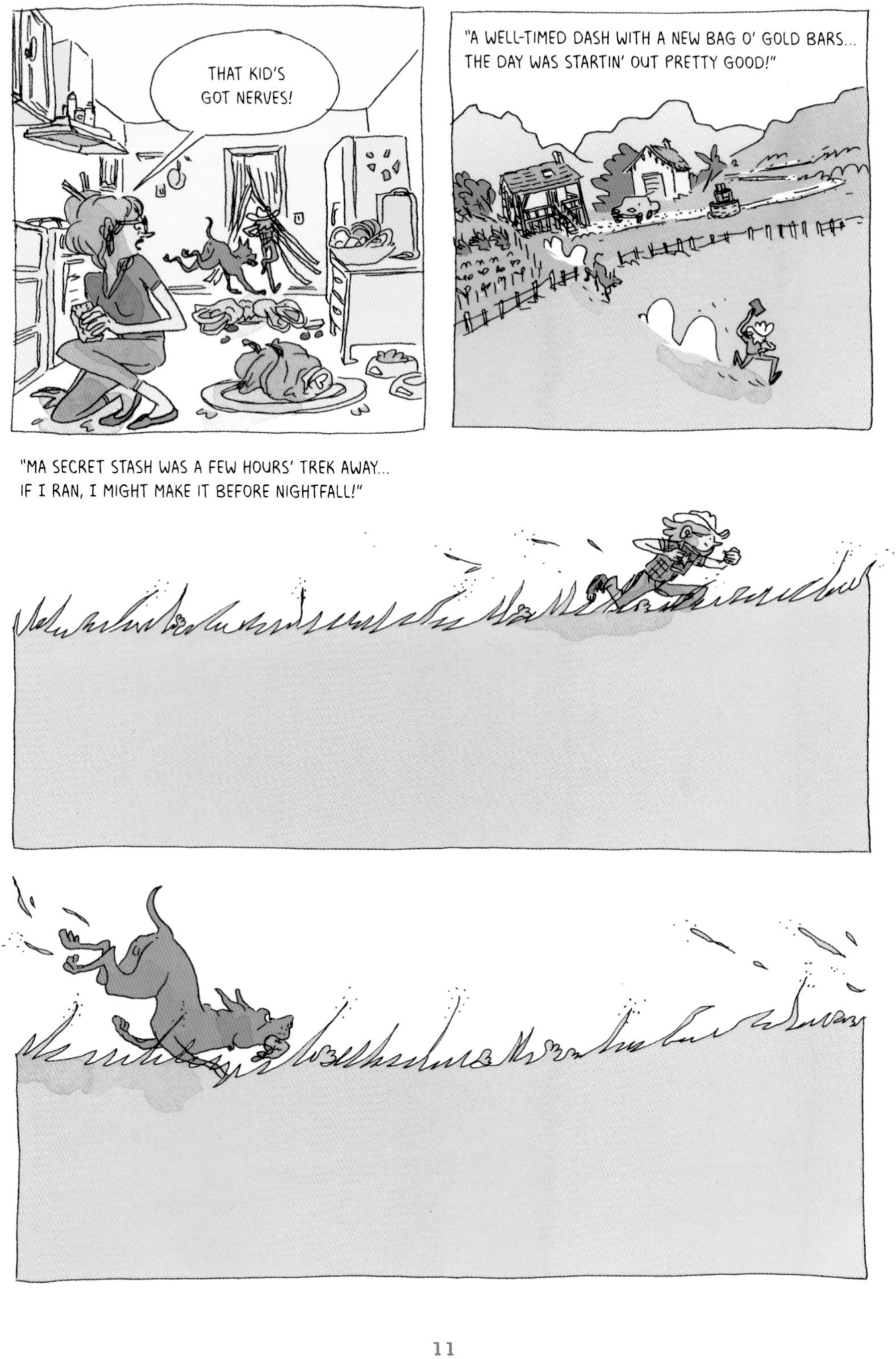
THAT KID'S GOT NERVES!
"A WELL-TIMED DASH WITH A NEW BAG O' GOLD BARS... THE DAY WAS STARTIN' OUT PRETTY GOOD!"
"MA SECRET STASH WAS A FEW HOURS' TREK AWAY... IF I RAN, I MIGHT MAKE IT BEFORE NIGHTFALL!"

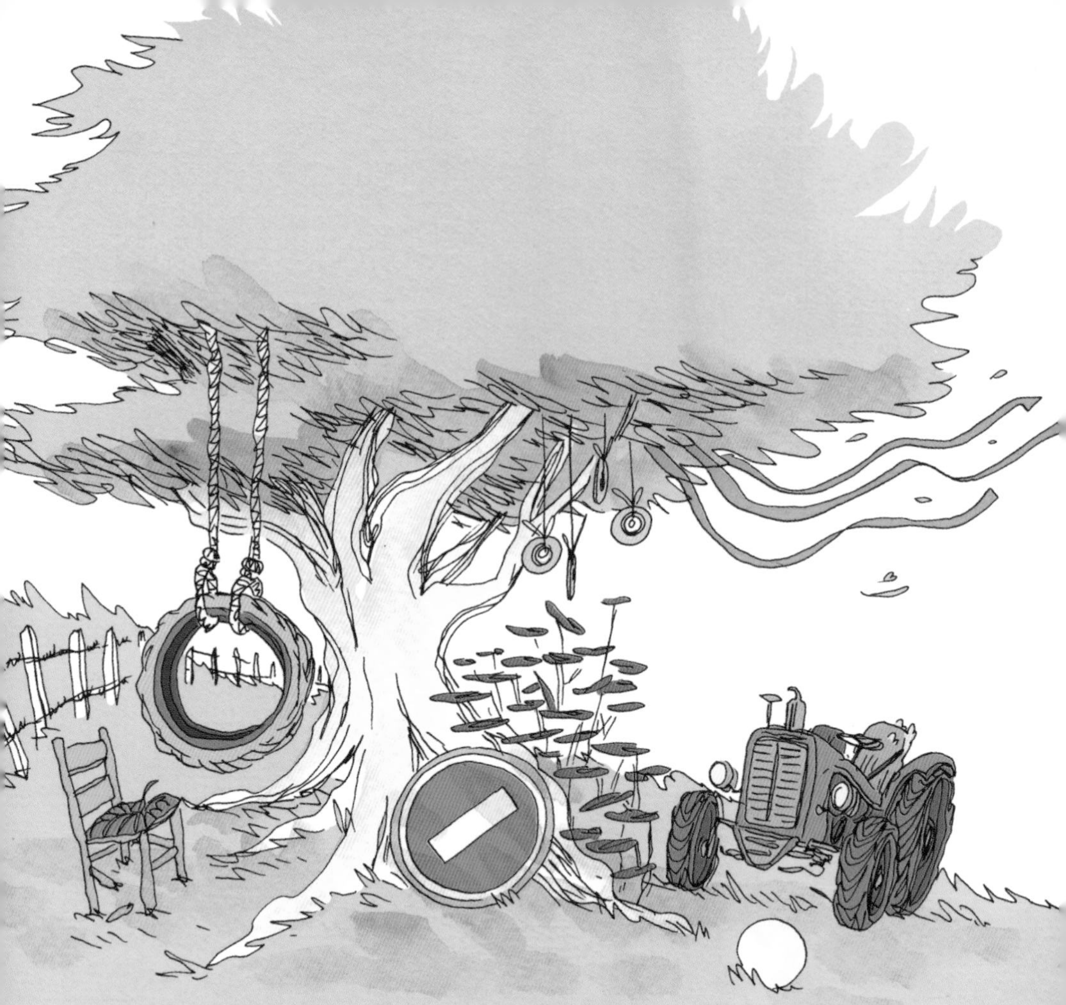

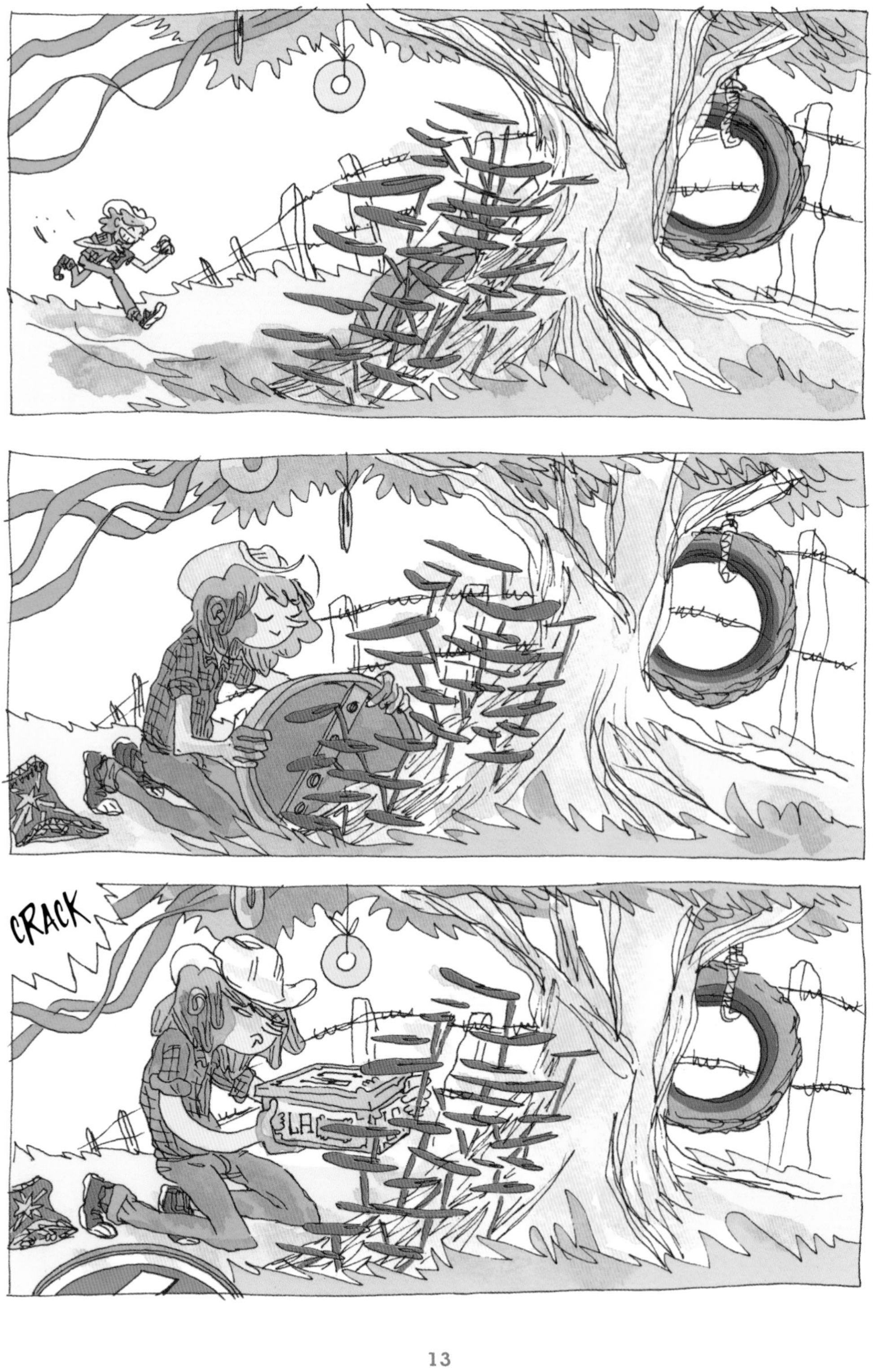
CRACK

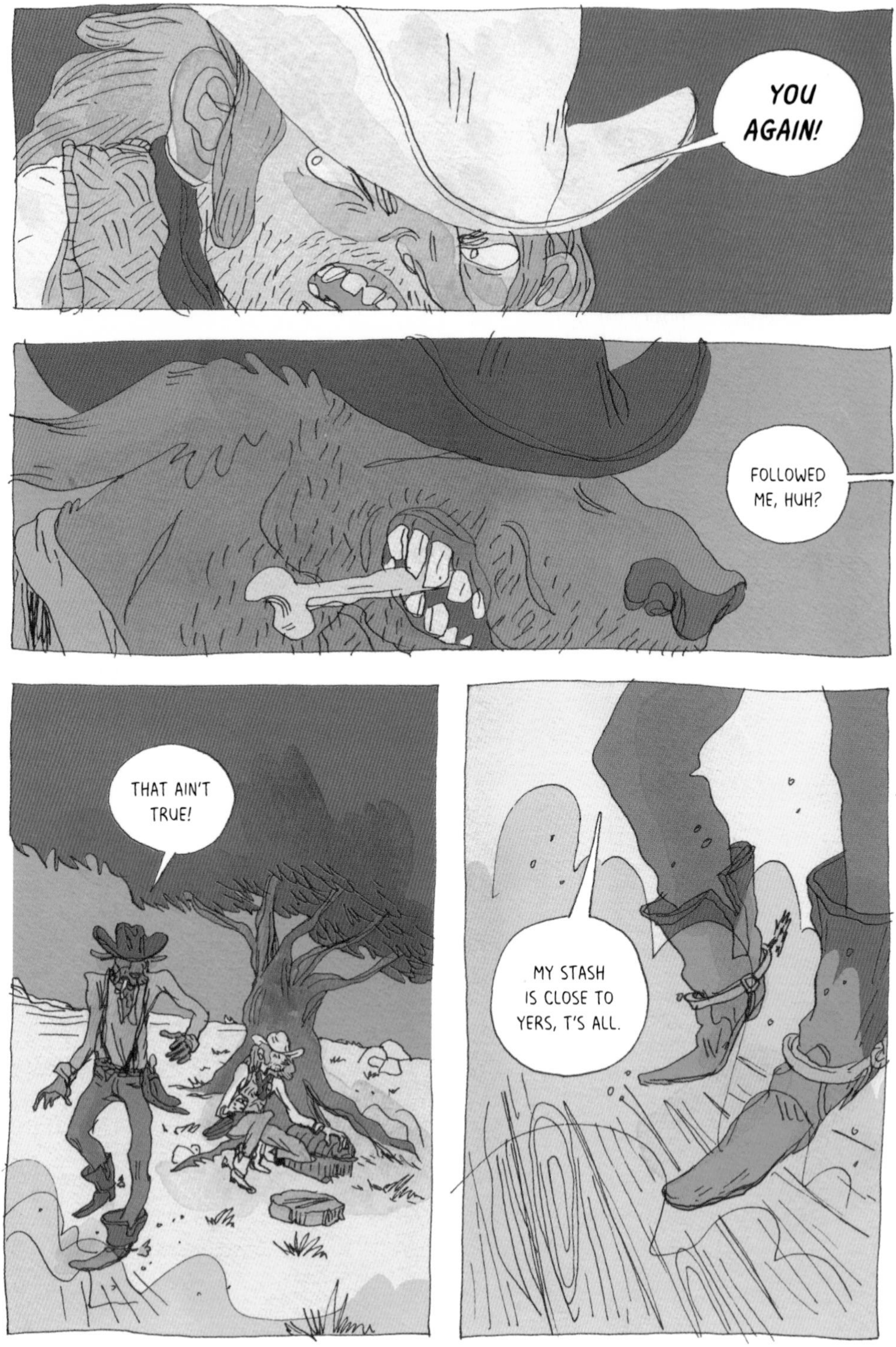
YOU AGAIN!
FOLLOWED ME, HUH?
THAT AIN'T TRUE!
MY STASH IS CLOSE TO YERS, T'S ALL.

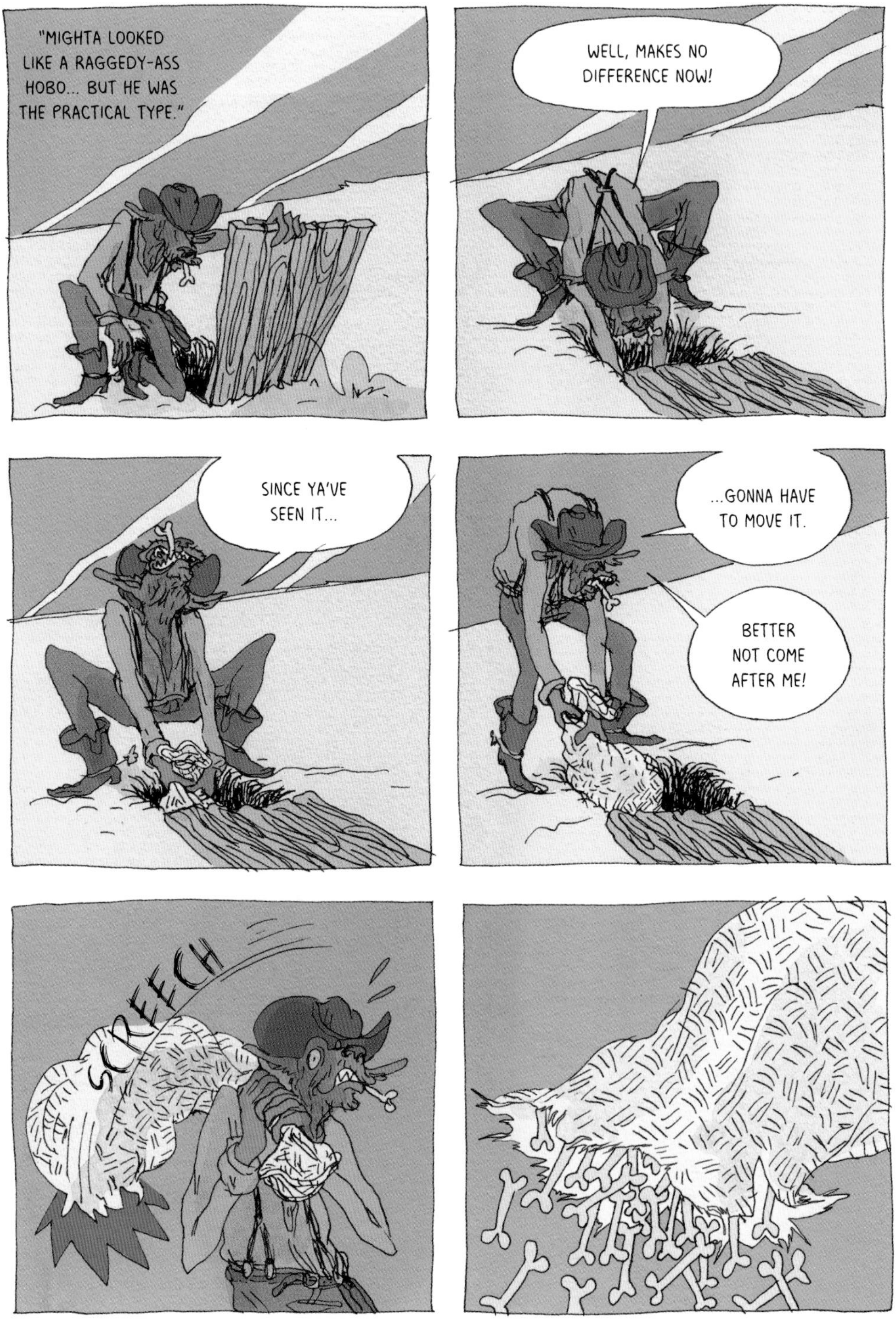
"MIGHTA LOOKED LIKE A RAGGEDY-ASS HOBO... BUT HE WAS THE PRACTICAL TYPE."
WELL, MAKES NO DIFFERENCE NOW!
SINCE YA'VE SEEN IT...
...GONNA HAVE TO MOVE IT.
BETTER NOT COME AFTER ME!
SCREECH

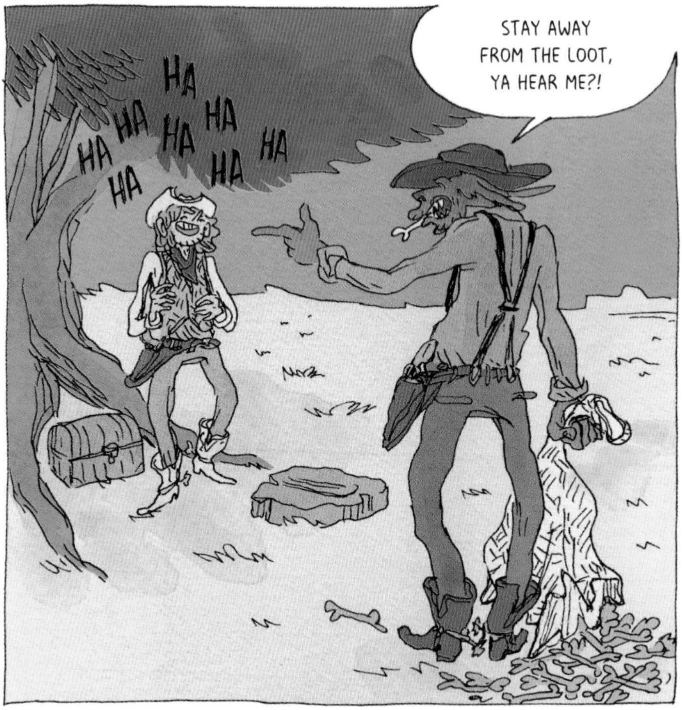
STAY AWAY FROM THE LOOT, YA HEAR ME?!
HA HA HA HA HA HA HA HA HA

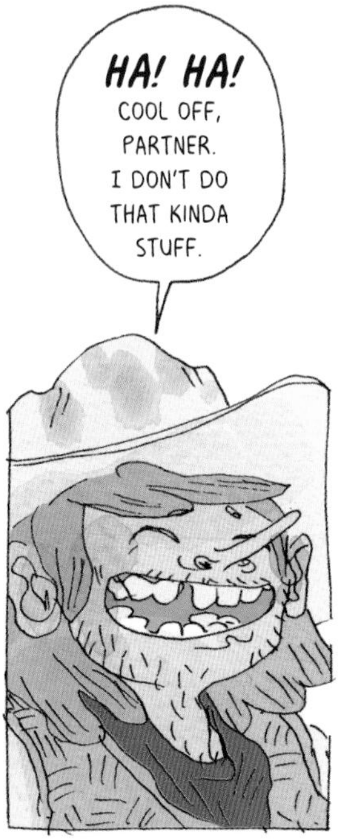
HA! HA! COOL OFF, PARTNER. I DON'T DO THAT KINDA STUFF.

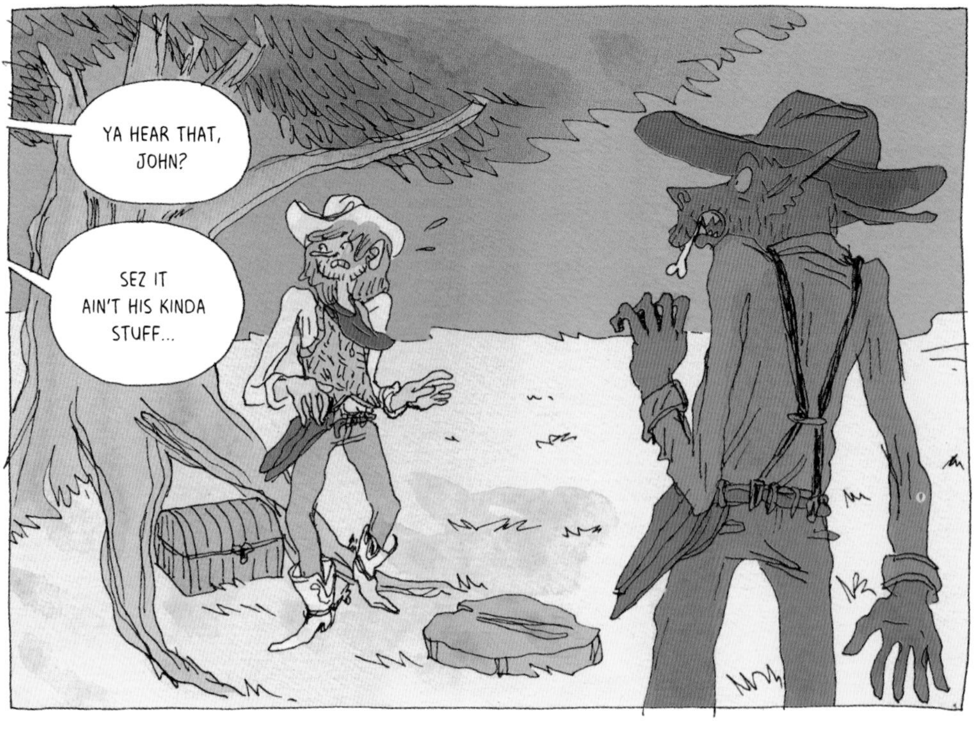
YA HEAR THAT, JOHN?
SEZ IT AIN'T HIS KINDA STUFF...

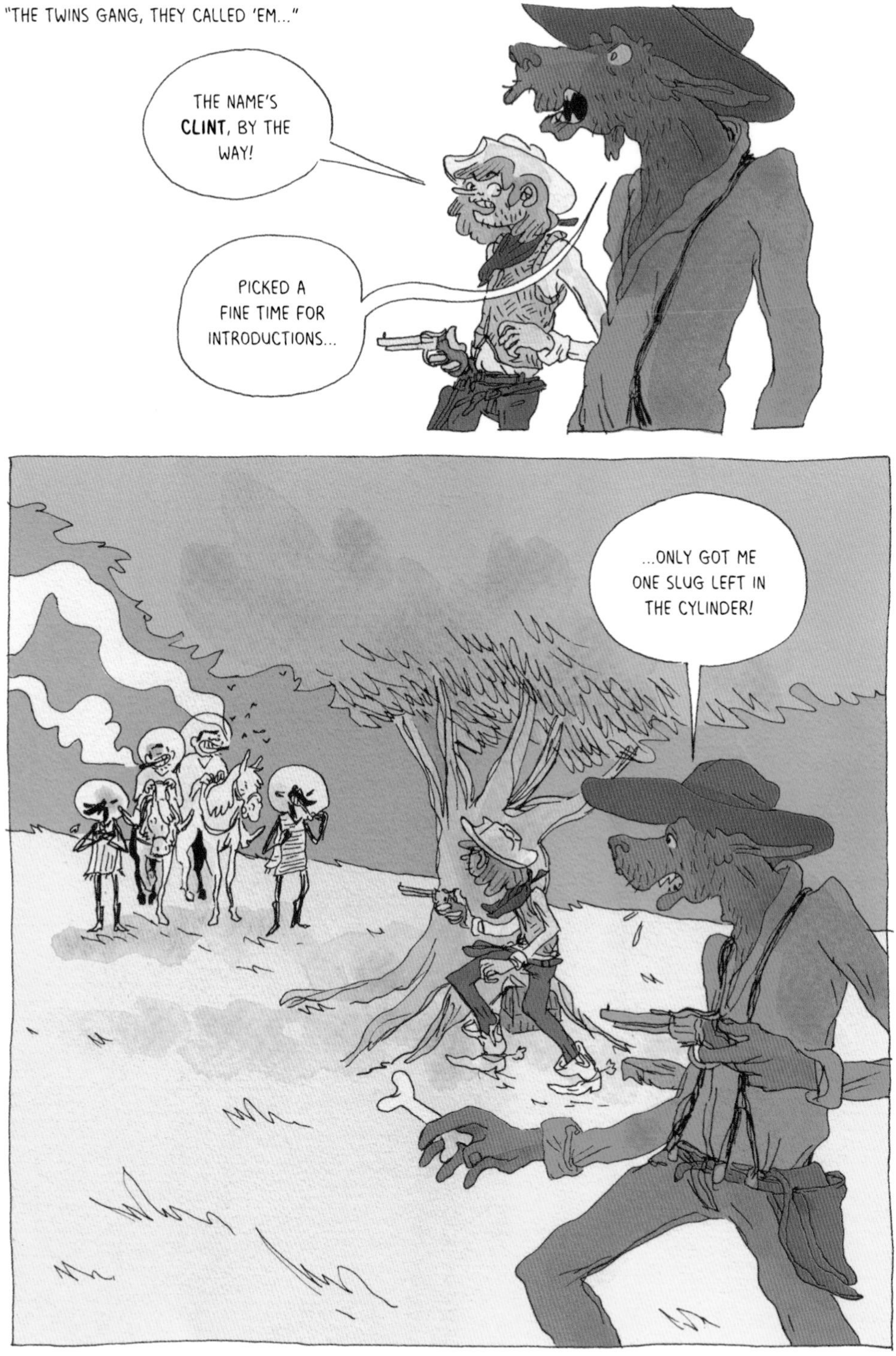
"THE TWINS GANG, THEY CALLED 'EM..."
THE NAME'S **CLINT**, BY THE WAY!
PICKED A FINE TIME FOR INTRODUCTIONS...
...ONLY GOT ME ONE SLUG LEFT IN THE CYLINDER!

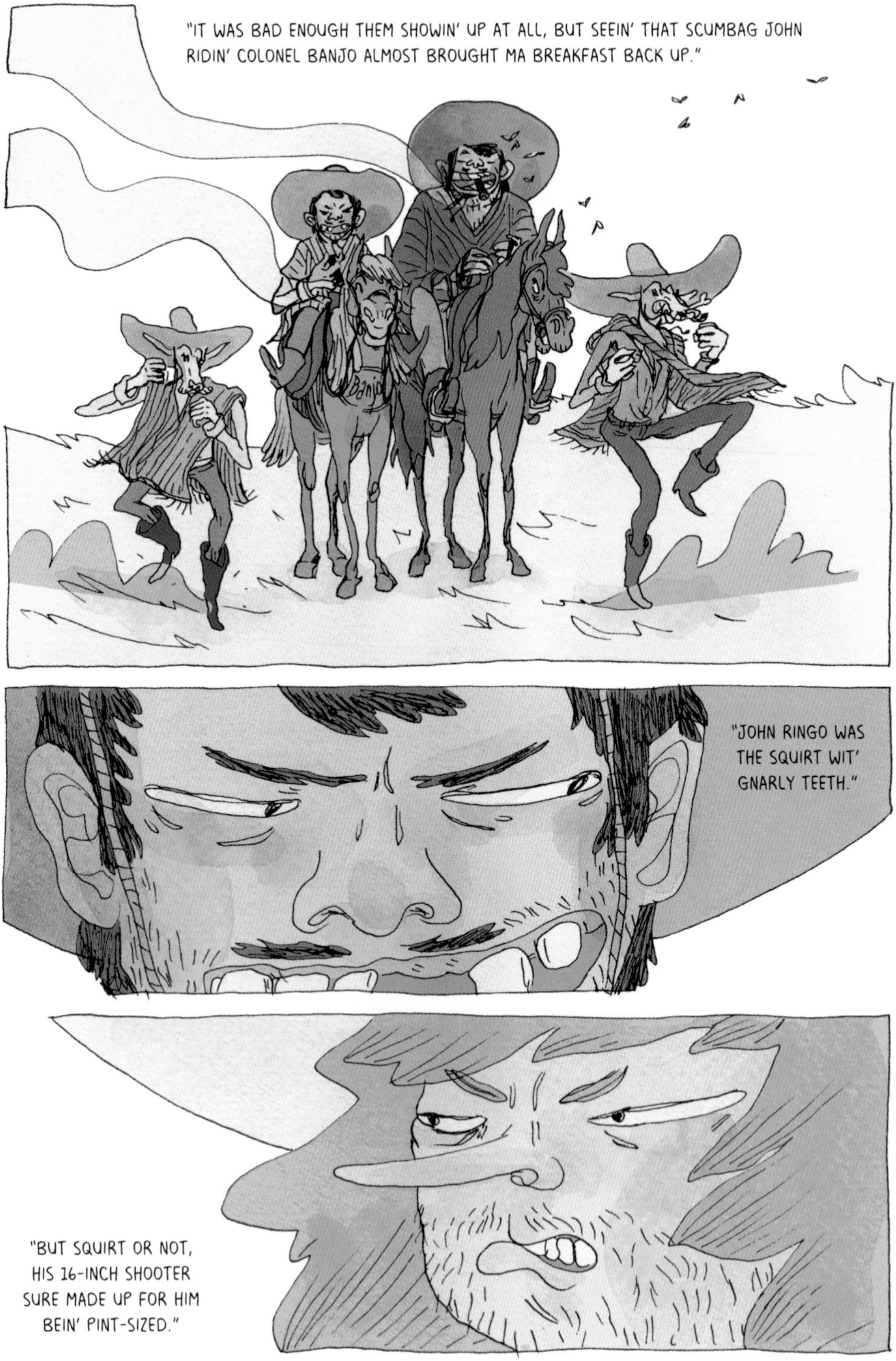
"IT WAS BAD ENOUGH THEM SHOWIN' UP AT ALL, BUT SEEIN' THAT SCUMBAG JOHN RIDIN' COLONEL BANJO ALMOST BROUGHT MA BREAKFAST BACK UP."
BANJO
"JOHN RINGO WAS THE SQUIRT WIT' GNARLY TEETH."
"BUT SQUIRT OR NOT, HIS 16-INCH SHOOTER SURE MADE UP FOR HIM BEIN' PINT-SIZED."

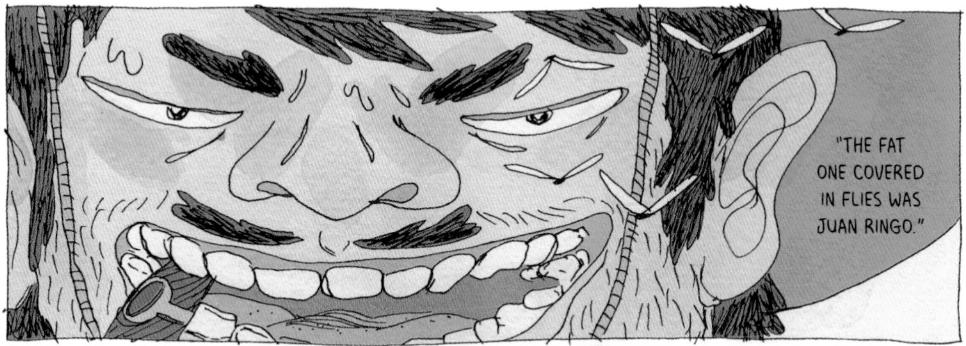
"THE FAT ONE COVERED IN FLIES WAS JUAN RINGO."

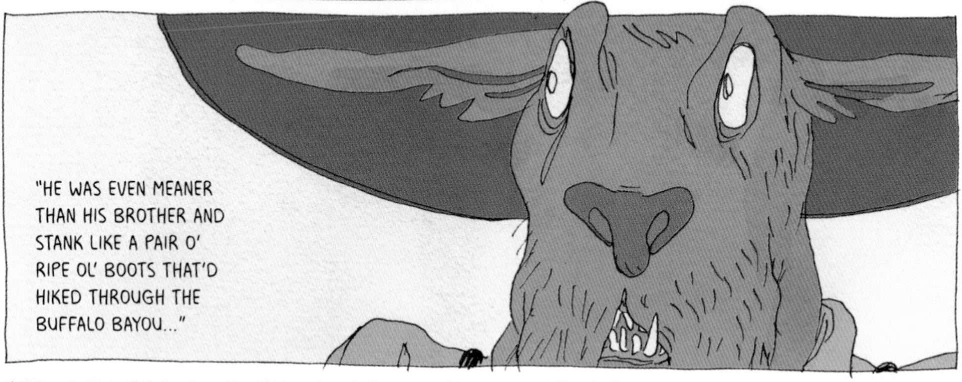
"HE WAS EVEN MEANER THAN HIS BROTHER AND STANK LIKE A PAIR O' RIPE OL' BOOTS THAT'D HIKED THROUGH THE BUFFALO BAYOU..."

"THEN YA HAD THEIR CRONIES, SPARKY 'N SPOT. CONSIDERIN' HOW OFTEN THEIR BUTTS GOT KICKED, I COULD NEVER SEE WHY THEY STAYED LOYAL."

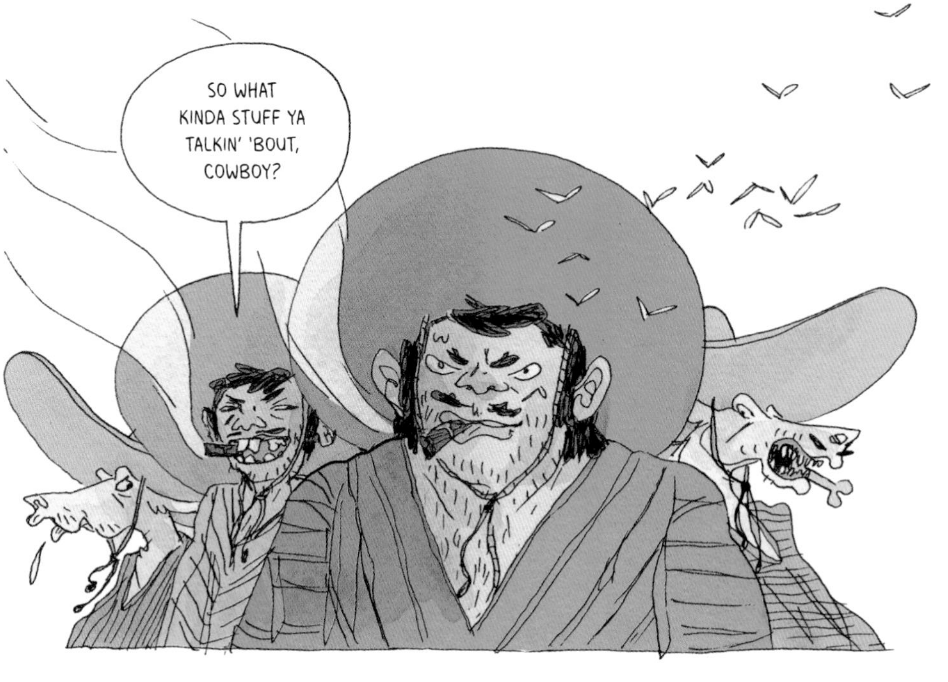
SO WHAT KINDA STUFF YA TALKIN' 'BOUT, COWBOY?

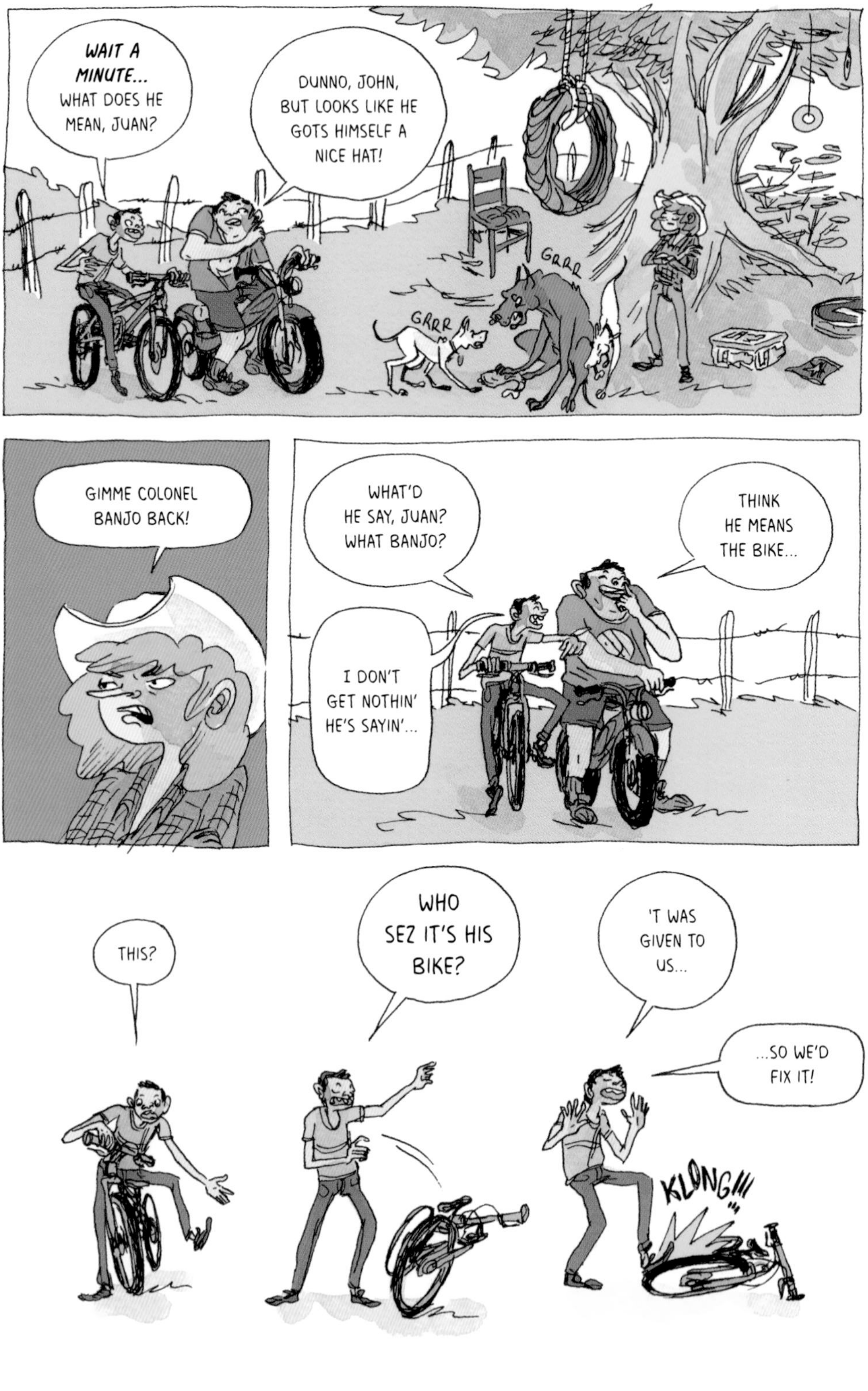
WAIT A MINUTE... WHAT DOES HE MEAN, JUAN?
DUNNO, JOHN, BUT LOOKS LIKE HE GOTS HIMSELF A NICE HAT!
GRRR
GRRR
GIMME COLONEL BANJO BACK!
WHAT'D HE SAY, JUAN? WHAT BANJO?
THINK HE MEANS THE BIKE...
I DON'T GET NOTHIN' HE'S SAYIN'...
THIS?
WHO SEZ IT'S HIS BIKE?
'T WAS GIVEN TO US...
...SO WE'D FIX IT!
KLONG!!!

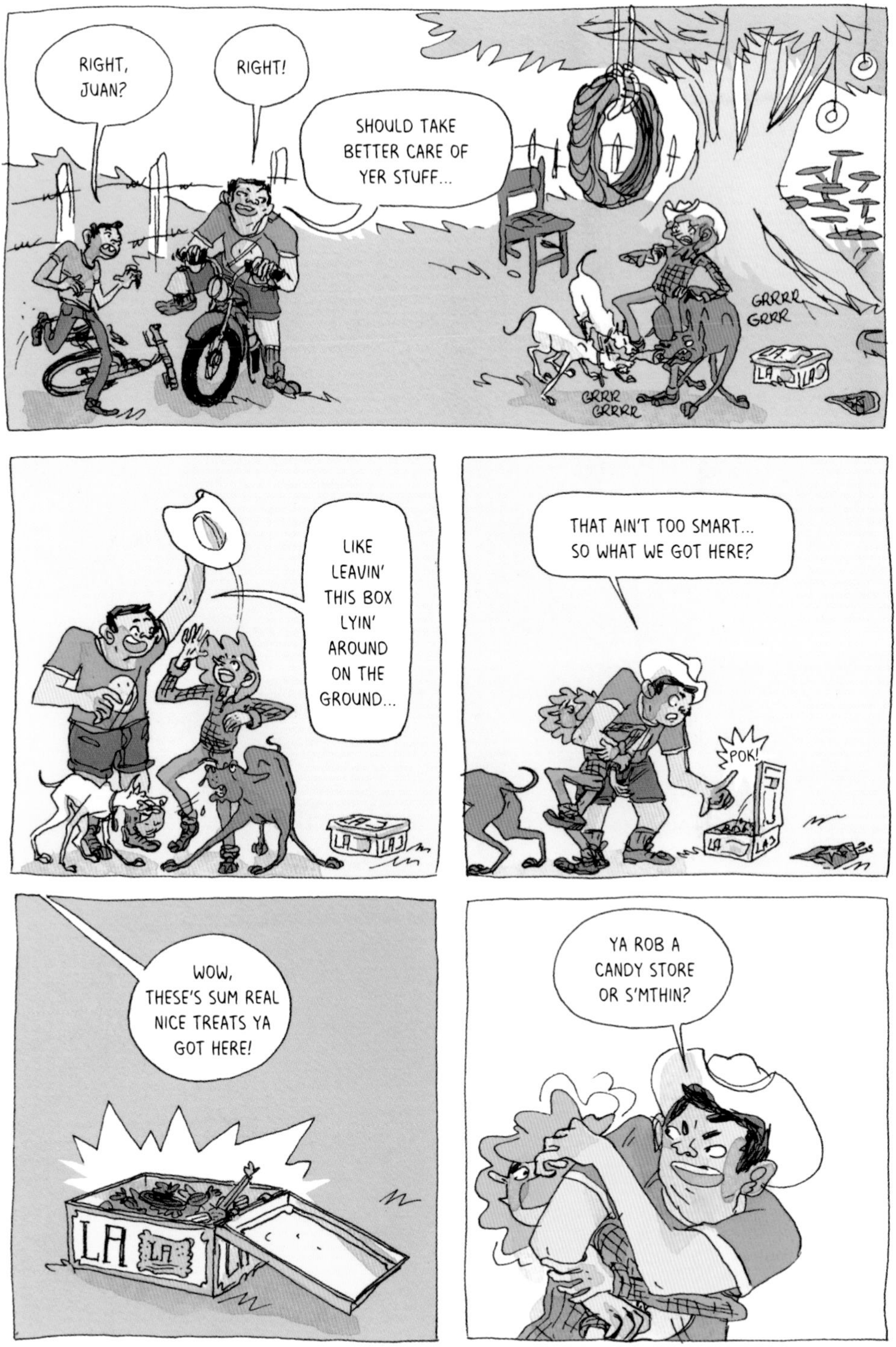
RIGHT, JUAN?
RIGHT!
SHOULD TAKE BETTER CARE OF YER STUFF...
GRRRR GRRR
GRRR GRRRR
LIKE LEAVIN' THIS BOX LYIN' AROUND ON THE GROUND...
THAT AIN'T TOO SMART... SO WHAT WE GOT HERE?
POK!
WOW, THESE'S SUM REAL NICE TREATS YA GOT HERE!
LA
YA ROB A CANDY STORE OR S'MTHIN?

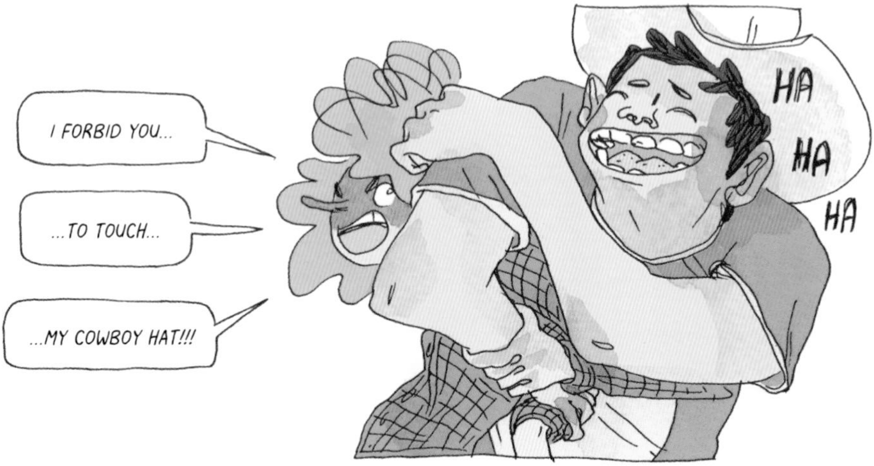
I FORBID YOU...
...TO TOUCH...
...MY COWBOY HAT!!!
HA
HA
HA

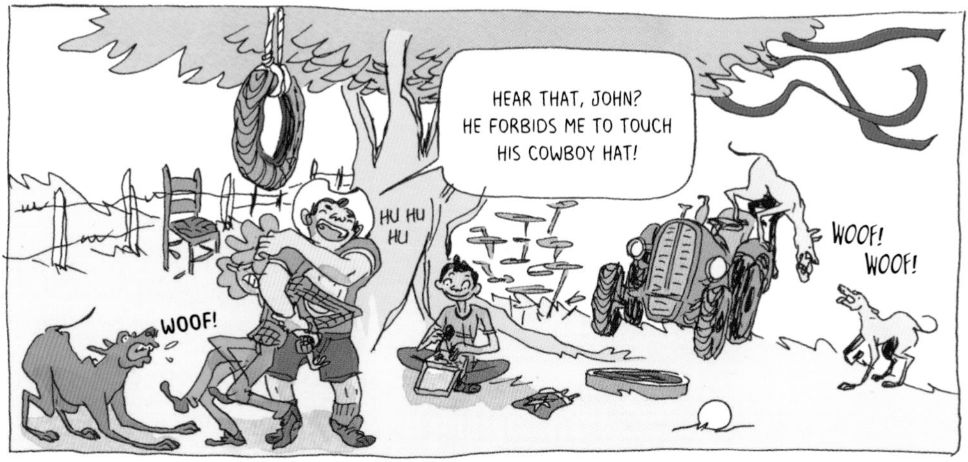
HEAR THAT, JOHN?
HE FORBIDS ME TO TOUCH
HIS COWBOY HAT!
HU HU
HU
WOOF!
WOOF!
WOOF!

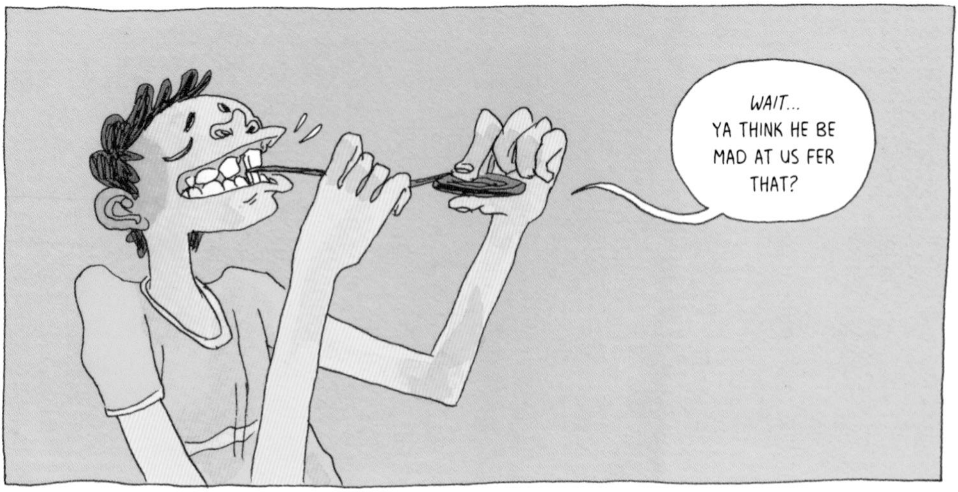
WAIT...
YA THINK HE BE
MAD AT US FER
THAT?

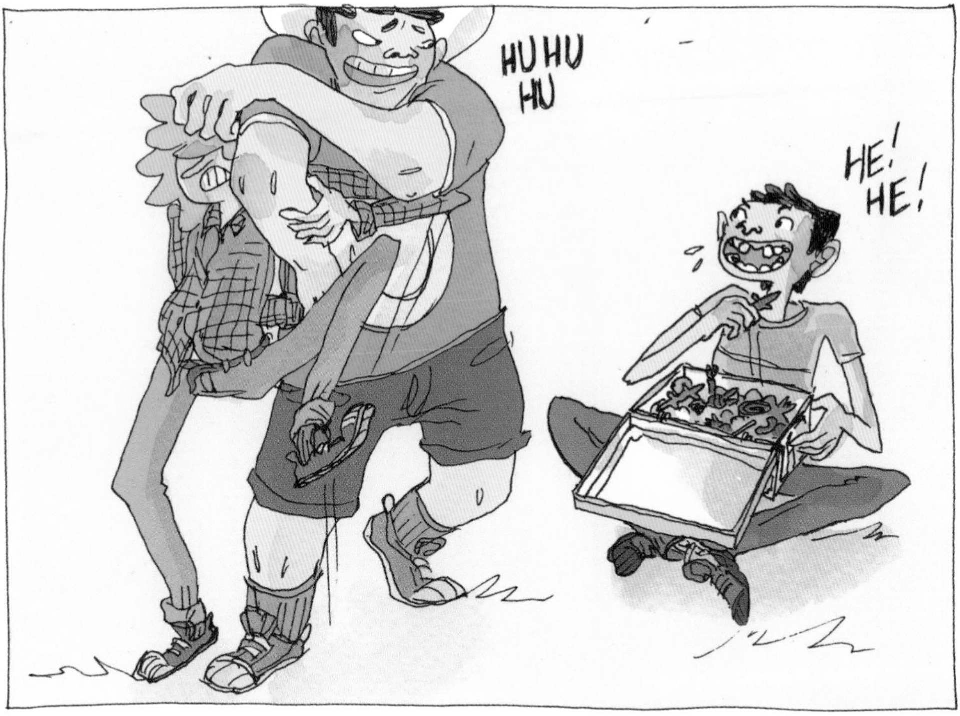
HU HU
HU
HE! HE!

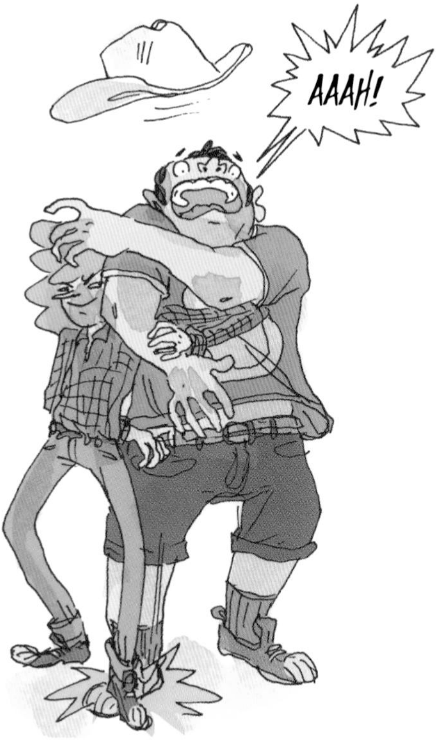
AAAH!

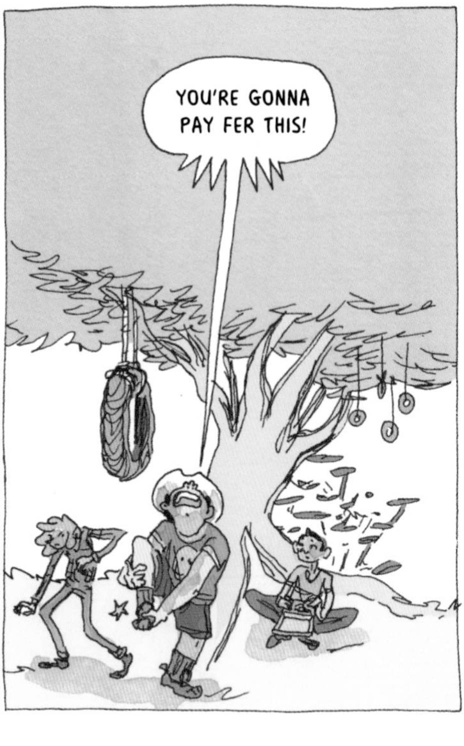
YOU'RE GONNA PAY FER THIS!

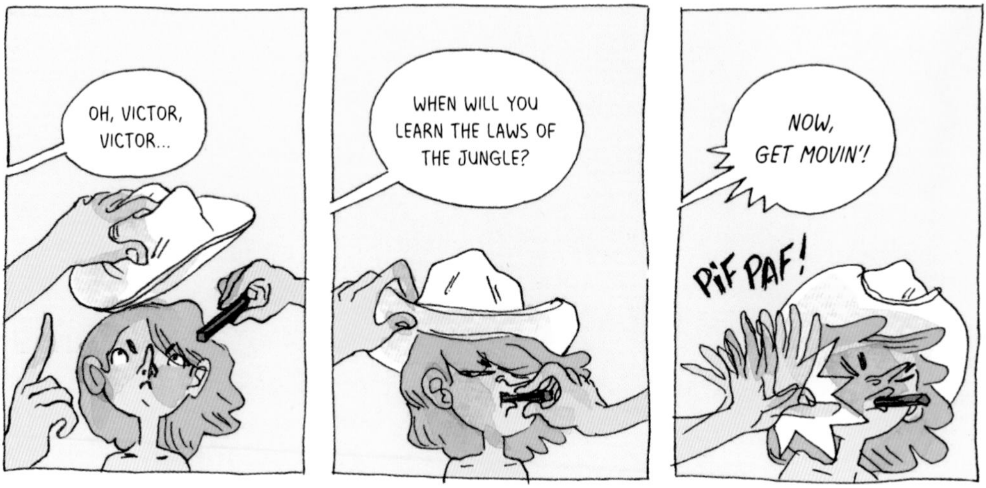
OH, VICTOR,
VICTOR...
WHEN WILL YOU
LEARN THE LAWS OF
THE JUNGLE?
NOW,
GET MOVIN'!
PIF PAF!

"I WAS LUCKY TO GET OFF SO LIGHTLY..."

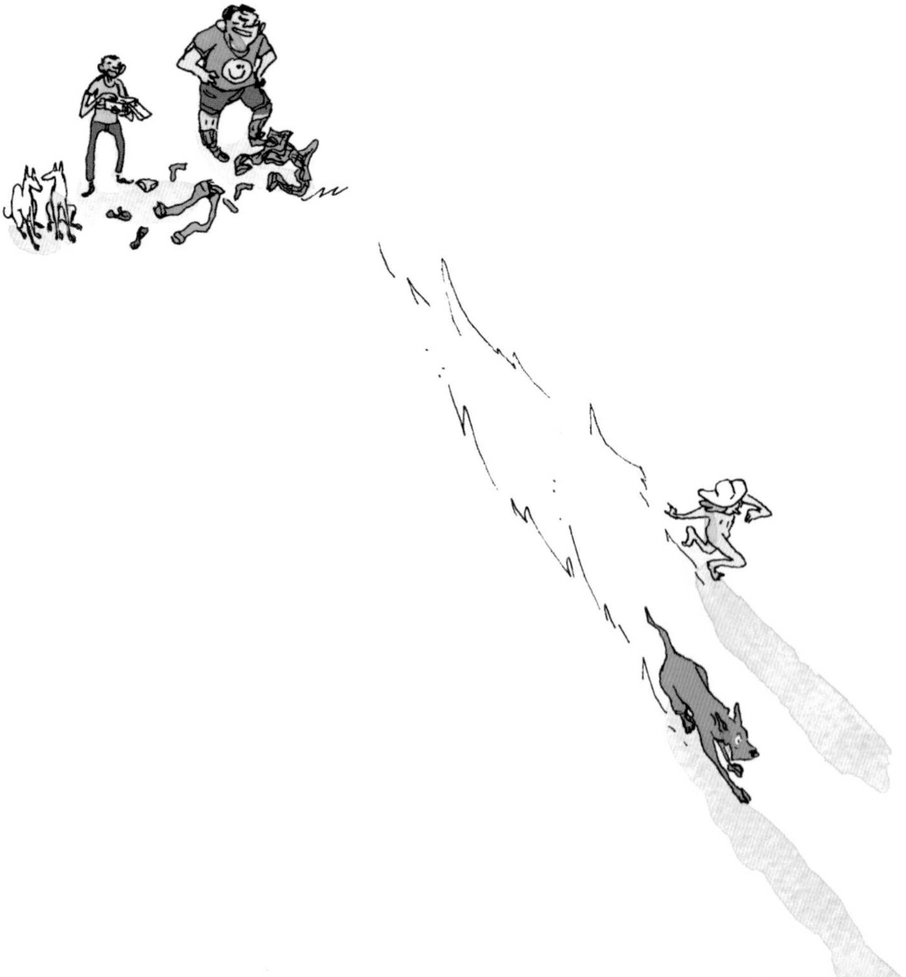

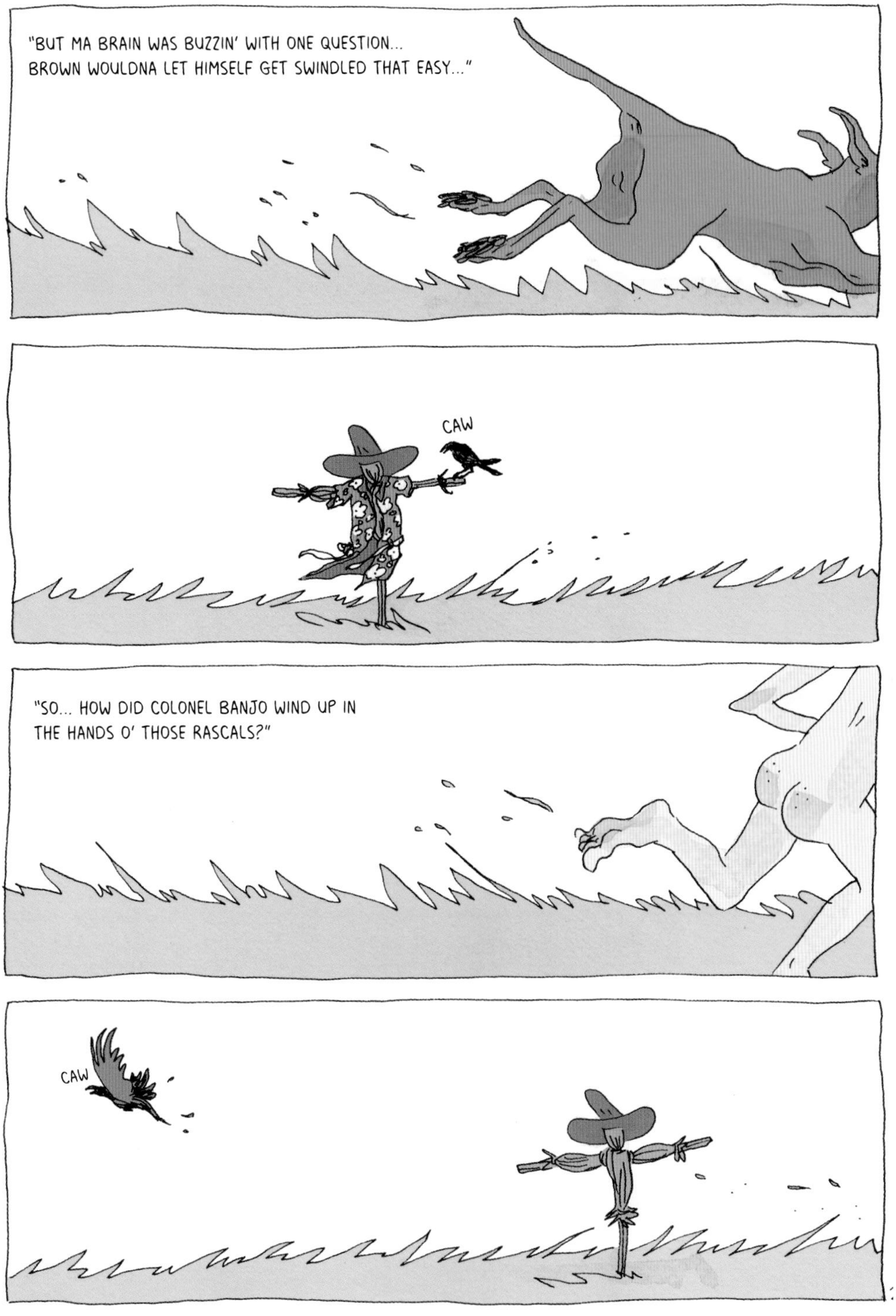
"BUT MA BRAIN WAS BUZZIN' WITH ONE QUESTION...
BROWN WOULDNA LET HIMSELF GET SWINDLED THAT EASY..."
CAW
"SO... HOW DID COLONEL BANJO WIND UP IN
THE HANDS O' THOSE RASCALS?"
CAW

"I STILL REMEMBER THE FIRST TIME I MET WILLY BROWN.
HE'D BEEN IN THE DESERT SO LONG HE KNEW ALL THE LIZARDS BY NAME..."

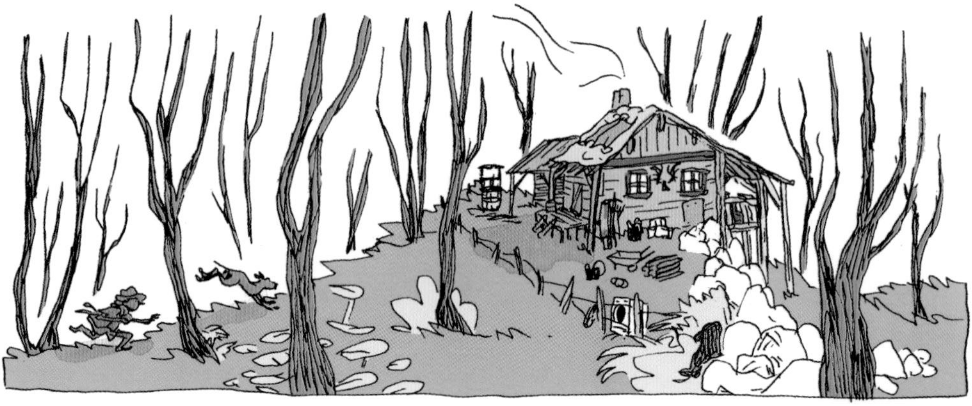

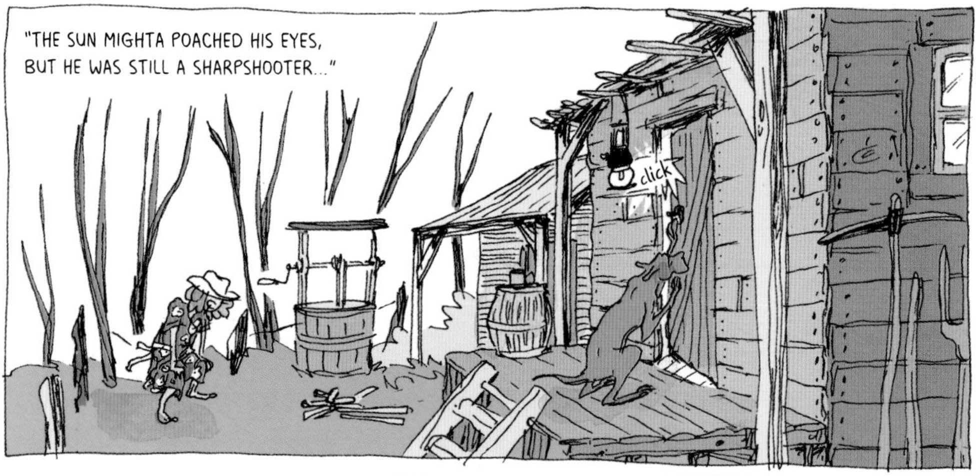
"THE SUN MIGHTA POACHED HIS EYES,
BUT HE WAS STILL A SHARPSHOOTER..."
click

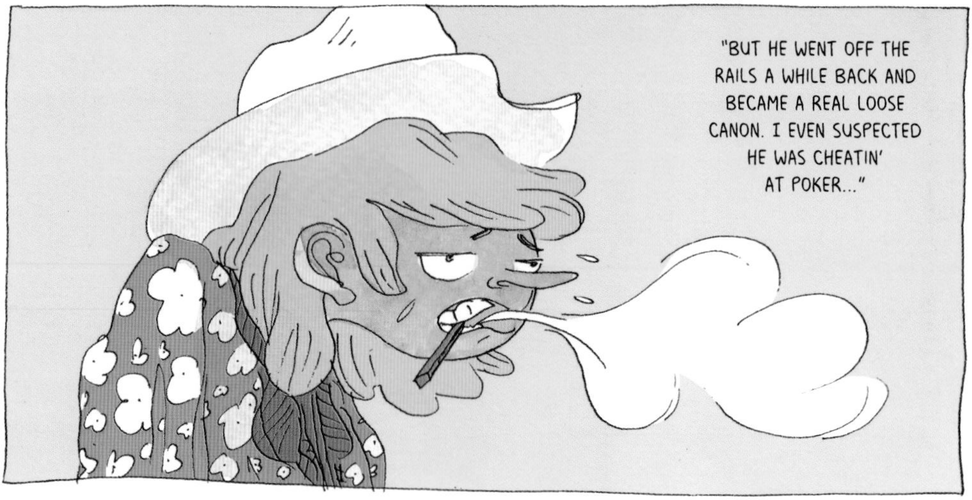
"BUT HE WENT OFF THE
RAILS A WHILE BACK AND
BECAME A REAL LOOSE
CANON. I EVEN SUSPECTED
HE WAS CHEATIN'
AT POKER..."

"INSIDE HIS SHACK, 'T SMELLED O' COFFIN VARNISH..."

"BROWN WAS IN ONE HELLUVA STATE AGAIN!"

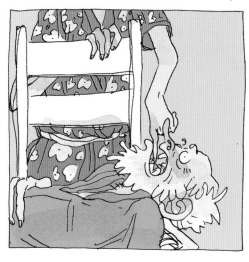

WASN'T ME! I SAW NOTHING!

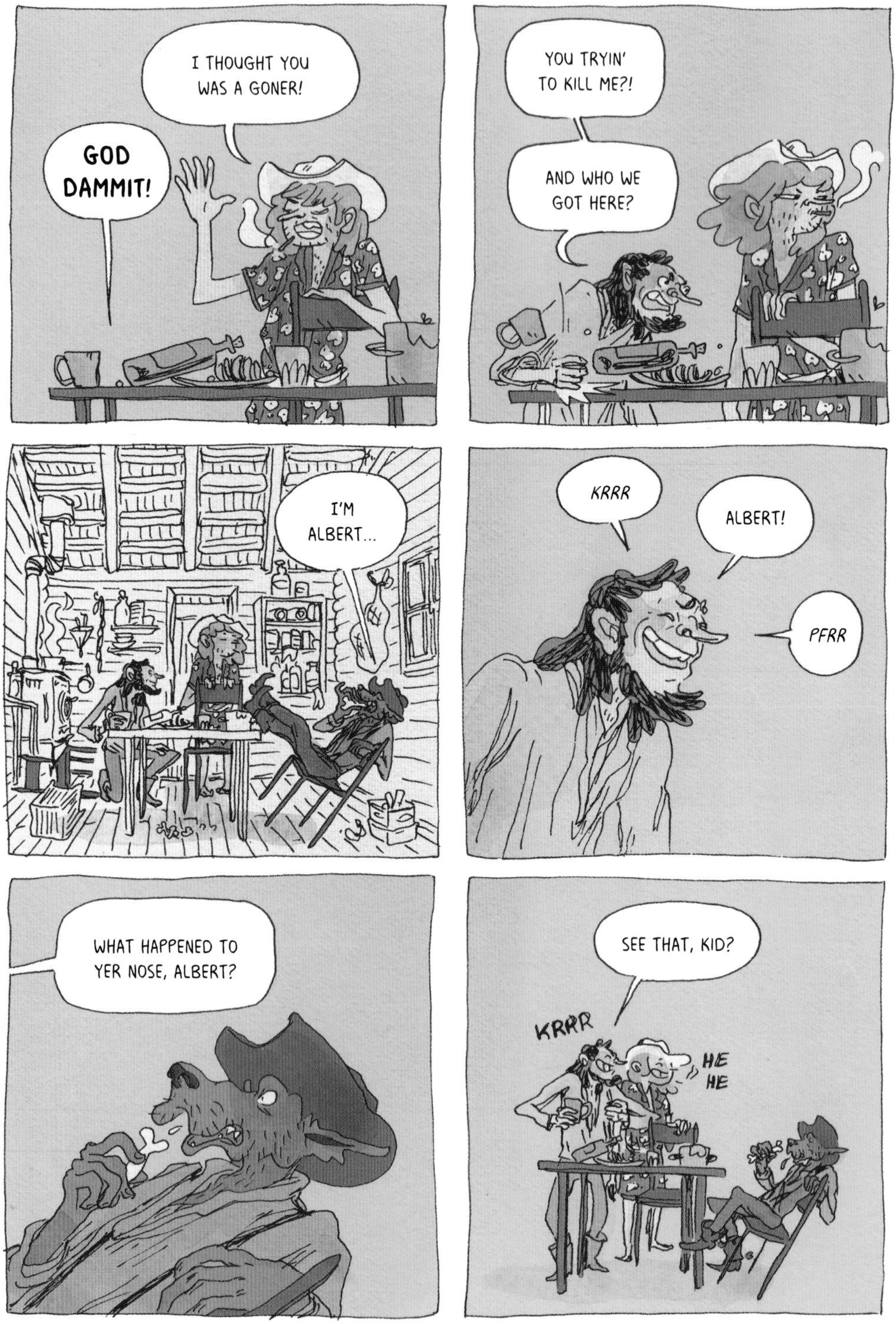
GOD DAMMIT!
I THOUGHT YOU WAS A GONER!
YOU TRYIN' TO KILL ME?!
AND WHO WE GOT HERE?
I'M ALBERT...
KRRR
ALBERT!
PFRR
WHAT HAPPENED TO YER NOSE, ALBERT?
SEE THAT, KID?
KRRR
HE HE

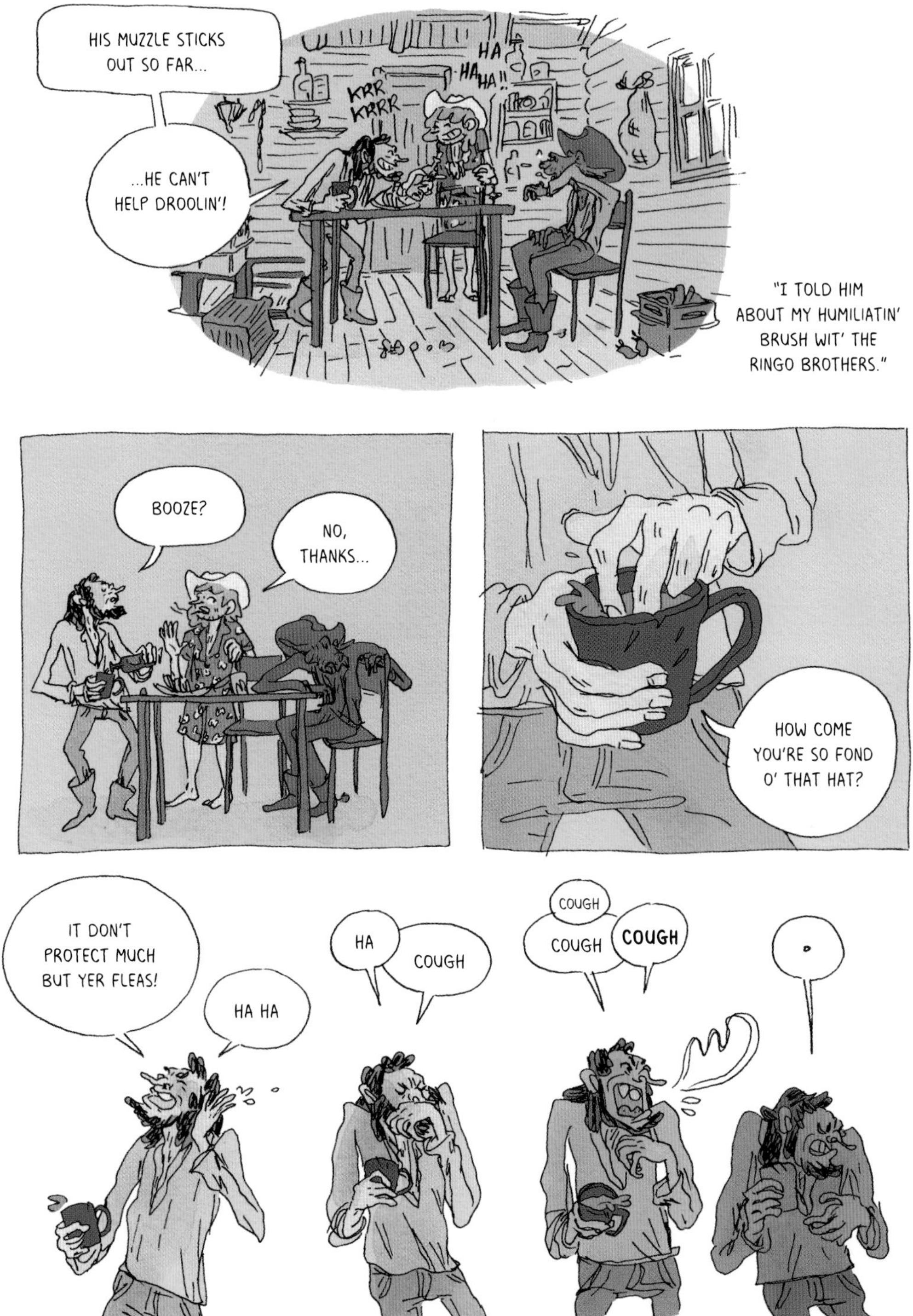
HIS MUZZLE STICKS OUT SO FAR...
...HE CAN'T HELP DROOLIN'!
KRR KRRR
HA HA HA!!
"I TOLD HIM ABOUT MY HUMILIATIN' BRUSH WIT' THE RINGO BROTHERS."
BOOZE?
NO, THANKS...
HOW COME YOU'RE SO FOND O' THAT HAT?
IT DON'T PROTECT MUCH BUT YER FLEAS!
HA HA
HA
COUGH
COUGH
COUGH
COUGH

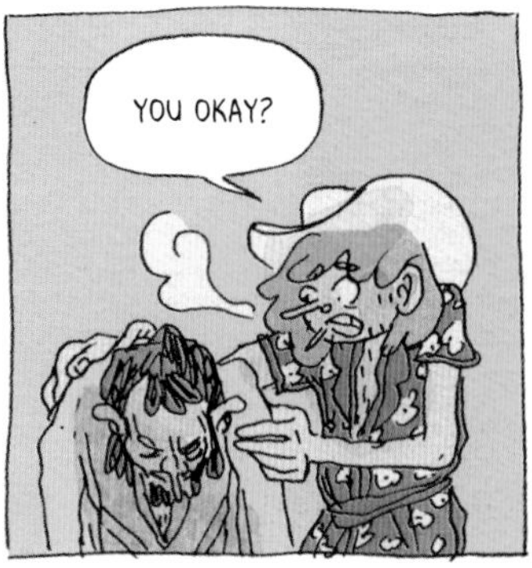
YOU OKAY?

"BROWN ADMITTED THEY STOLE MY COLONEL BANJO WHILE HE WAS NAPPIN' IN THE SHADE O' SOME COWS OUT IN THE FIELD."

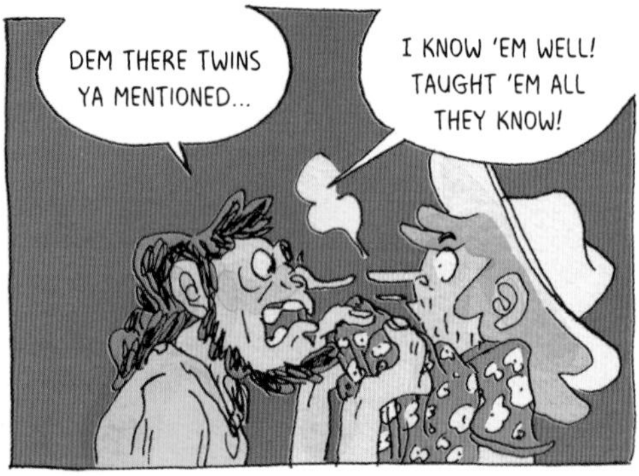
DEM THERE TWINS YA MENTIONED...
I KNOW 'EM WELL! TAUGHT 'EM ALL THEY KNOW!

"WHAT VEXED BROWN THE MOST WAS THAT NOBODY'D EVER DARED CONNIN' HIM BEFORE, AND IT MADE HIM FEEL OLD!"

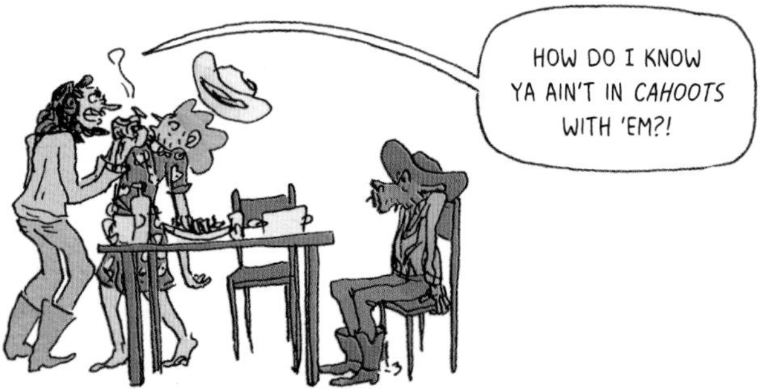
HOW DO I KNOW YA AIN'T IN *CAHOOTS* WITH 'EM?!

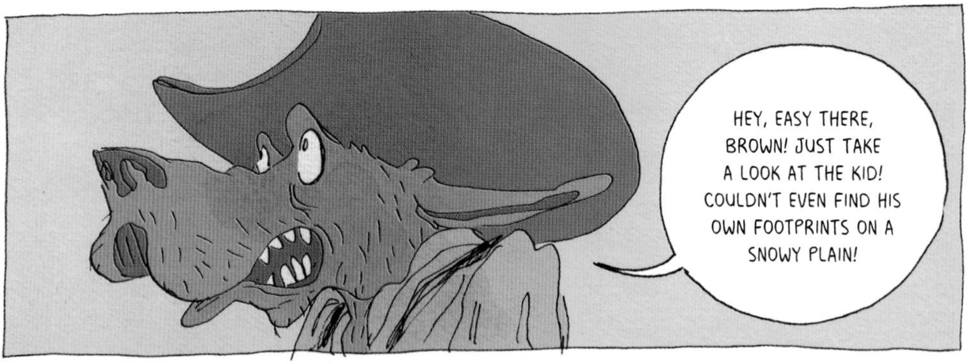
HEY, EASY THERE, BROWN! JUST TAKE A LOOK AT THE KID! COULDN'T EVEN FIND HIS OWN FOOTPRINTS ON A SNOWY PLAIN!

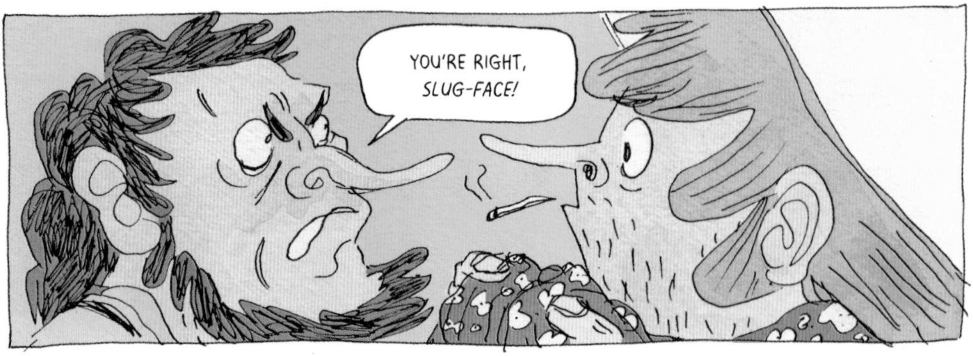
YOU'RE RIGHT, *SLUG-FACE!*

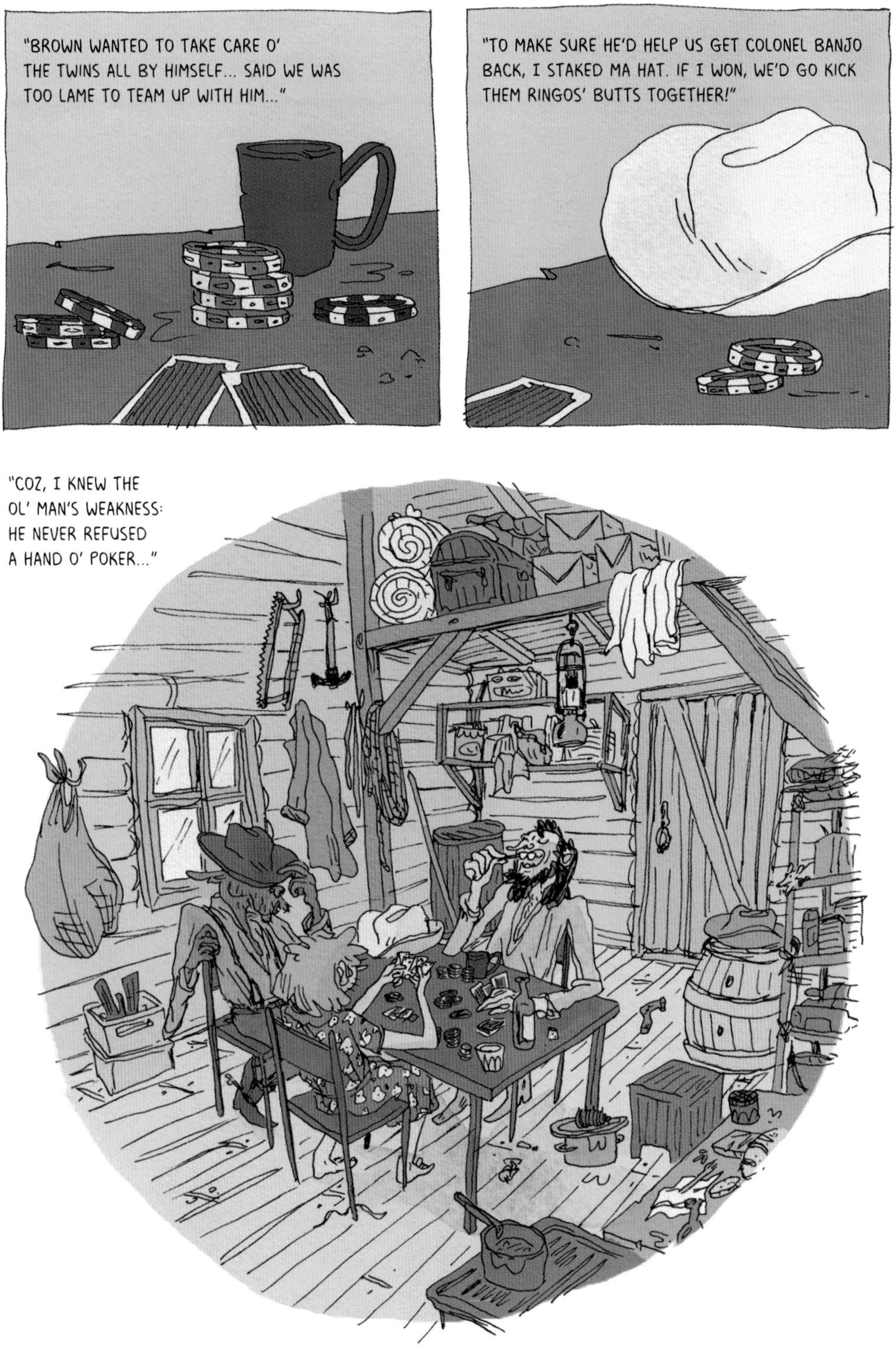
"BROWN WANTED TO TAKE CARE O' THE TWINS ALL BY HIMSELF... SAID WE WAS TOO LAME TO TEAM UP WITH HIM..."
"TO MAKE SURE HE'D HELP US GET COLONEL BANJO BACK, I STAKED MA HAT. IF I WON, WE'D GO KICK THEM RINGOS' BUTTS TOGETHER!"
"COZ, I KNEW THE OL' MAN'S WEAKNESS: HE NEVER REFUSED A HAND O' POKER..."

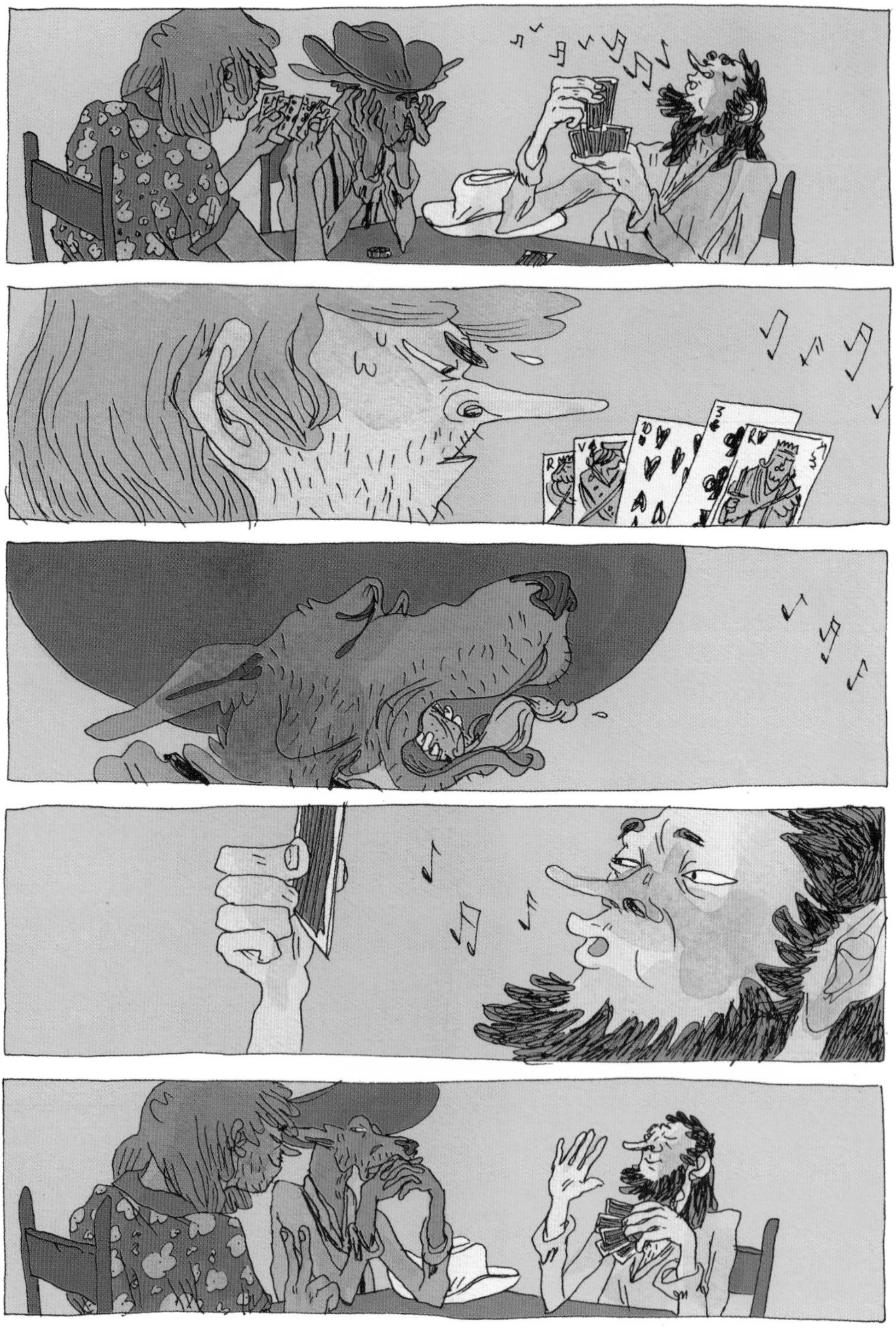

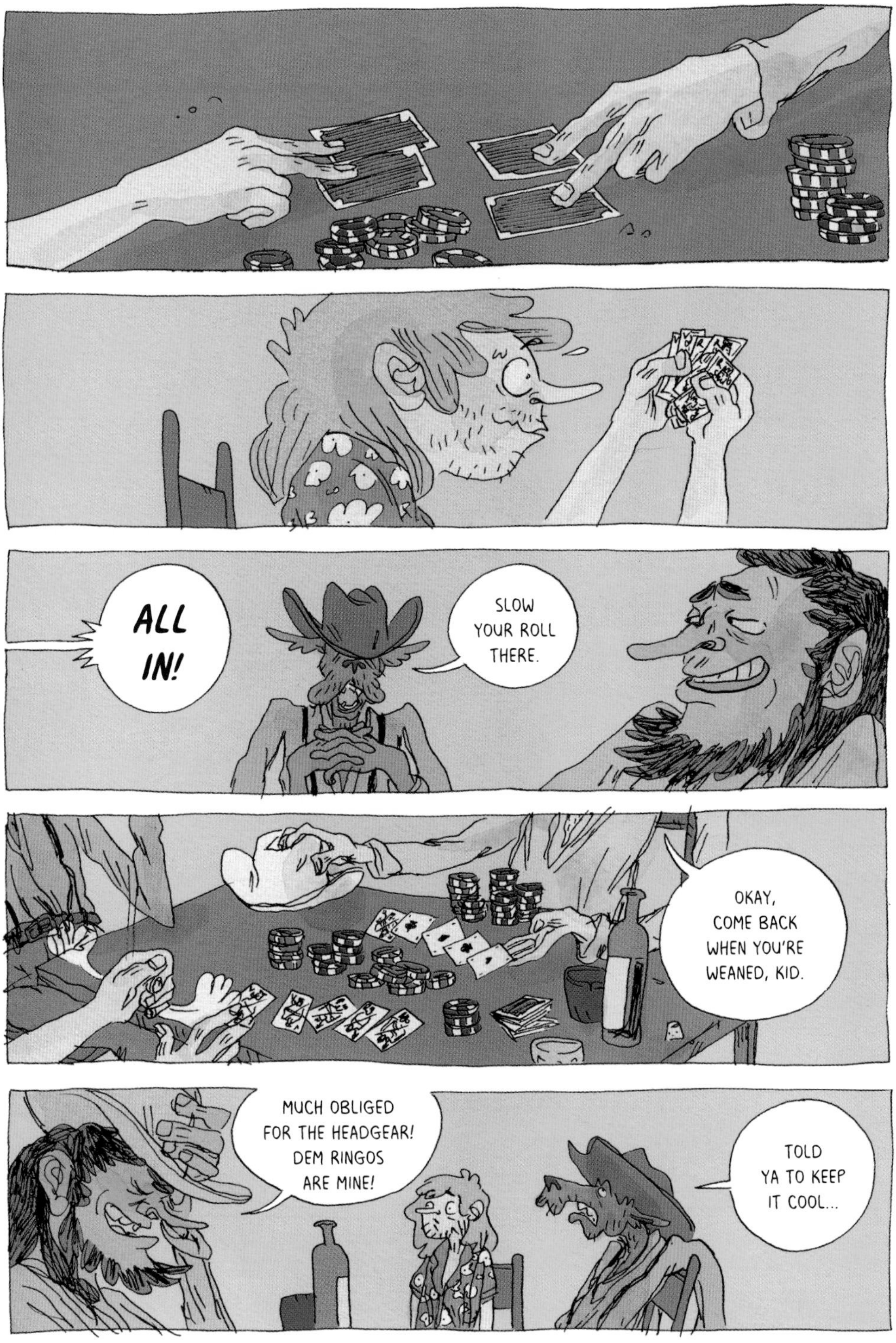
ALL IN!
SLOW YOUR ROLL THERE.
OKAY, COME BACK WHEN YOU'RE WEANED, KID.
MUCH OBLIGED FOR THE HEADGEAR! DEM RINGOS ARE MINE!
TOLD YA TO KEEP IT COOL...

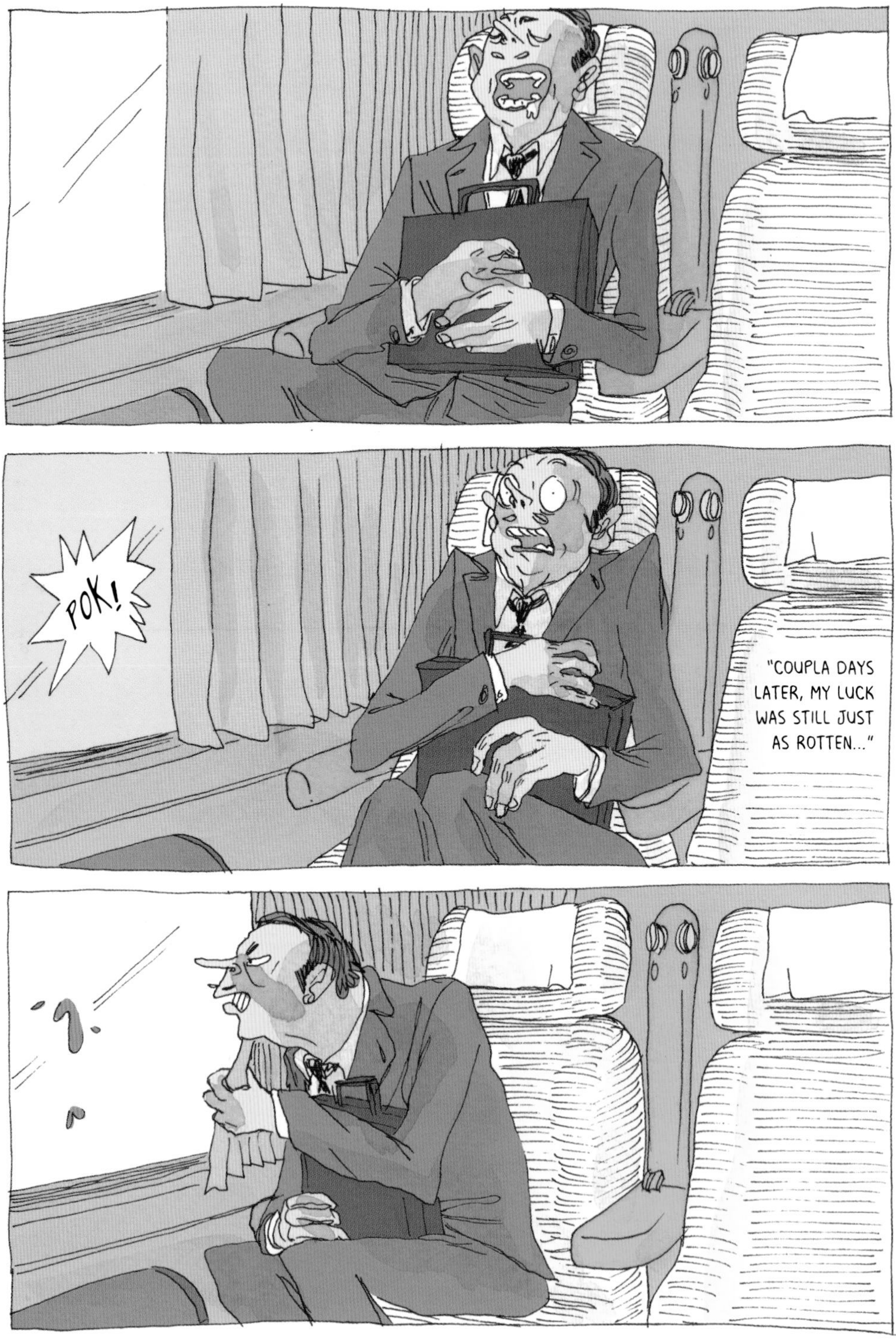
POK!
"COUPLA DAYS LATER, MY LUCK WAS STILL JUST AS ROTTEN..."

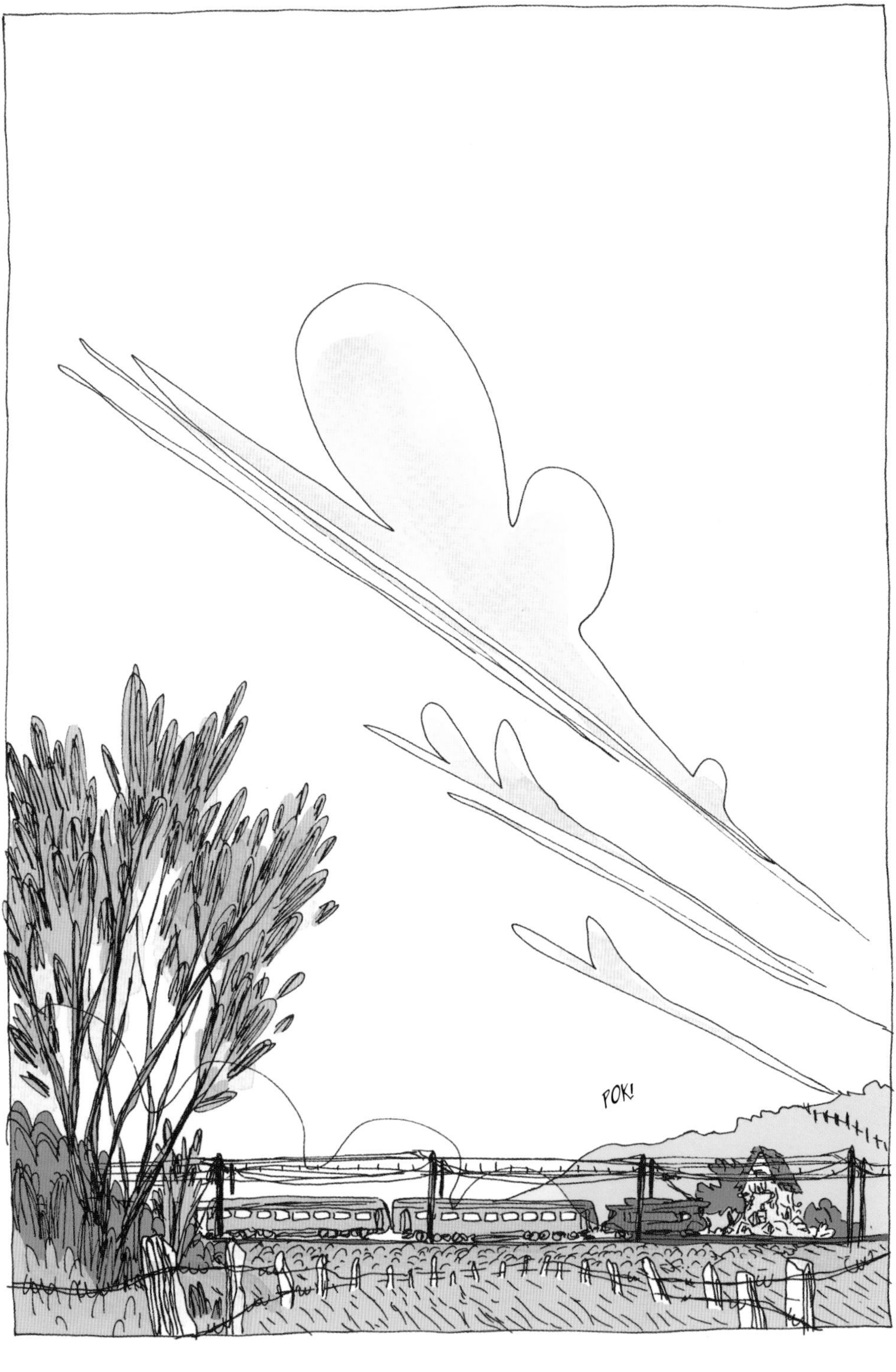
POK!

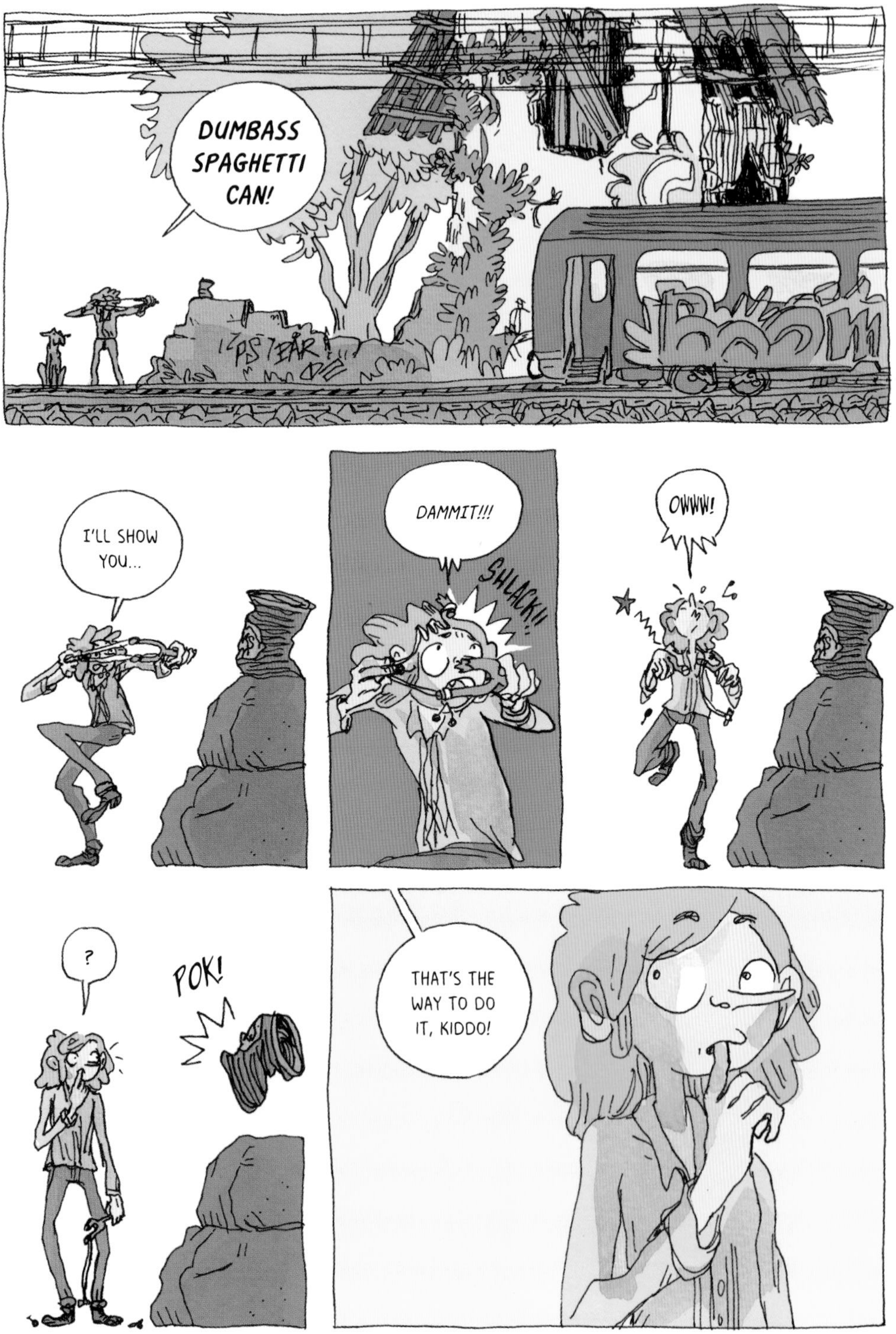
DUMBASS SPAGHETTI CAN!
I'LL SHOW YOU...
DAMMIT!!!
SHLACK!!
OWWW!
?
POK!
THAT'S THE WAY TO DO IT, KIDDO!

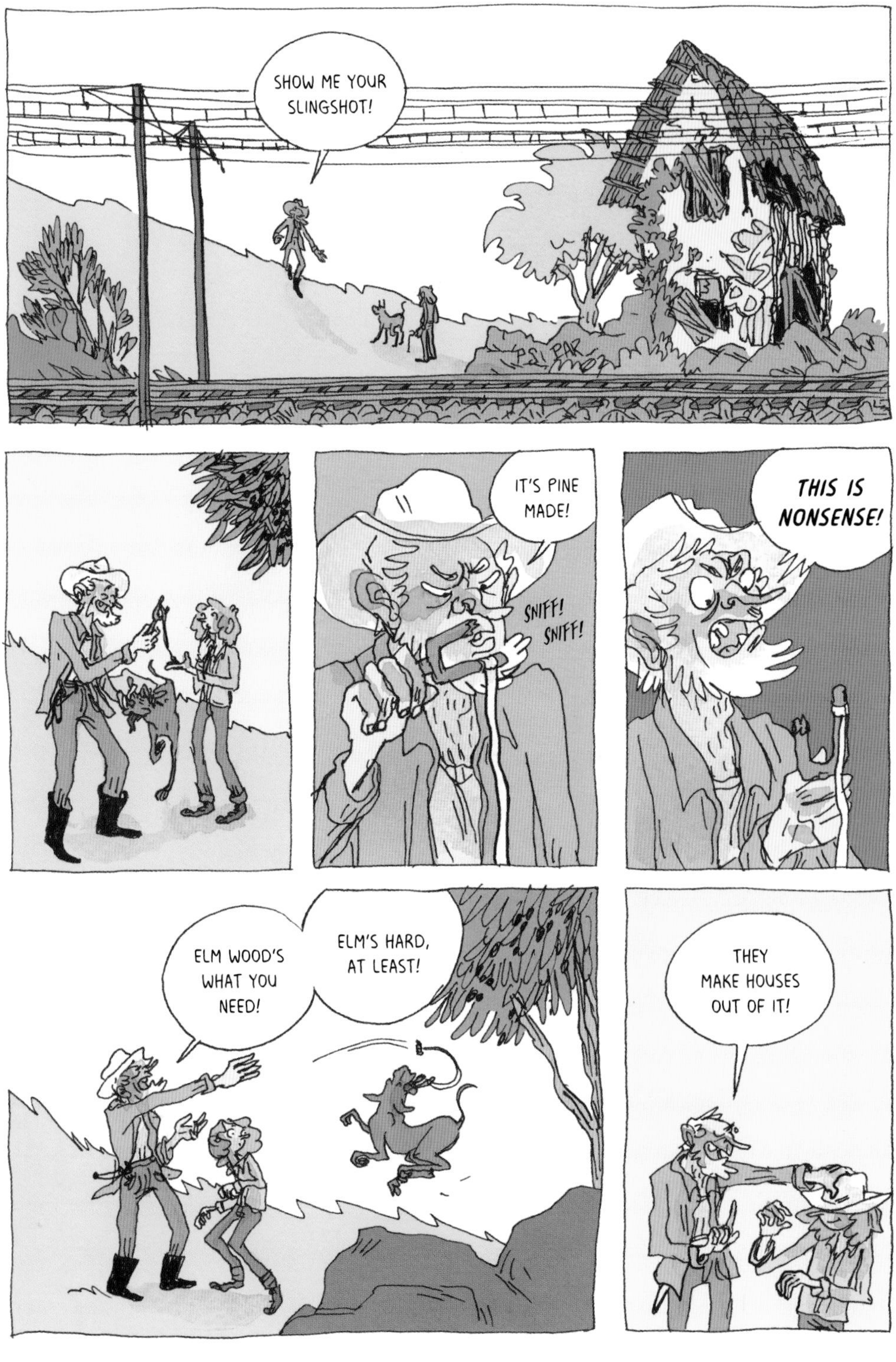
SHOW ME YOUR SLINGSHOT!
IT'S PINE MADE!
SNIFF! SNIFF!
THIS IS NONSENSE!
ELM WOOD'S WHAT YOU NEED!
ELM'S HARD, AT LEAST!
THEY MAKE HOUSES OUT OF IT!

"I NEVER REALLY UNDERSTOOD WHY BROWN CHANGED HIS MIND..."

"THEY SAY WHEN A COWBOY'S TOO OLD TO SET A BAD EXAMPLE, HE HANDS OUT GOOD ADVICE..."

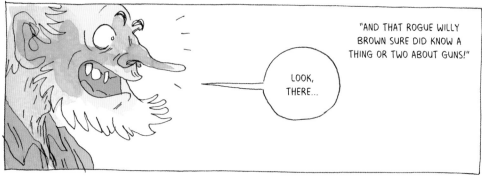

"AND THAT ROGUE WILLY BROWN SURE DID KNOW A THING OR TWO ABOUT GUNS!"

LOOK, THERE...

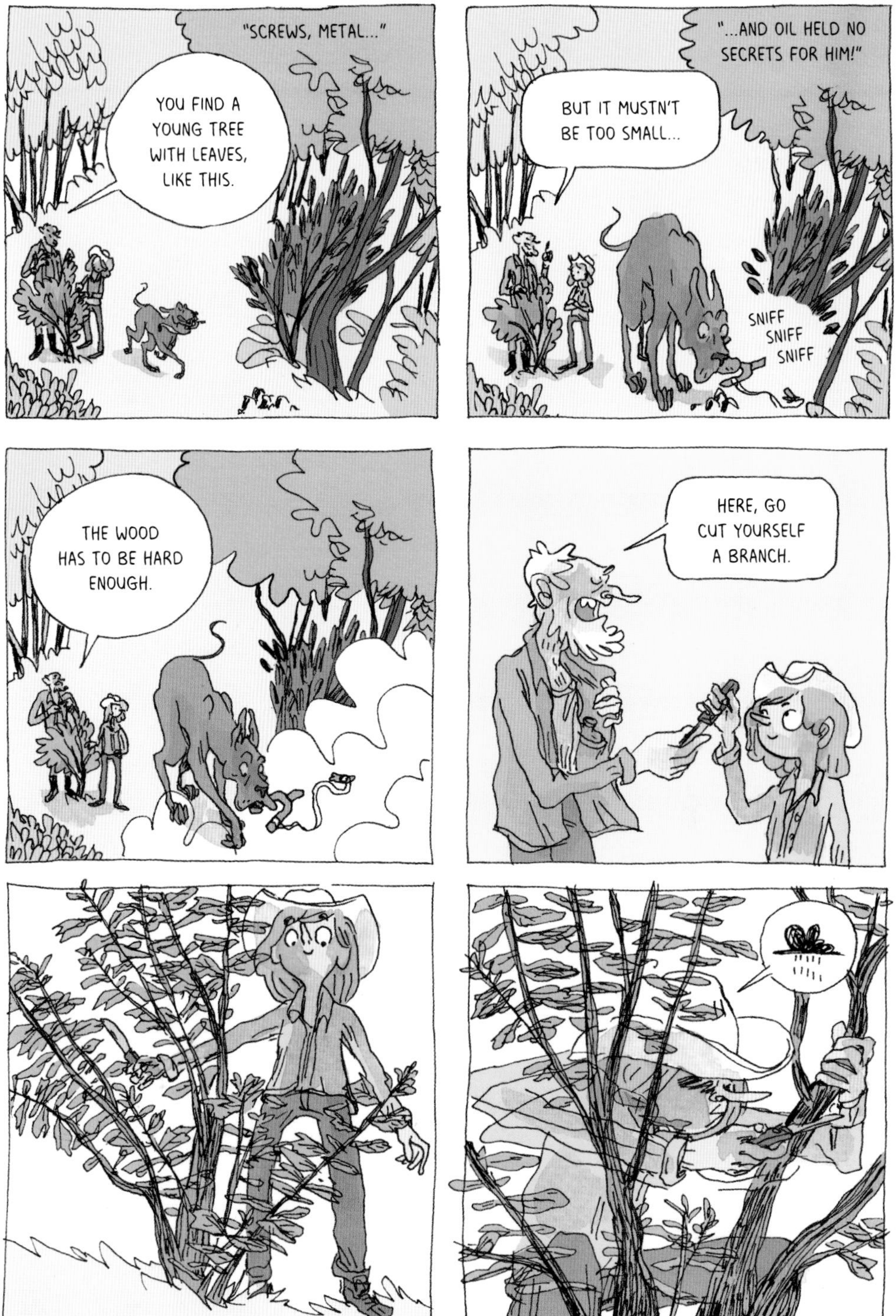
"SCREWS, METAL..."
YOU FIND A YOUNG TREE WITH LEAVES, LIKE THIS.
"...AND OIL HELD NO SECRETS FOR HIM!"
BUT IT MUSTN'T BE TOO SMALL...
SNIFF SNIFF SNIFF
THE WOOD HAS TO BE HARD ENOUGH.
HERE, GO CUT YOURSELF A BRANCH.

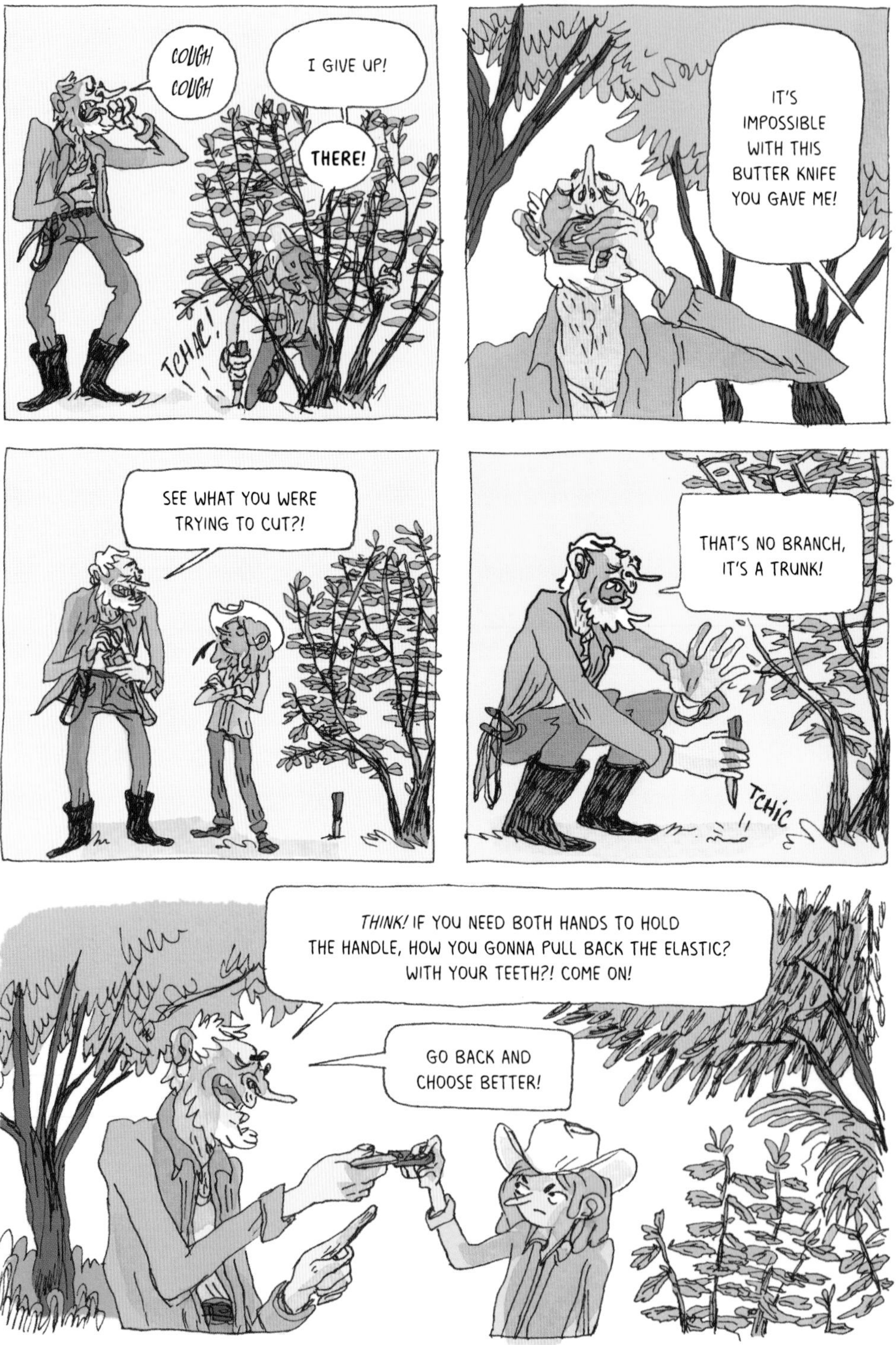
COUGH COUGH
I GIVE UP!
THERE!
TCHAC!
IT'S IMPOSSIBLE WITH THIS BUTTER KNIFE YOU GAVE ME!
SEE WHAT YOU WERE TRYING TO CUT?!
THAT'S NO BRANCH, IT'S A TRUNK!
TCHIC
*THINK!* IF YOU NEED BOTH HANDS TO HOLD THE HANDLE, HOW YOU GONNA PULL BACK THE ELASTIC? WITH YOUR TEETH?! COME ON!
GO BACK AND CHOOSE BETTER!

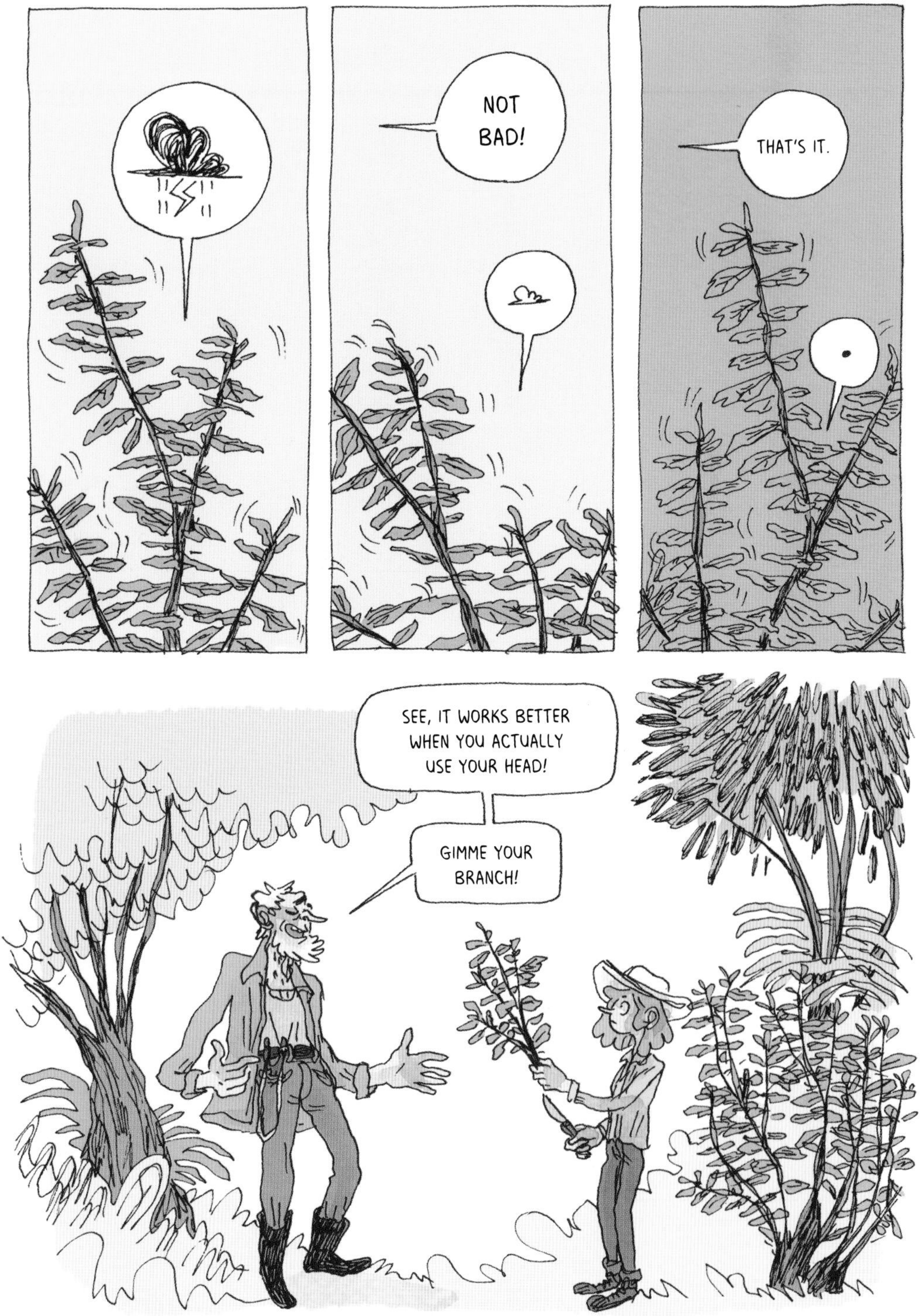
NOT BAD!
THAT'S IT.
SEE, IT WORKS BETTER WHEN YOU ACTUALLY USE YOUR HEAD!
GIMME YOUR BRANCH!

"THERE AIN'T MUCH THAT CAN IMPRESS ME..."

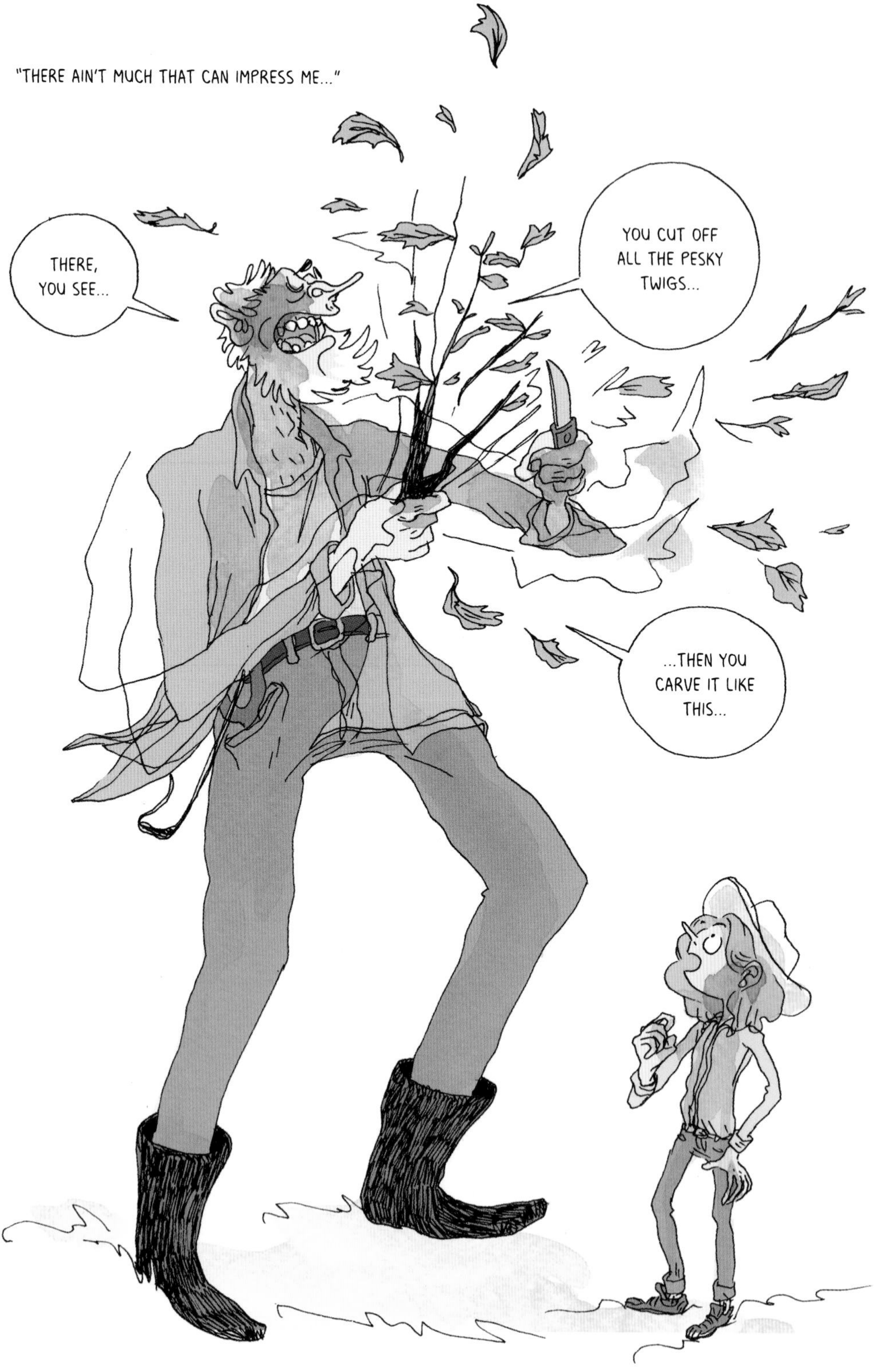
THERE, YOU SEE...
YOU CUT OFF ALL THE PESKY TWIGS...
...THEN YOU CARVE IT LIKE THIS...

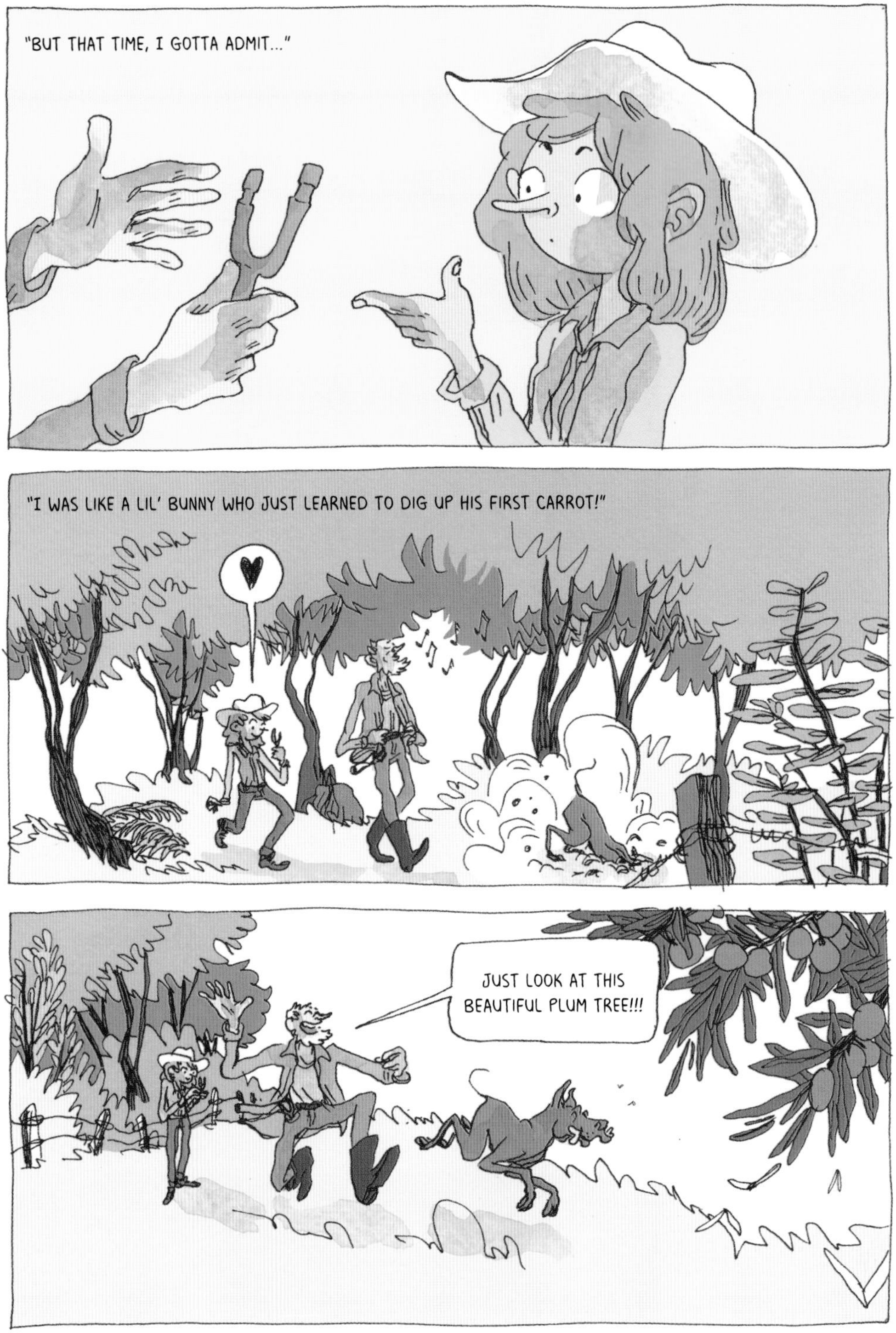
"BUT THAT TIME, I GOTTA ADMIT..."
"I WAS LIKE A LIL' BUNNY WHO JUST LEARNED TO DIG UP HIS FIRST CARROT!"
JUST LOOK AT THIS BEAUTIFUL PLUM TREE!!!

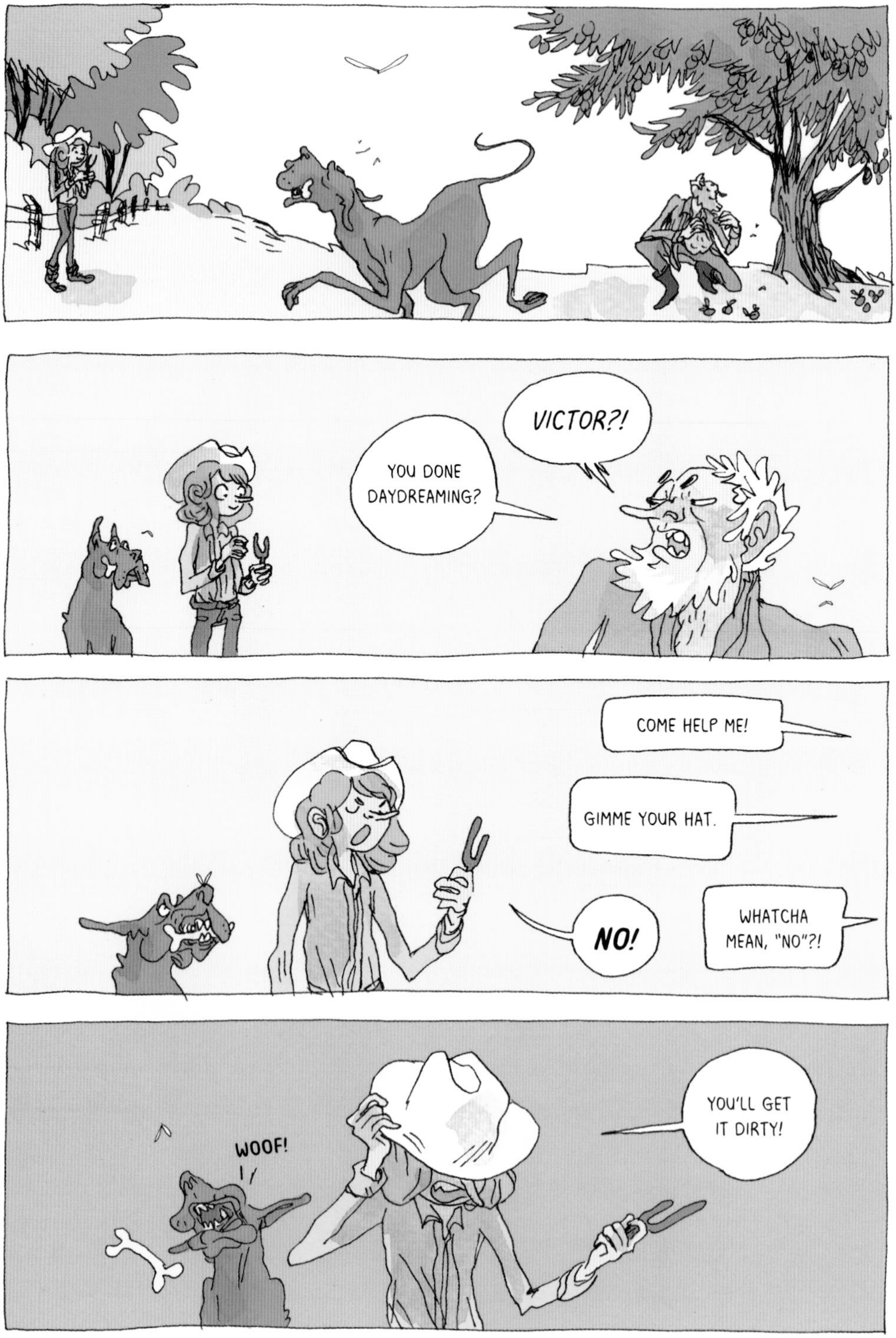
VICTOR?!
YOU DONE DAYDREAMING?
COME HELP ME!
GIMME YOUR HAT.
NO!
WHATCHA MEAN, "NO"?!
WOOF!
YOU'LL GET IT DIRTY!

FTB

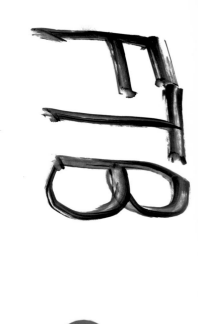

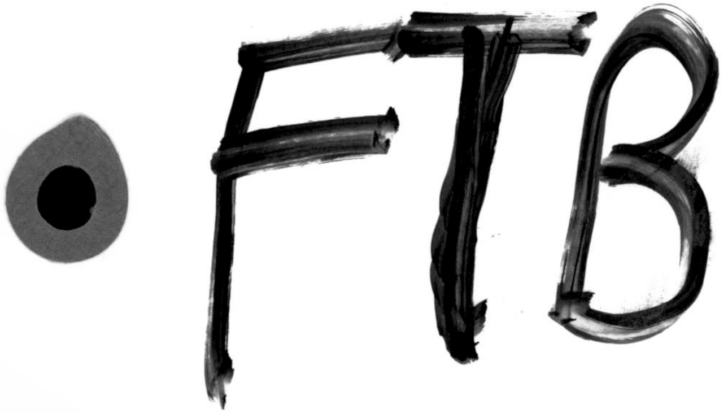
FTB

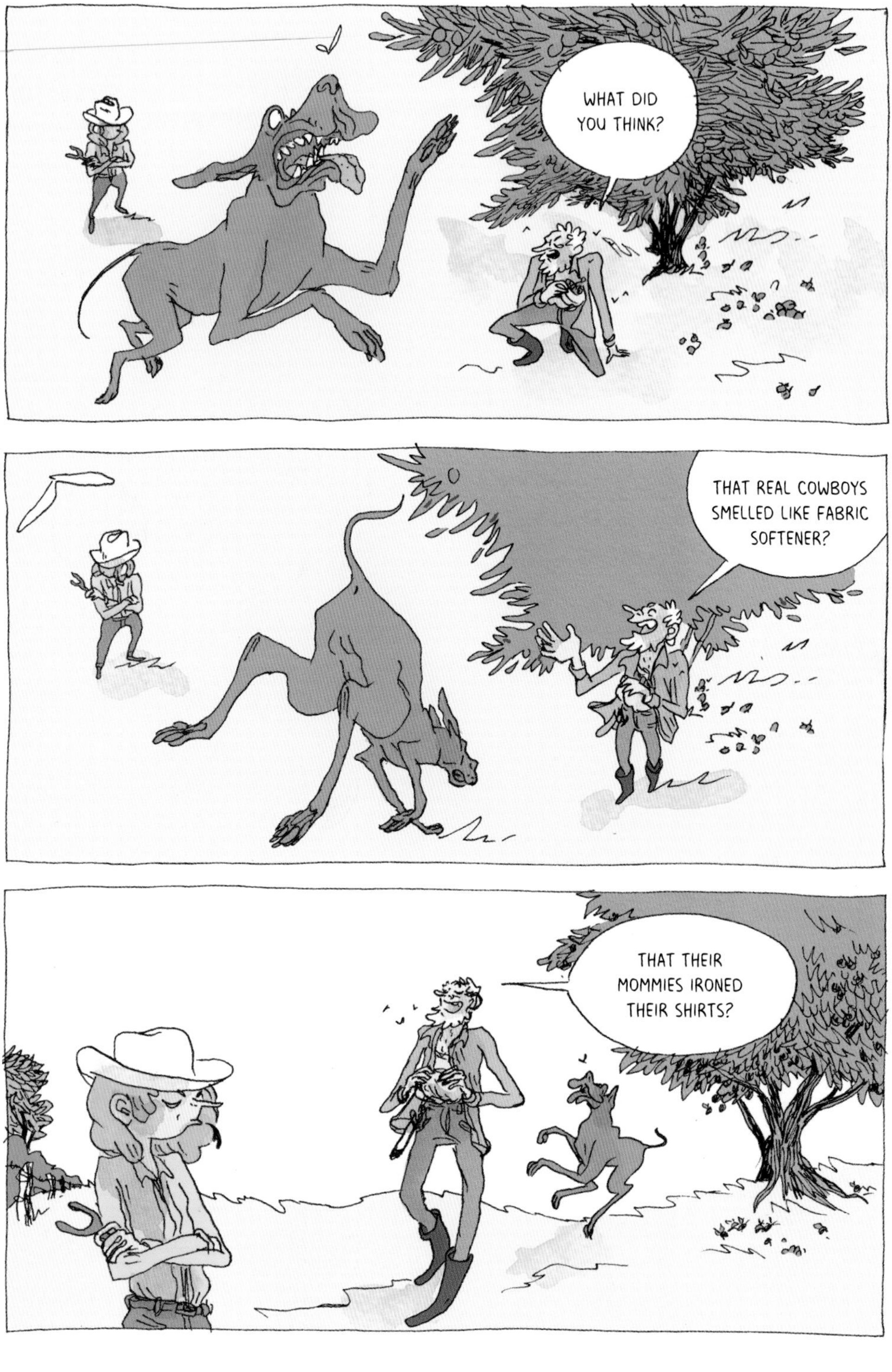
WHAT DID YOU THINK?
THAT REAL COWBOYS SMELLED LIKE FABRIC SOFTENER?
THAT THEIR MOMMIES IRONED THEIR SHIRTS?

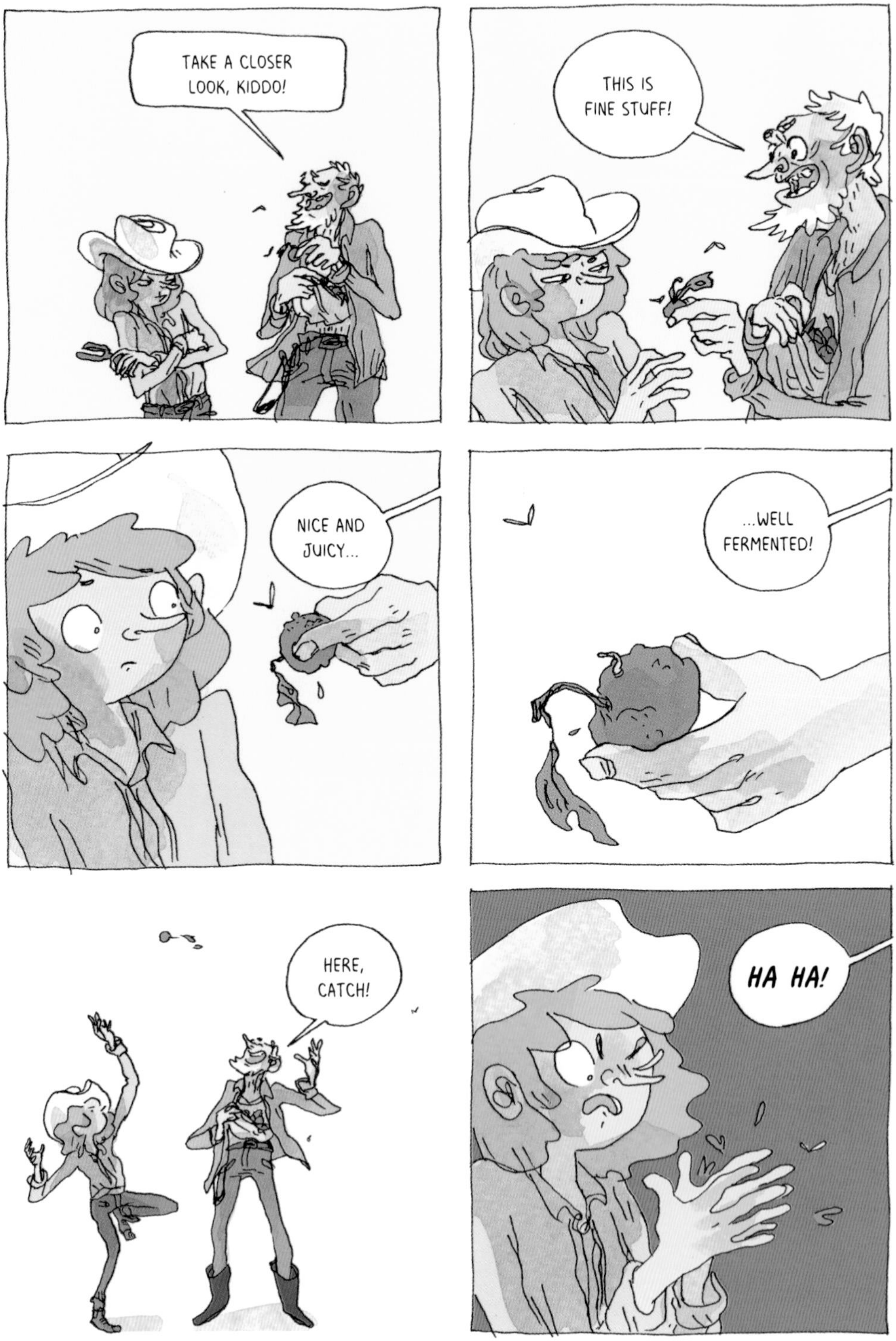
TAKE A CLOSER LOOK, KIDDO!
THIS IS FINE STUFF!
NICE AND JUICY...
...WELL FERMENTED!
HERE, CATCH!
HA HA!

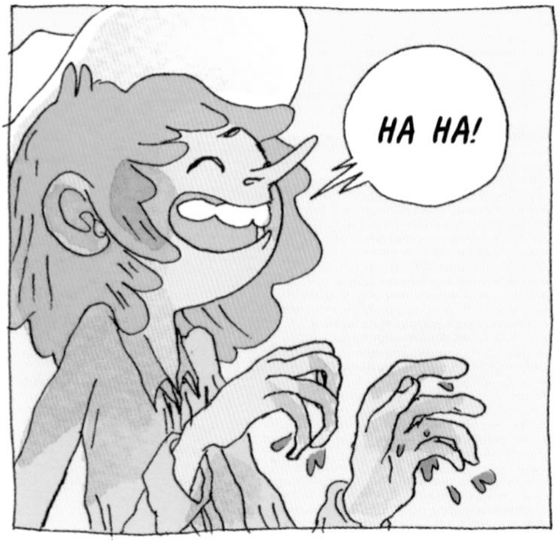
HA HA!

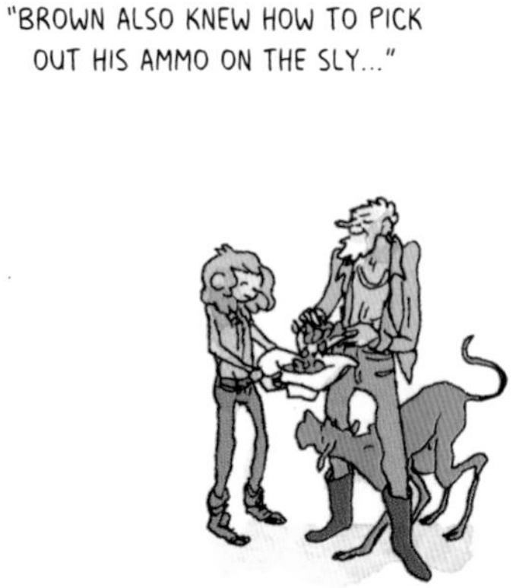
"BROWN ALSO KNEW HOW TO PICK OUT HIS AMMO ON THE SLY..."

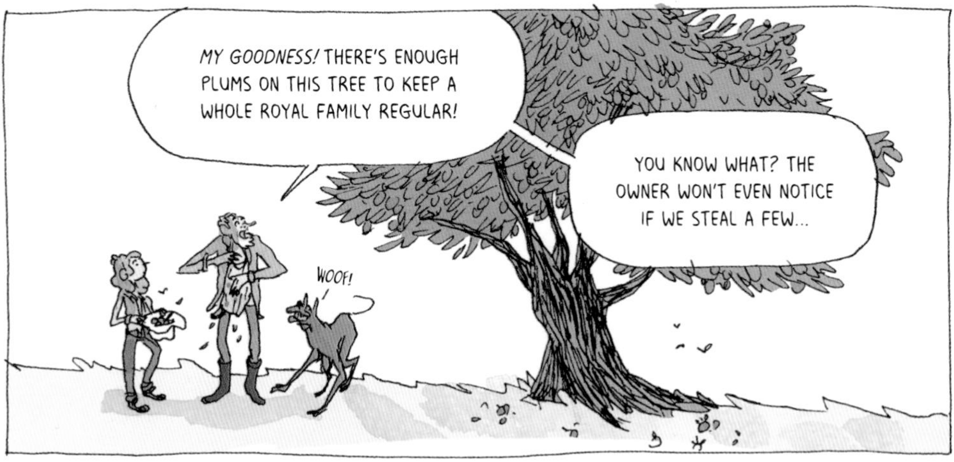
MY GOODNESS! THERE'S ENOUGH PLUMS ON THIS TREE TO KEEP A WHOLE ROYAL FAMILY REGULAR!
YOU KNOW WHAT? THE OWNER WON'T EVEN NOTICE IF WE STEAL A FEW...
WOOF!

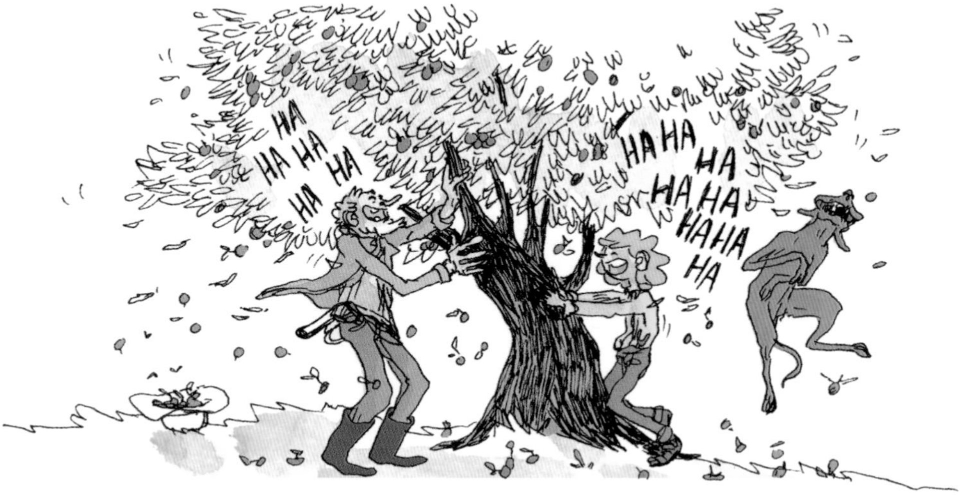
HA HA HA HA HA HA
HA HA HA HA HA HA HA HA HA

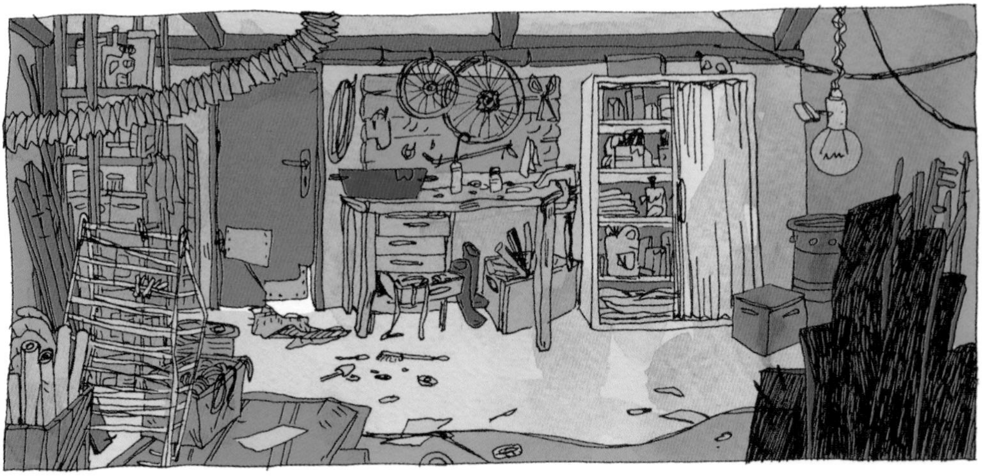

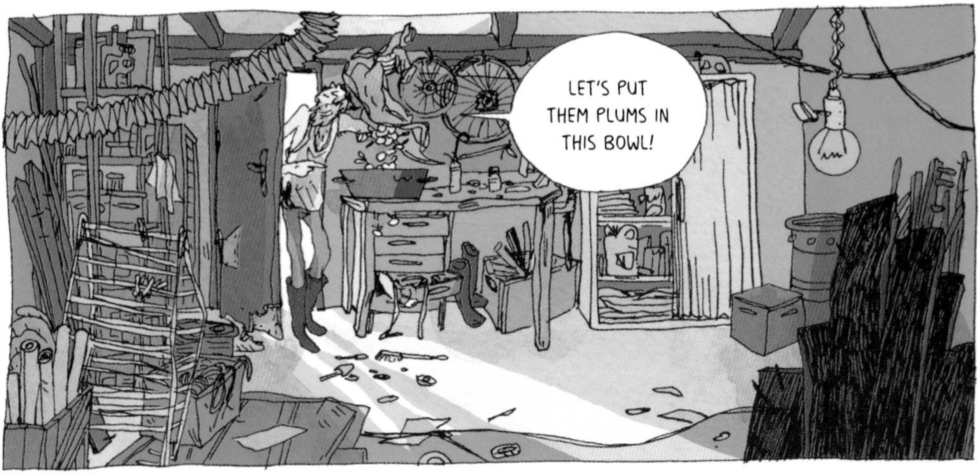
LET'S PUT THEM PLUMS IN THIS BOWL!

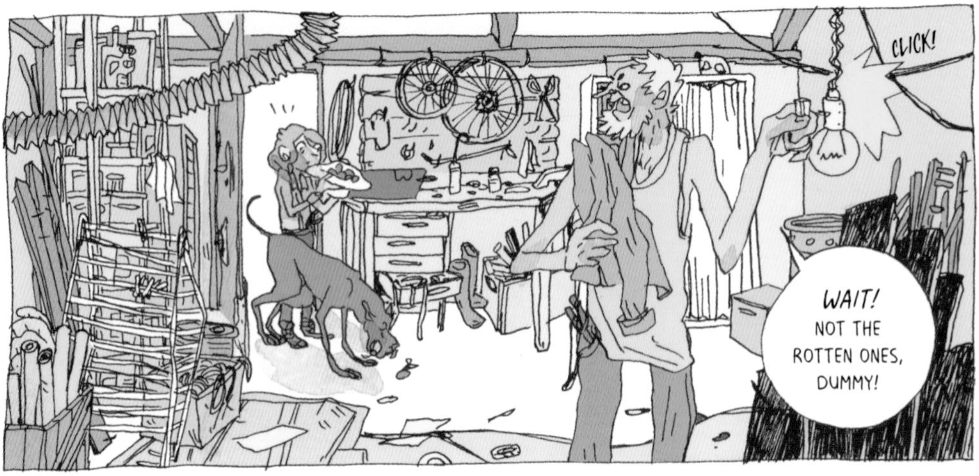
CLICK!
WAIT! NOT THE ROTTEN ONES, DUMMY!

YOU'LL MAKE MY JAM TASTE OFF...

*JEEZ!* GODDAMN MESS IN HERE!!!

*COUGH* *COUGH*

*THERE*, FOUND IT! BRING ME YOUR BRANCH.

YOU'LL SEE, KIDDO...

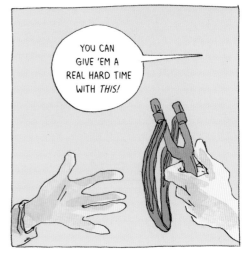

YOU CAN GIVE 'EM A REAL HARD TIME WITH *THIS!*

49

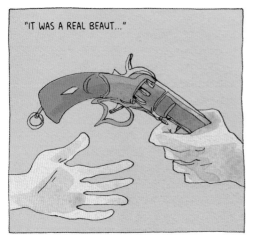

"IT WAS A REAL BEAUT..."

"...LIGHT AS A FEATHER, BUT IT LOOKED ROCK SOLID!"

YOU'RE PRETTY GOOD FOR AN OLD-TIMER!

YEAH, NOT TOO BAD...

GIVE IT HERE! I'LL SHOW Y'ALL!

LET'S HEAD OUT!

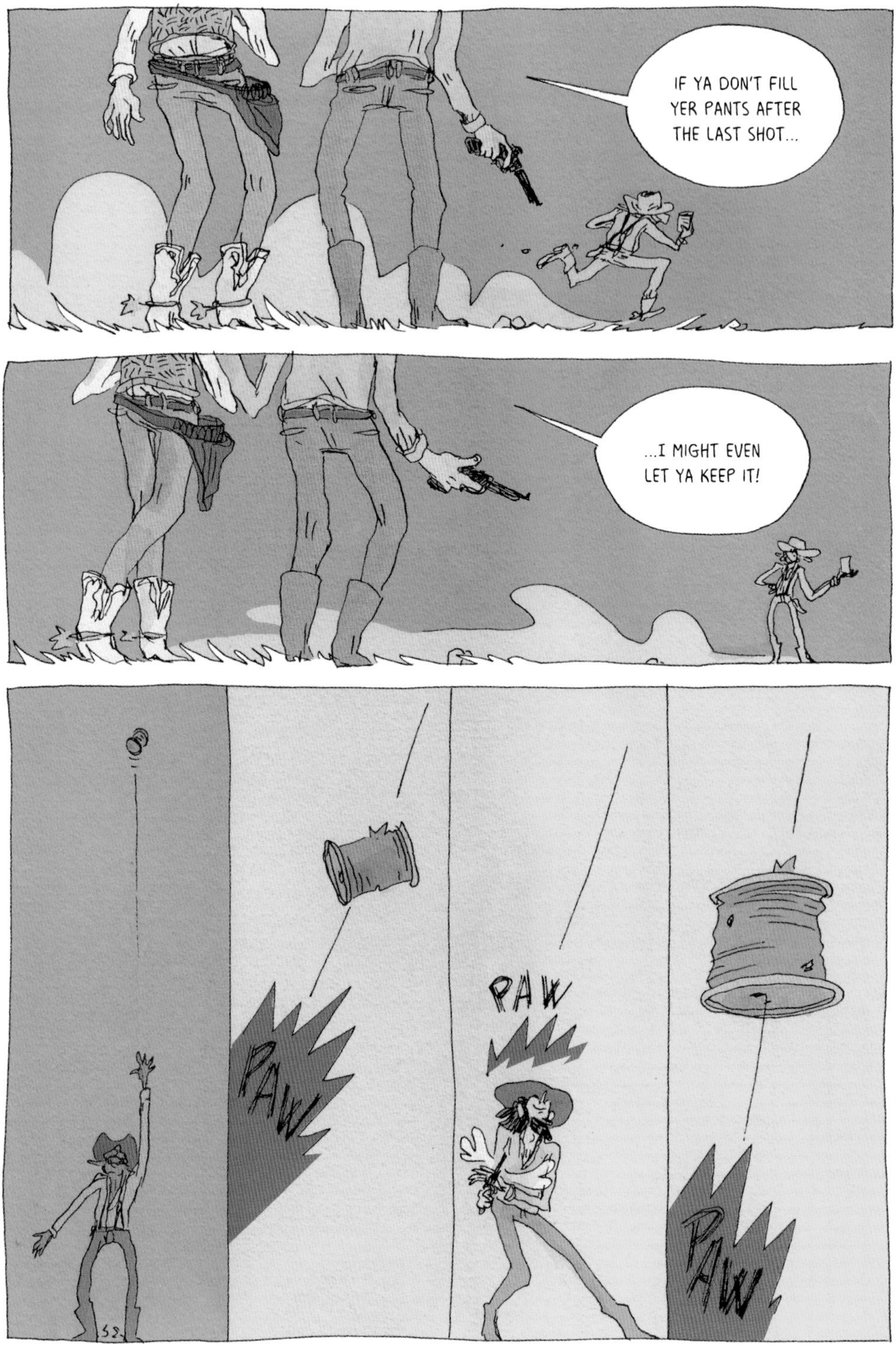
IF YA DON'T FILL YER PANTS AFTER THE LAST SHOT...
...I MIGHT EVEN LET YA KEEP IT!
PAW
PAW
PAW

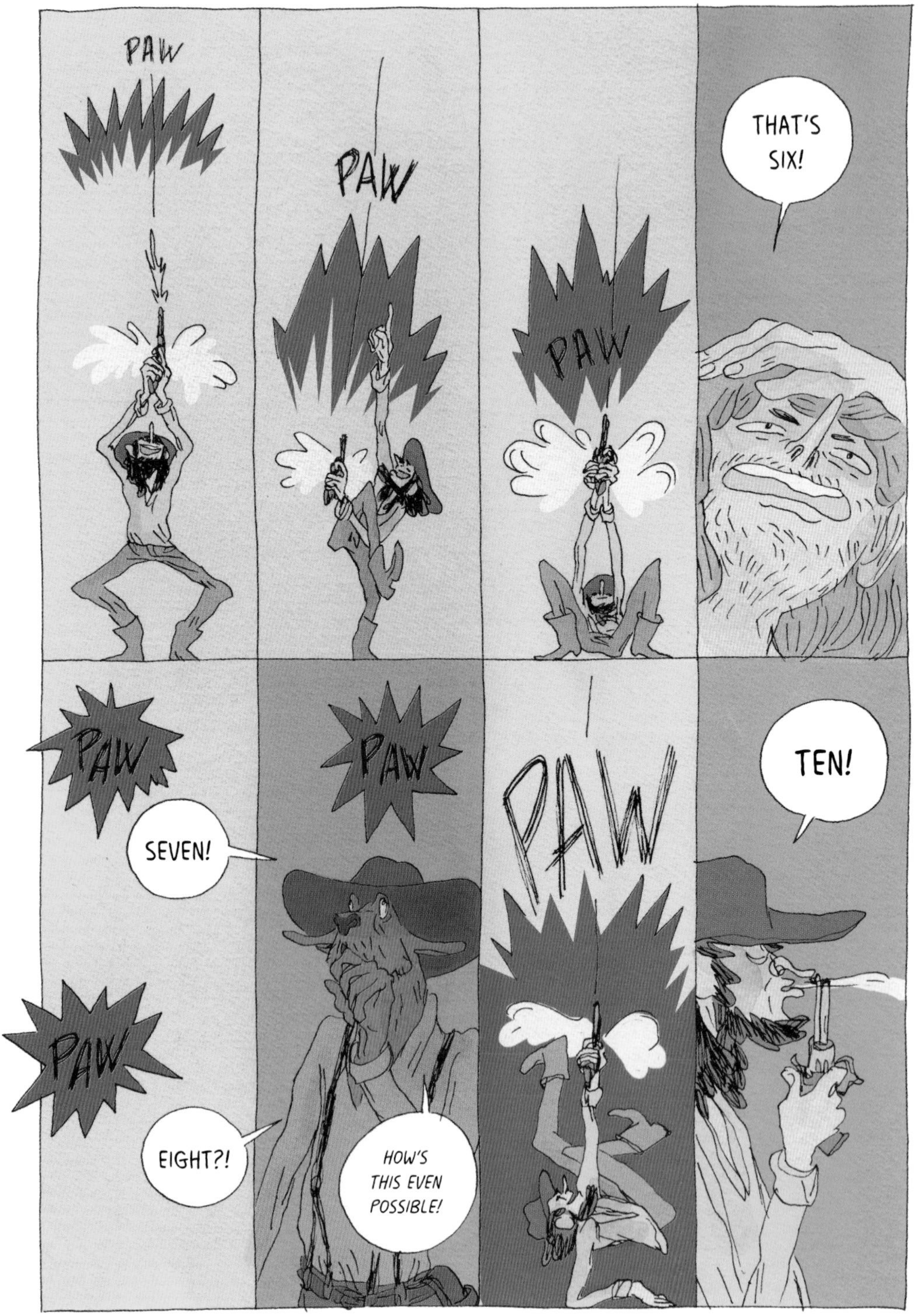
PAW
PAW
PAW
THAT'S SIX!
PAW
SEVEN!
PAW
EIGHT?!
PAW
HOW'S THIS EVEN POSSIBLE!
PAW
TEN!

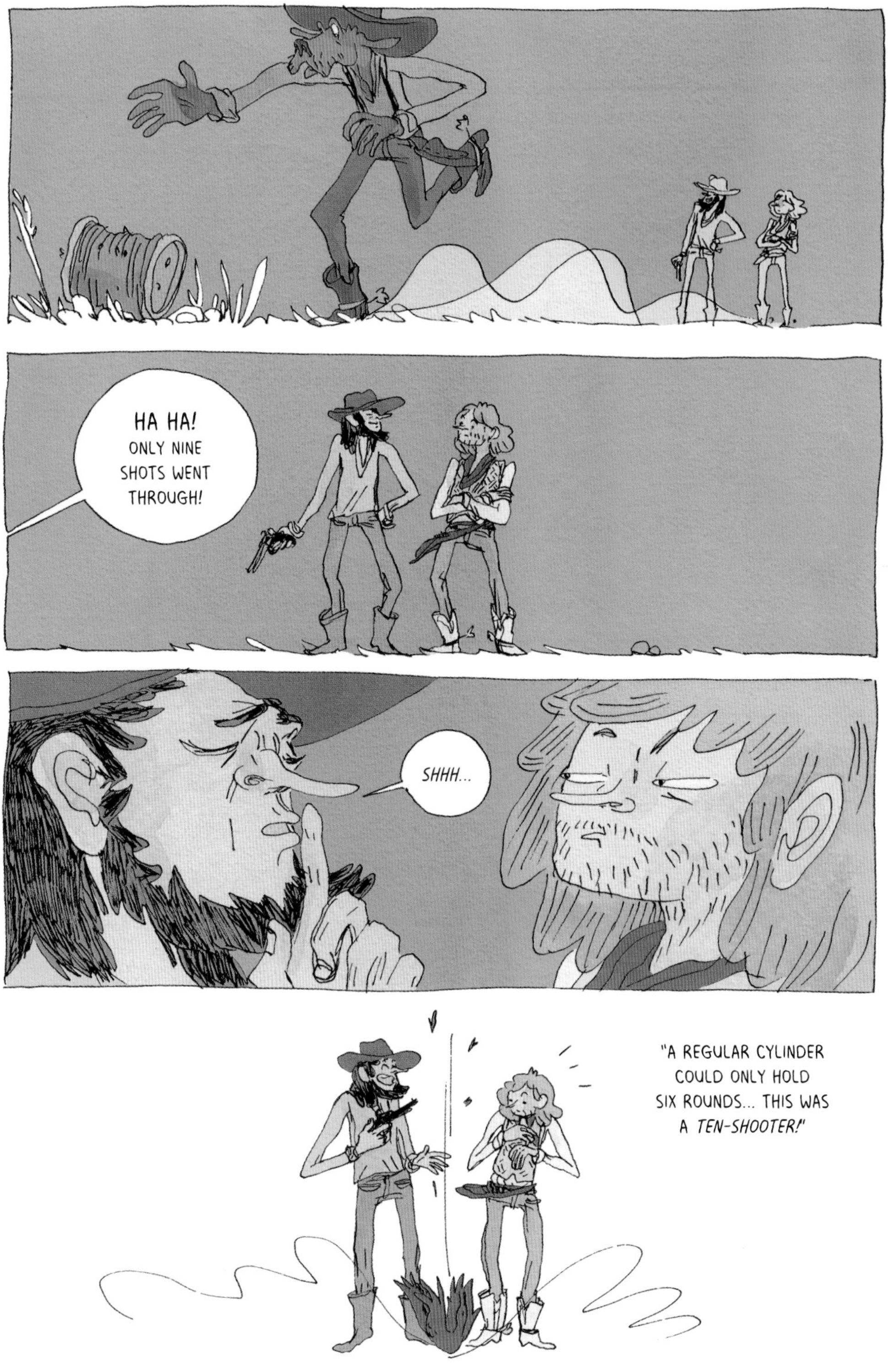
HA HA! ONLY NINE SHOTS WENT THROUGH!
SHHH...
"A REGULAR CYLINDER COULD ONLY HOLD SIX ROUNDS... THIS WAS A *TEN-SHOOTER!*"

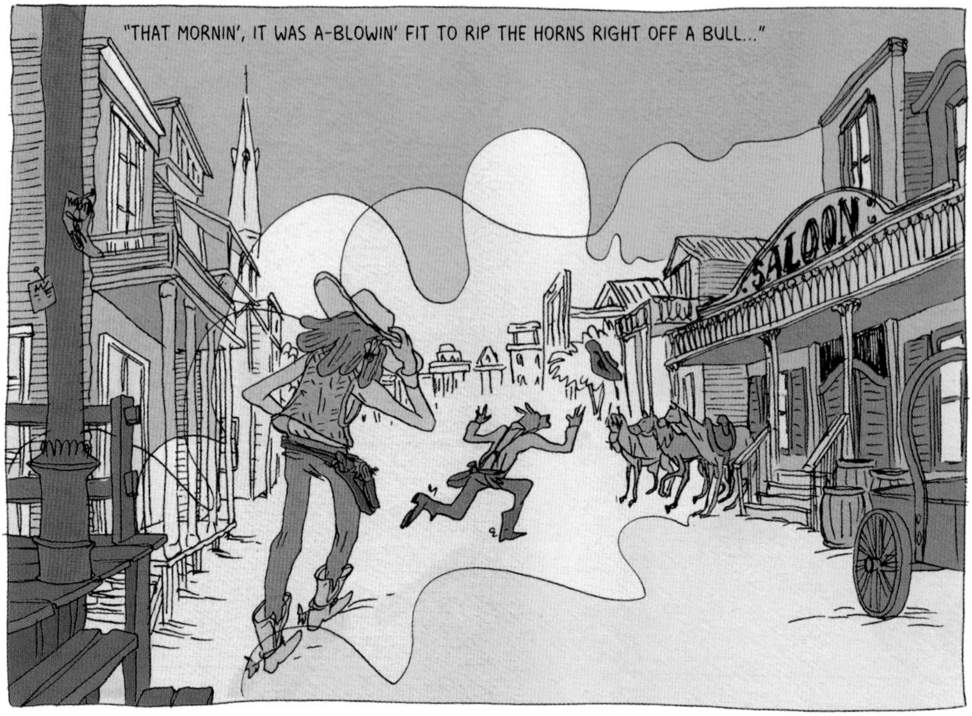
"THAT MORNIN', IT WAS A-BLOWIN' FIT TO RIP THE HORNS RIGHT OFF A BULL..."
SALOON

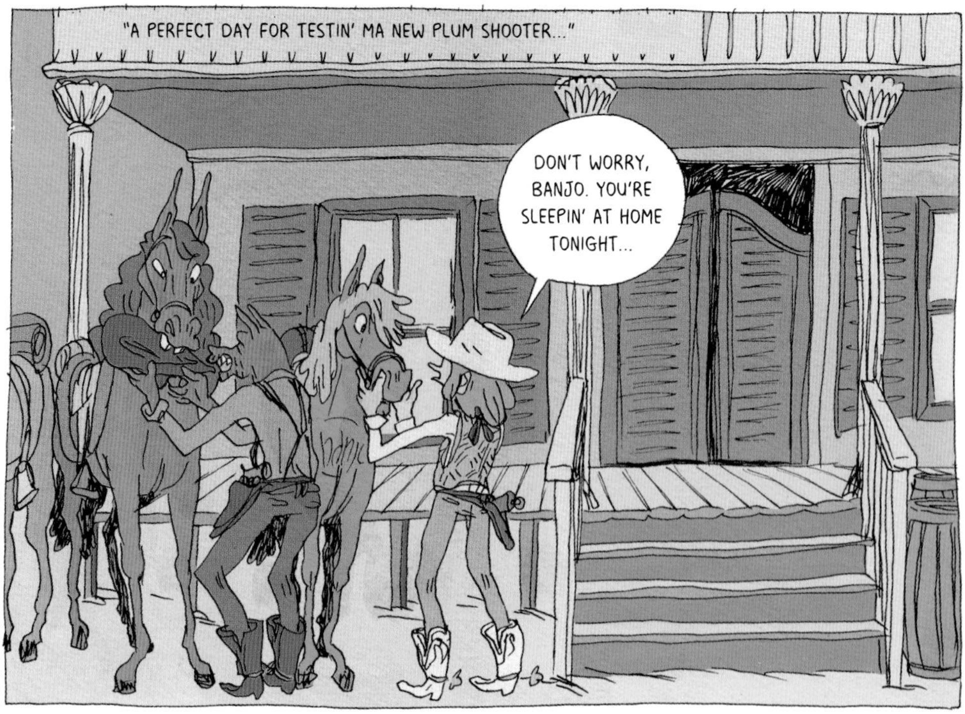
"A PERFECT DAY FOR TESTIN' MA NEW PLUM SHOOTER..."
DON'T WORRY, BANJO. YOU'RE SLEEPIN' AT HOME TONIGHT...

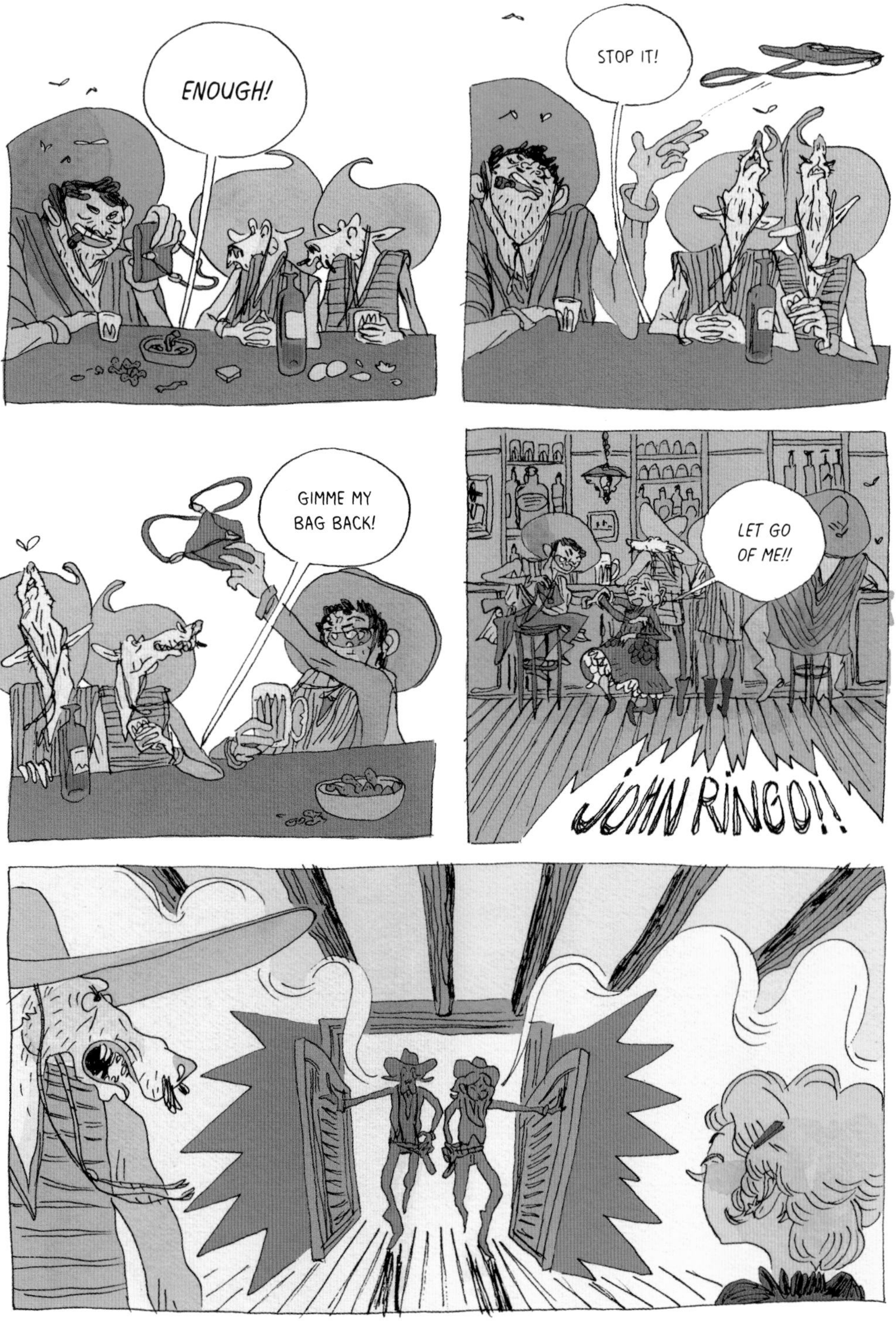
ENOUGH!
STOP IT!
GIMME MY BAG BACK!
LET GO OF ME!!
JOHN RINGO!!

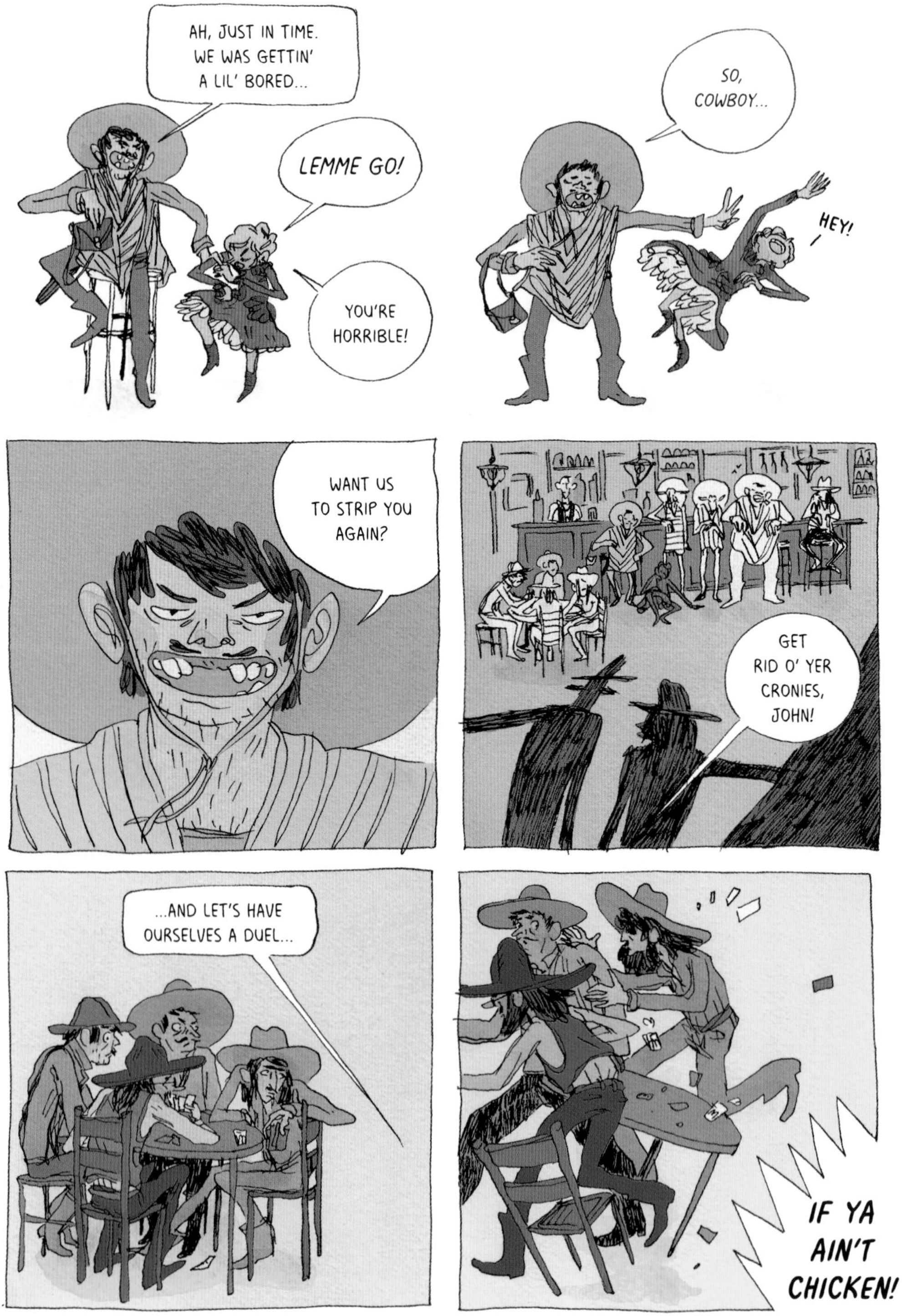
AH, JUST IN TIME. WE WAS GETTIN' A LIL' BORED...
LEMME GO!
YOU'RE HORRIBLE!
SO, COWBOY...
HEY!
WANT US TO STRIP YOU AGAIN?
GET RID O' YER CRONIES, JOHN!
...AND LET'S HAVE OURSELVES A DUEL...
IF YA AIN'T CHICKEN!

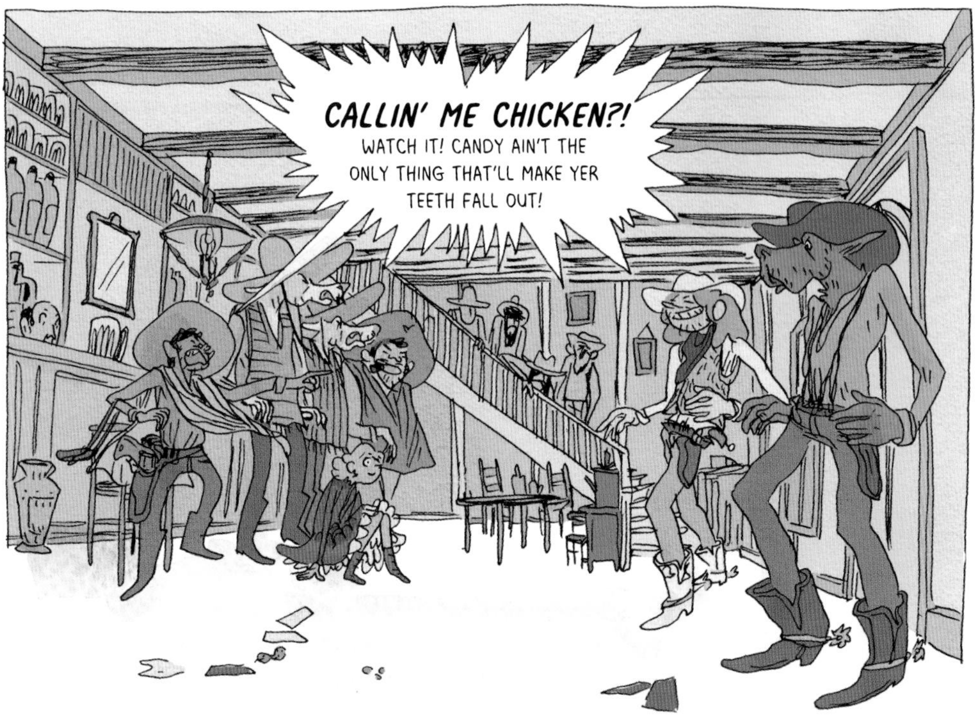
CALLIN' ME CHICKEN?!
WATCH IT! CANDY AIN'T THE ONLY THING THAT'LL MAKE YER TEETH FALL OUT!

"I'D NEVER EVEN GLIMPSED JOHN'S GUN, AND I WAS ABOUT TO FIND OUT WHY!"

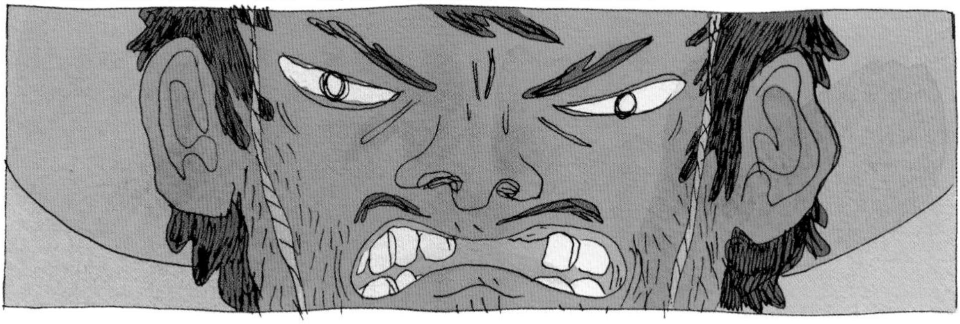

"HIS SHOOTER WAS SO HEAVY THAT, TO SAVE TIME, HE FIRED WITHOUT DRAWIN' IT FROM THE HOLSTER..."

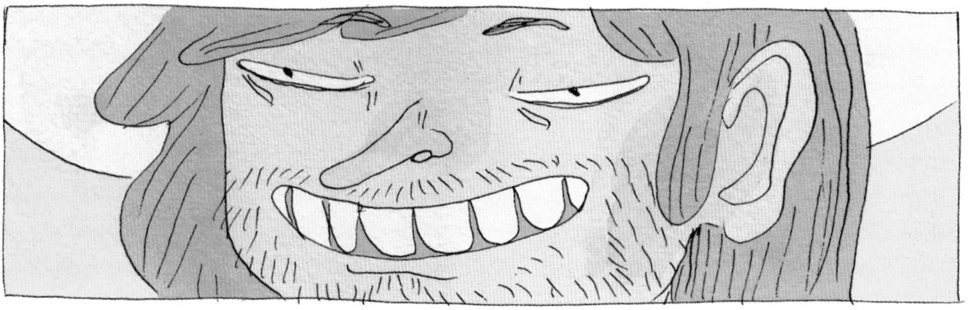

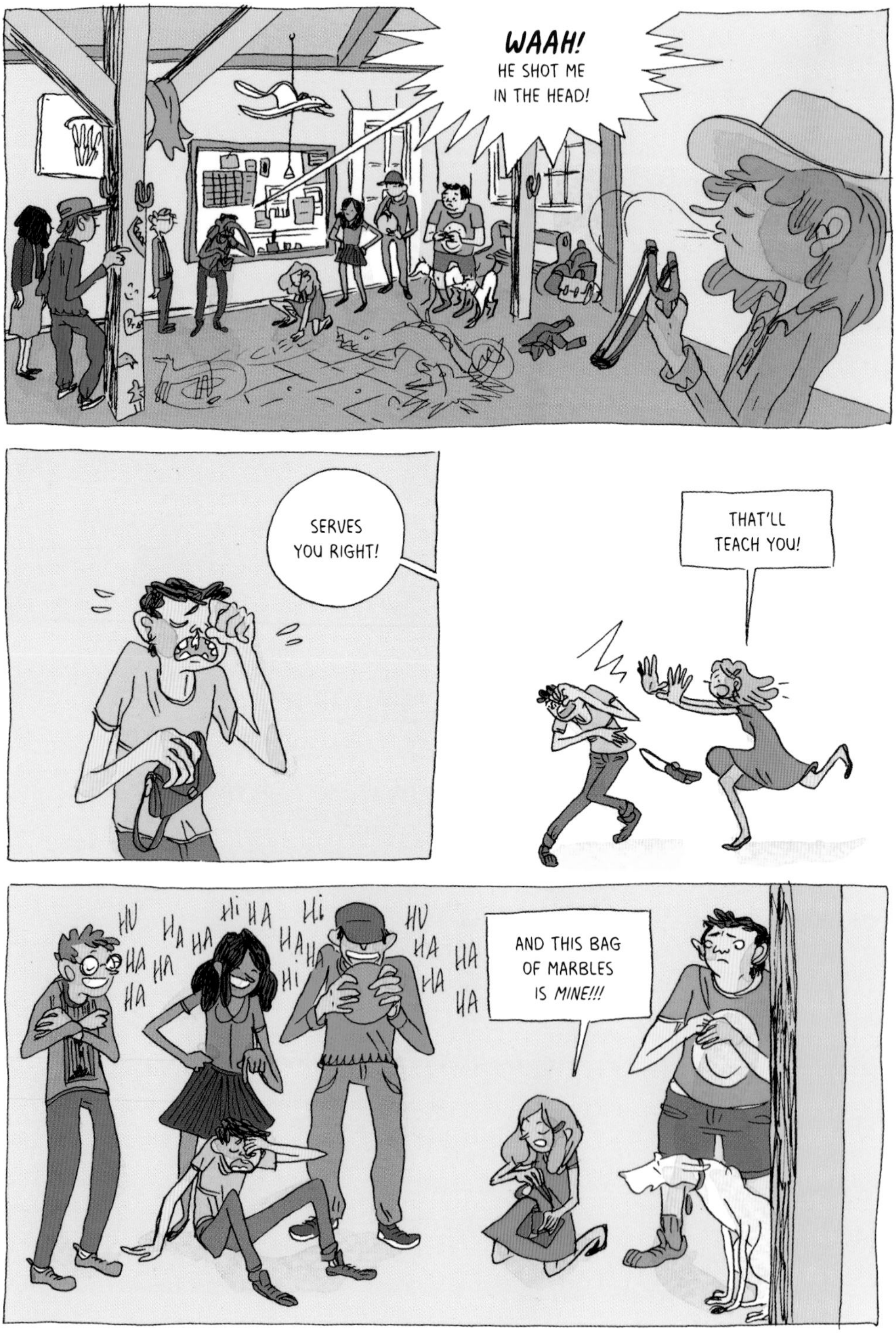
WAAH!
HE SHOT ME IN THE HEAD!
SERVES YOU RIGHT!
THAT'LL TEACH YOU!
HU HA HA HA HA HA HA Hi HA Hi HA HA Hi HA HU HA HA HA HA
AND THIS BAG OF MARBLES IS MINE!!!

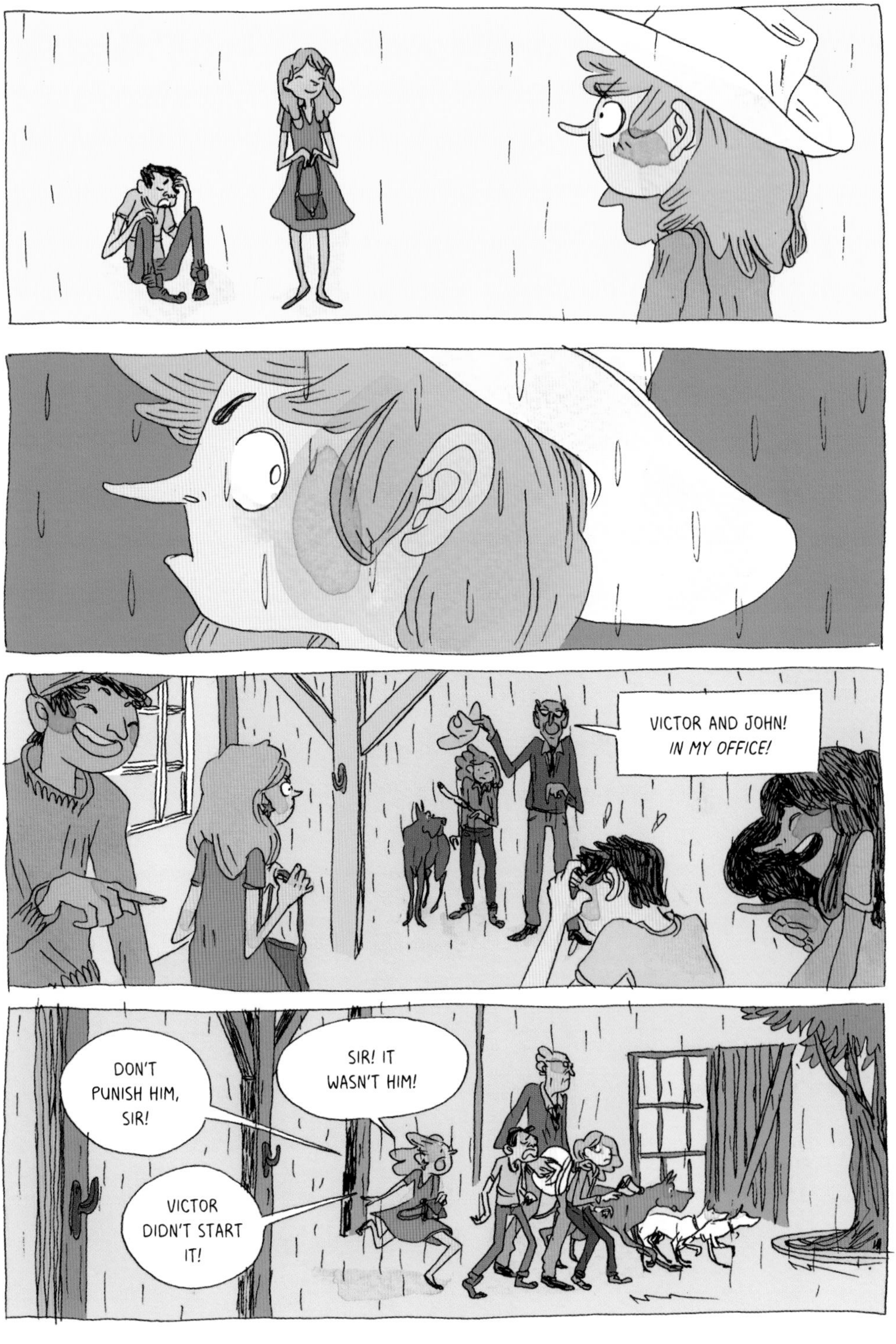

VICTOR AND JOHN! IN MY OFFICE!
DON'T PUNISH HIM, SIR!
SIR! IT WASN'T HIM!
VICTOR DIDN'T START IT!

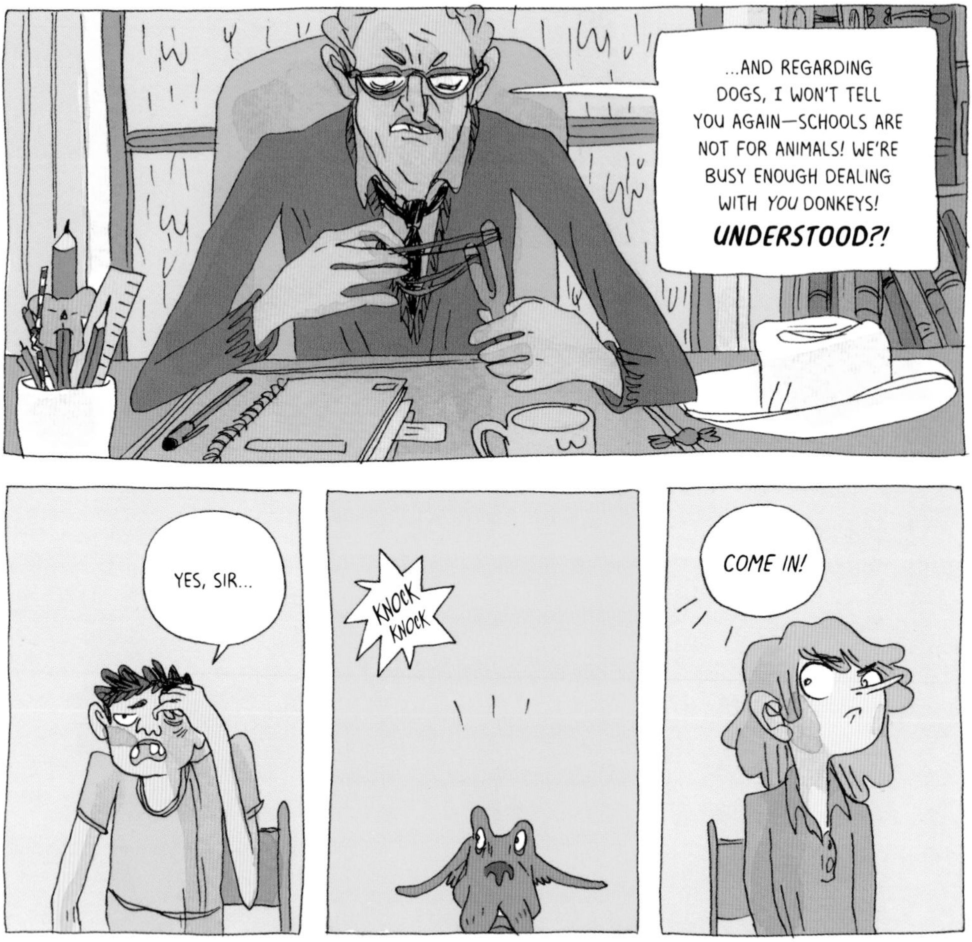
...AND REGARDING DOGS, I WON'T TELL YOU AGAIN—SCHOOLS ARE NOT FOR ANIMALS! WE'RE BUSY ENOUGH DEALING WITH *YOU* DONKEYS! **UNDERSTOOD?!**
YES, SIR...
KNOCK KNOCK
COME IN!

"GOOD THING ABOUT RAIN IS THAT SOME FOLKS GET TO HAVE A SHOWER FOR ONCE!"

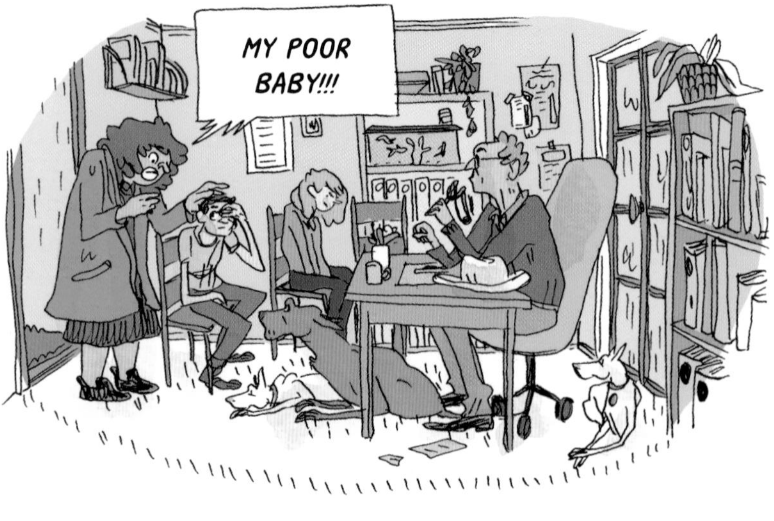
MY POOR BABY!!!

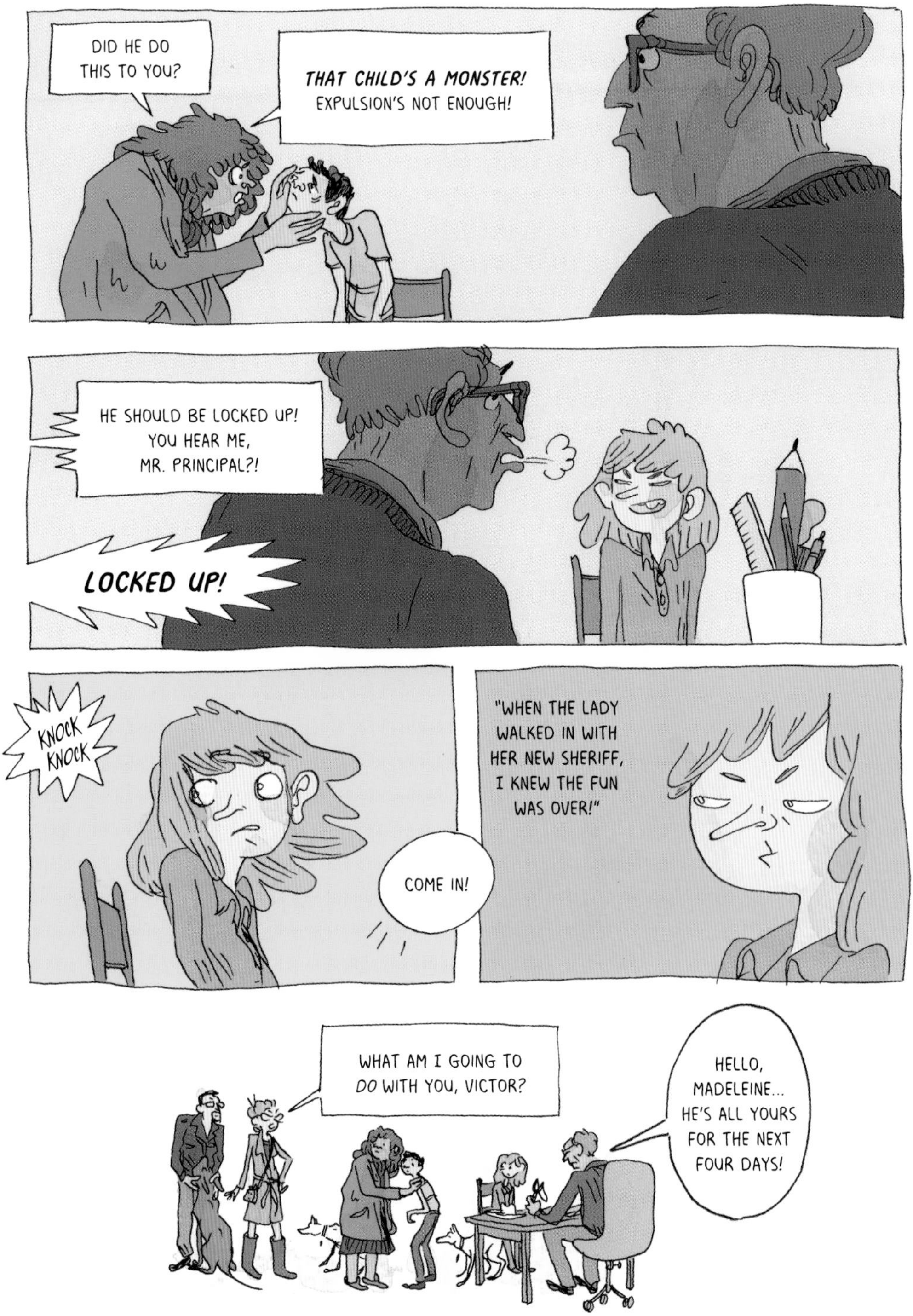

DID HE DO THIS TO YOU?
*THAT CHILD'S A MONSTER!* EXPULSION'S NOT ENOUGH!
HE SHOULD BE LOCKED UP! YOU HEAR ME, MR. PRINCIPAL?!
*LOCKED UP!*
KNOCK KNOCK
COME IN!
"WHEN THE LADY WALKED IN WITH HER NEW SHERIFF, I KNEW THE FUN WAS OVER!"
WHAT AM I GOING TO *DO* WITH YOU, VICTOR?
HELLO, MADELEINE... HE'S ALL YOURS FOR THE NEXT FOUR DAYS!

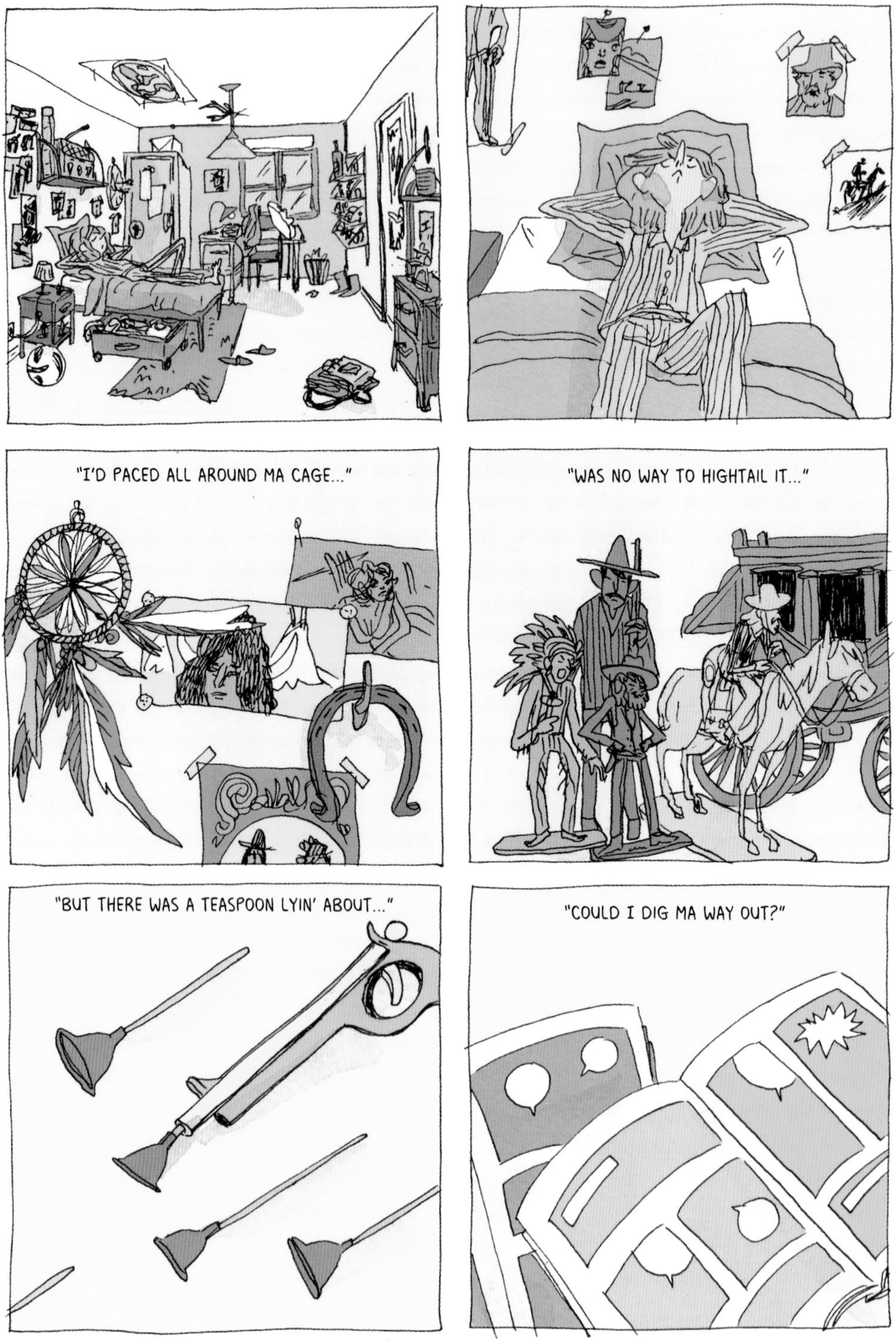
"I'D PACED ALL AROUND MA CAGE..."
"WAS NO WAY TO HIGHTAIL IT..."
"BUT THERE WAS A TEASPOON LYIN' ABOUT..."
"COULD I DIG MA WAY OUT?"

"IN THE END, THE FLOOR WAS TOO HARD!"

"STILL NO NEWS FROM BROWN, O' COURSE..."

"NOR THE DOG-FACED FELLER..."

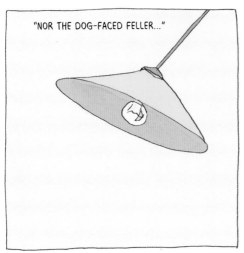

63

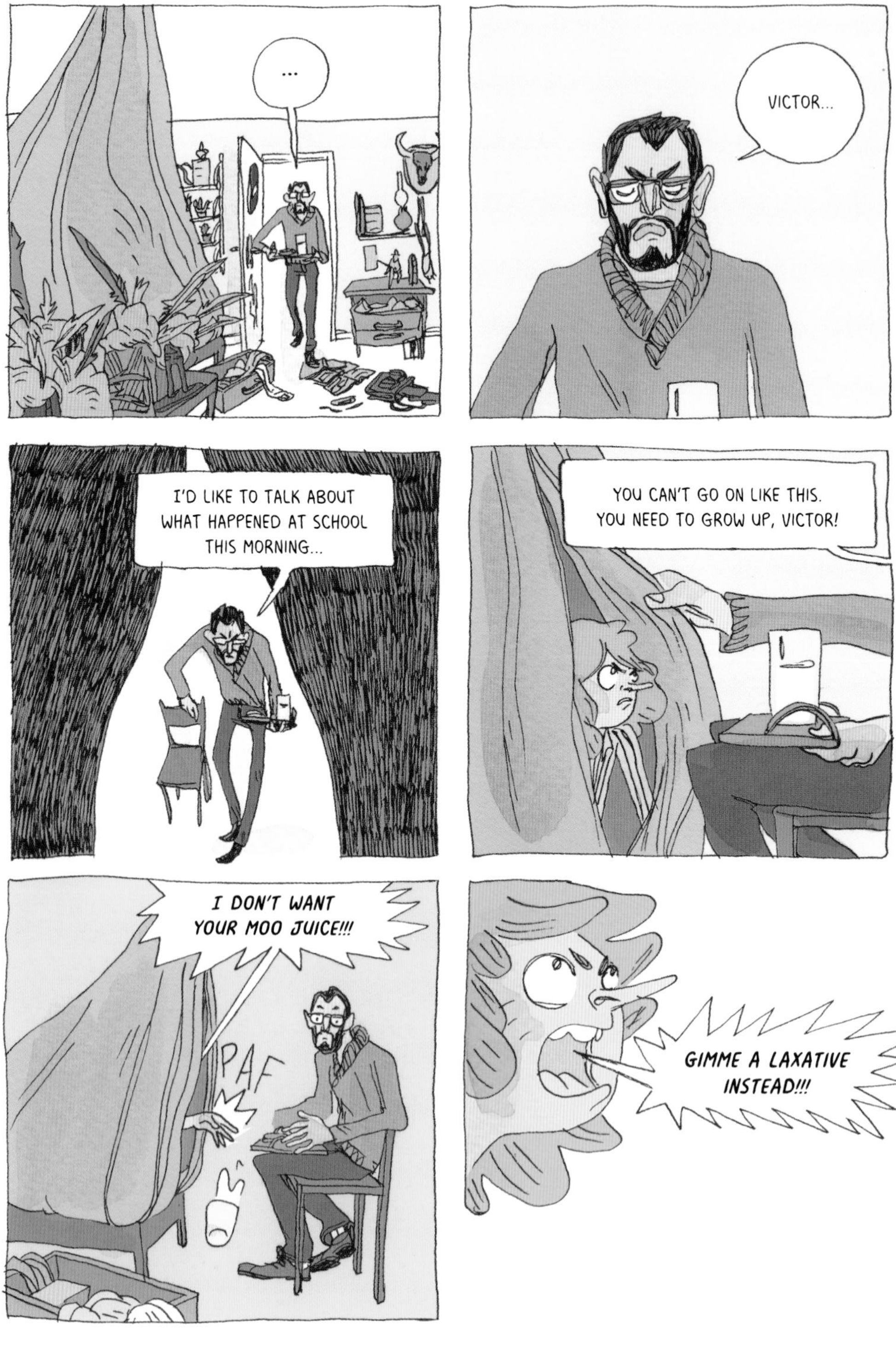
...
VICTOR...
I'D LIKE TO TALK ABOUT WHAT HAPPENED AT SCHOOL THIS MORNING...
YOU CAN'T GO ON LIKE THIS. YOU NEED TO GROW UP, VICTOR!
I DON'T WANT YOUR MOO JUICE!!!
PAF
GIMME A LAXATIVE INSTEAD!!!

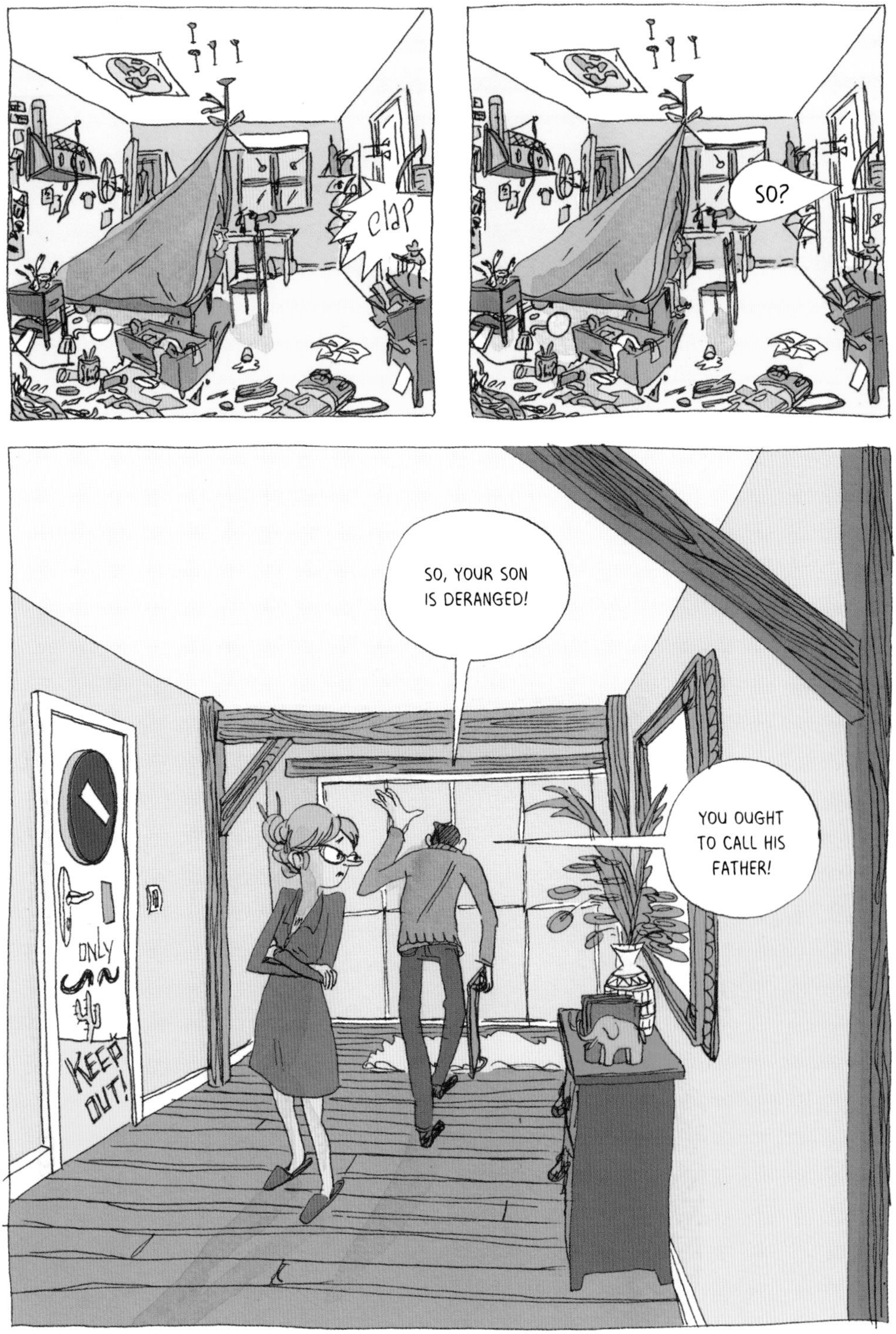
CLAP
SO?
SO, YOUR SON IS DERANGED!
YOU OUGHT TO CALL HIS FATHER!
ONLY
KEEP OUT!

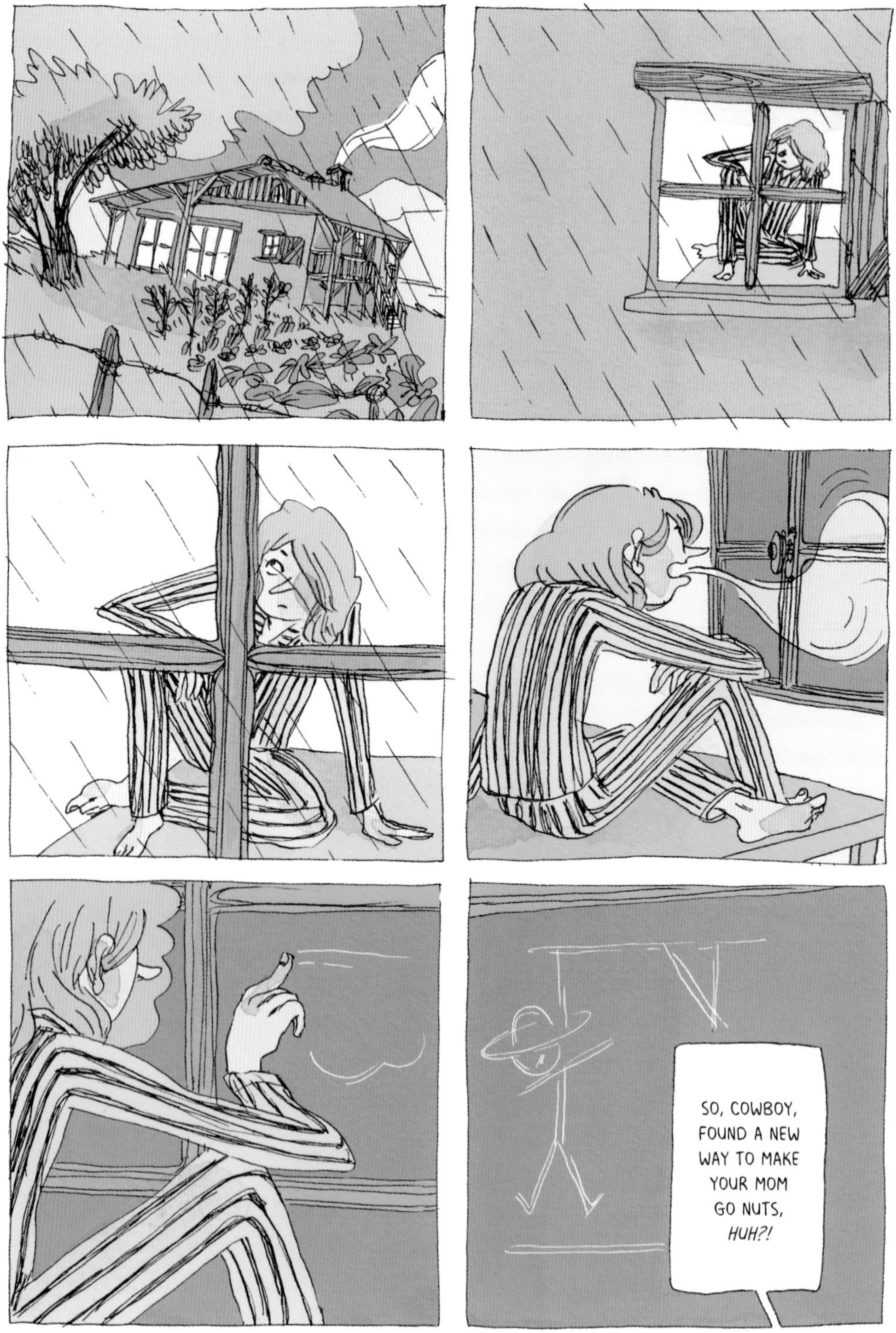
SO, COWBOY, FOUND A NEW WAY TO MAKE YOUR MOM GO NUTS, *HUH?!*

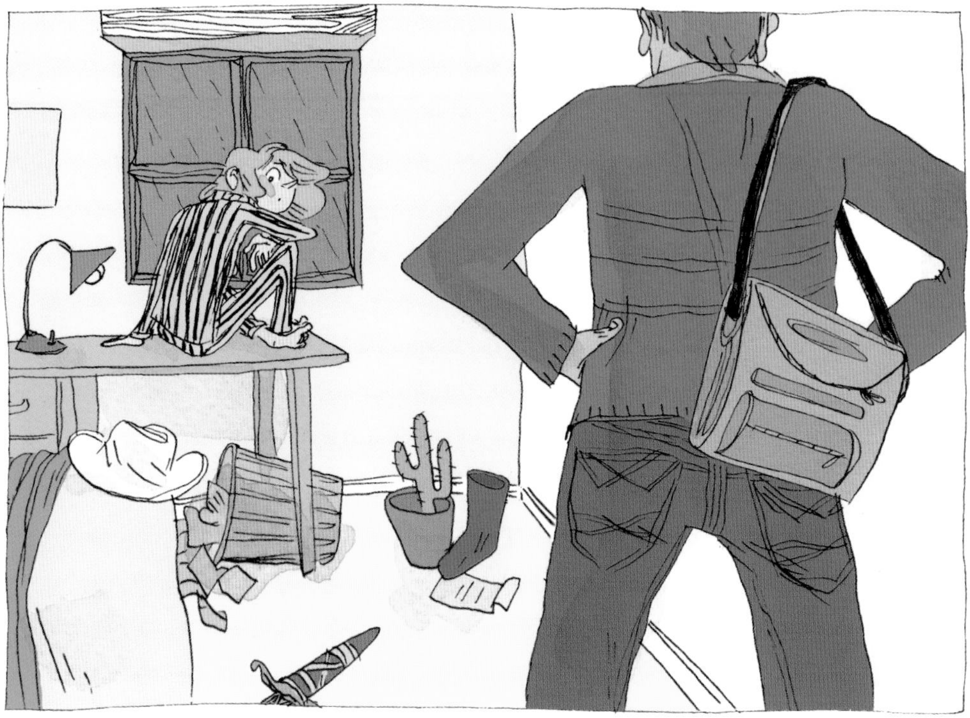

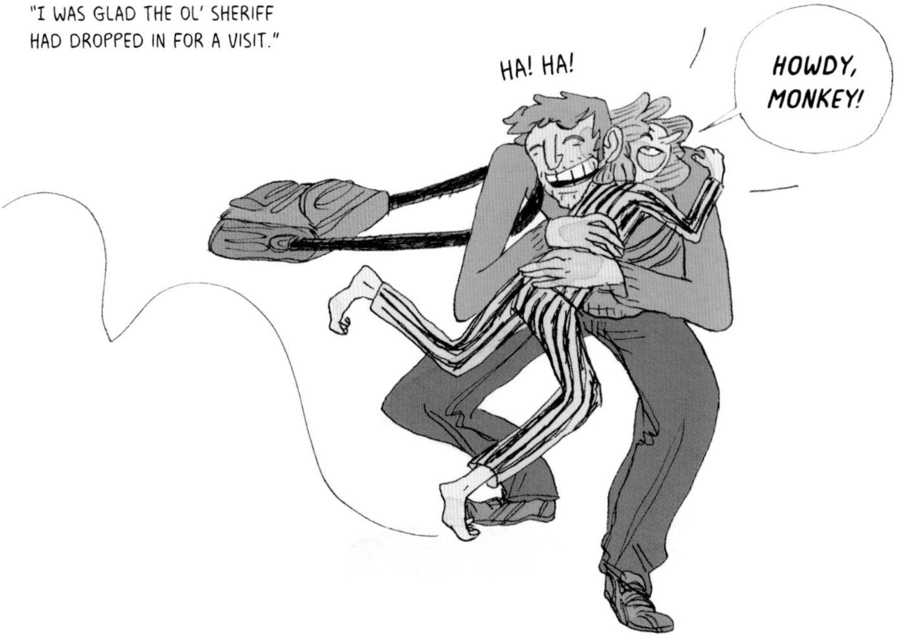
"I WAS GLAD THE OL' SHERIFF
HAD DROPPED IN FOR A VISIT."
HA! HA!
HOWDY,
MONKEY!

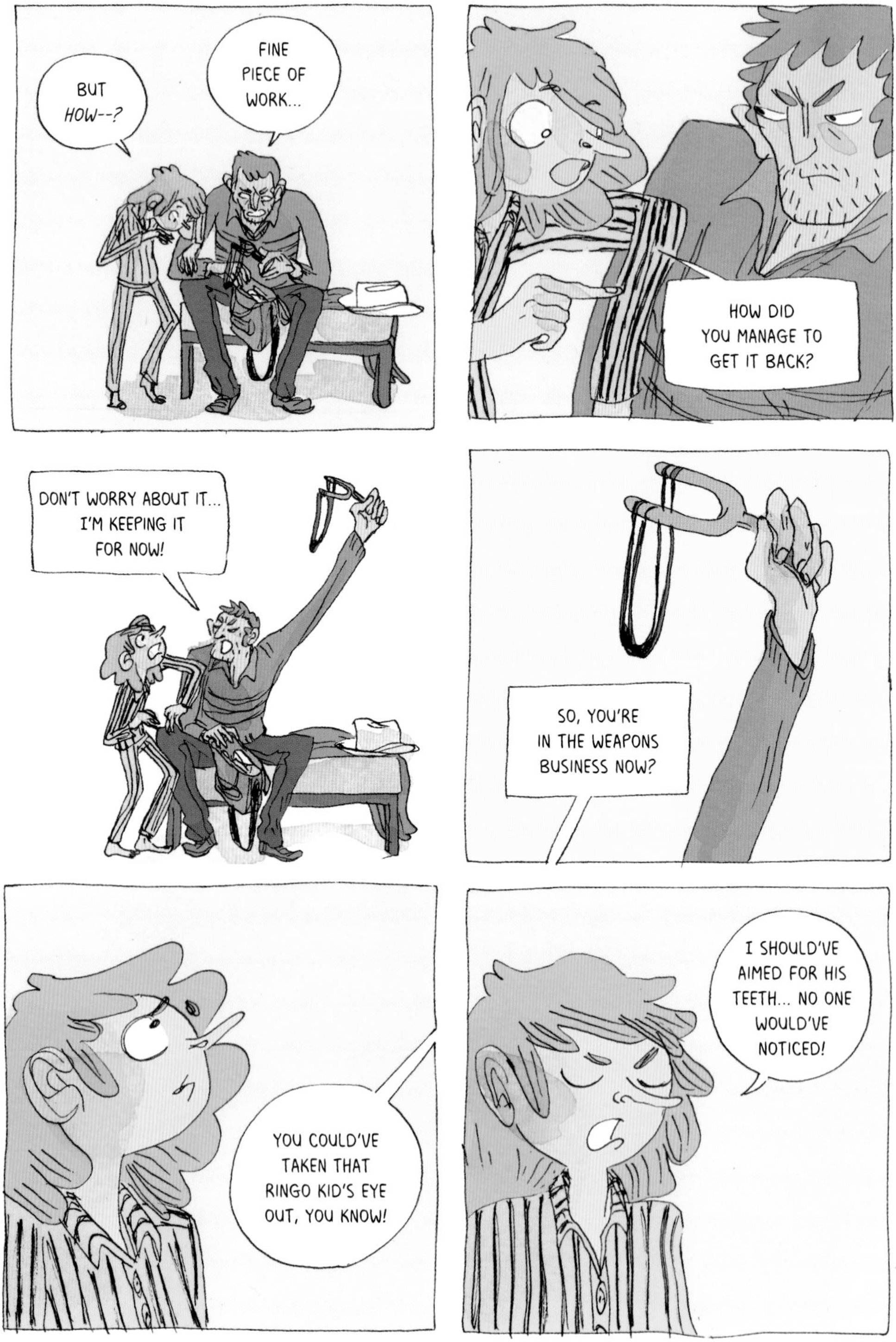
FINE PIECE OF WORK...
BUT HOW--?
HOW DID YOU MANAGE TO GET IT BACK?
DON'T WORRY ABOUT IT... I'M KEEPING IT FOR NOW!
SO, YOU'RE IN THE WEAPONS BUSINESS NOW?
YOU COULD'VE TAKEN THAT RINGO KID'S EYE OUT, YOU KNOW!
I SHOULD'VE AIMED FOR HIS TEETH... NO ONE WOULD'VE NOTICED!

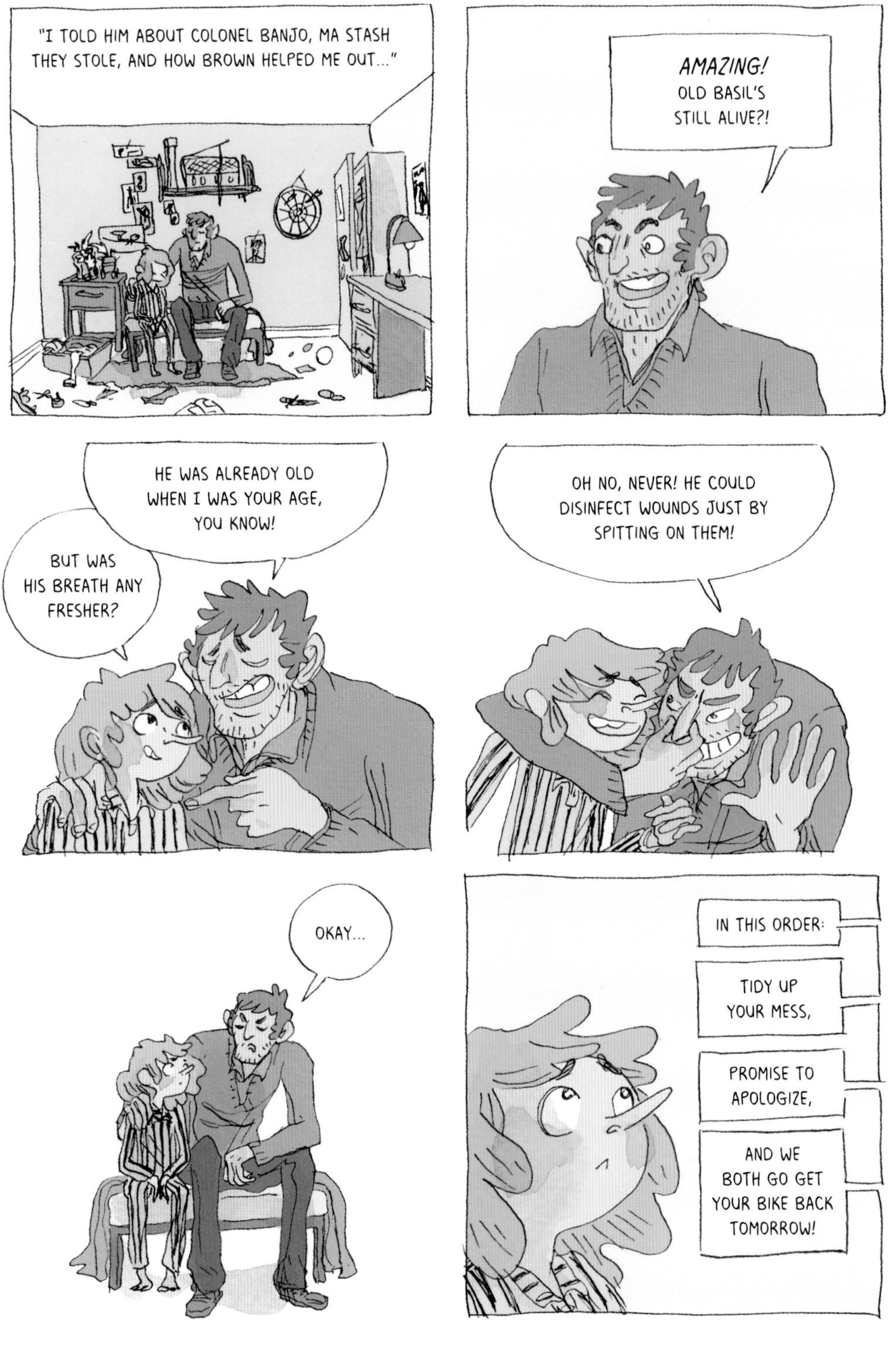
"I TOLD HIM ABOUT COLONEL BANJO, MA STASH THEY STOLE, AND HOW BROWN HELPED ME OUT..."
AMAZING! OLD BASIL'S STILL ALIVE?!
HE WAS ALREADY OLD WHEN I WAS YOUR AGE, YOU KNOW!
BUT WAS HIS BREATH ANY FRESHER?
OH NO, NEVER! HE COULD DISINFECT WOUNDS JUST BY SPITTING ON THEM!
OKAY...
IN THIS ORDER:
TIDY UP YOUR MESS,
PROMISE TO APOLOGIZE,
AND WE BOTH GO GET YOUR BIKE BACK TOMORROW!

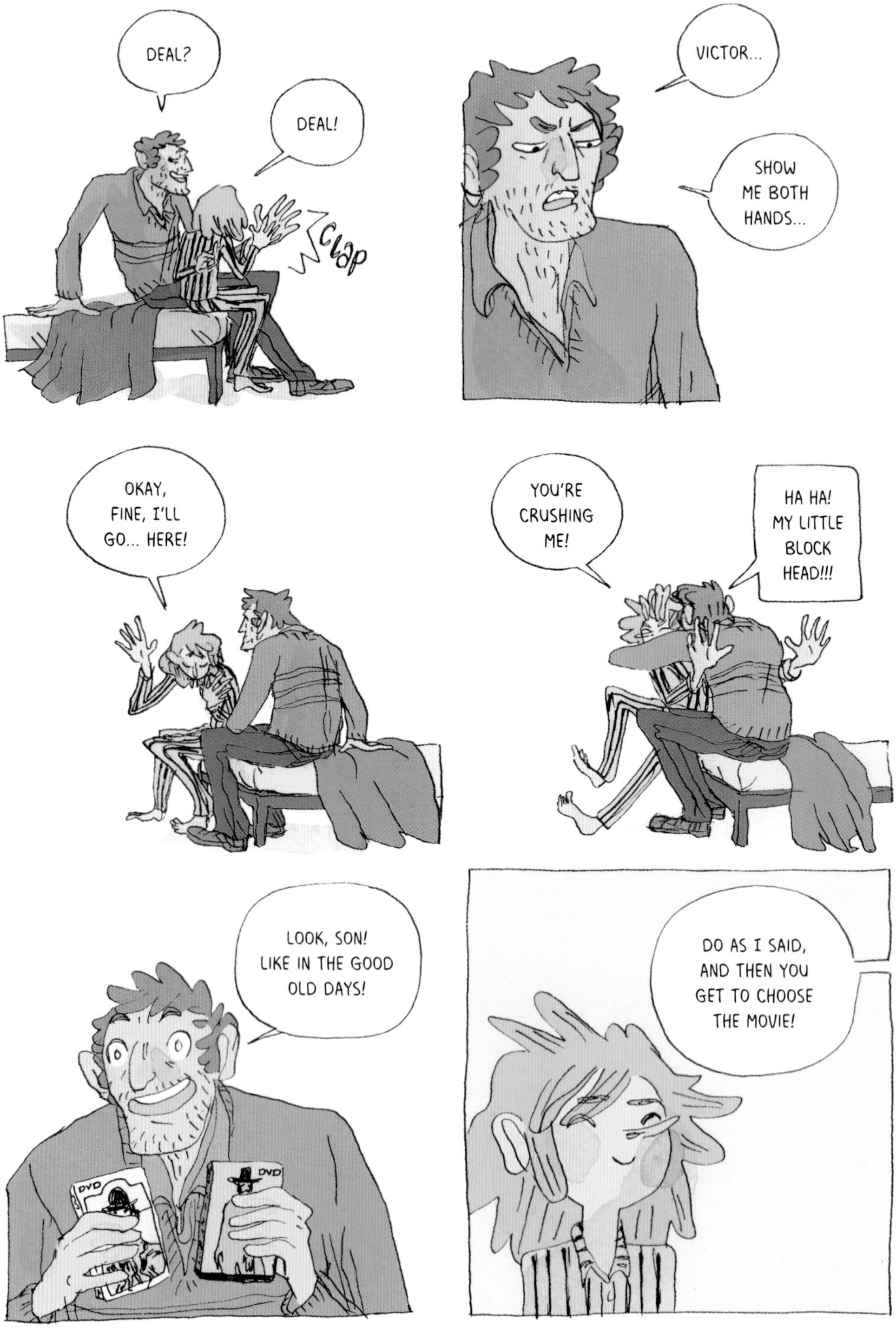
DEAL?
DEAL!
CLAP
VICTOR...
SHOW ME BOTH HANDS...
OKAY, FINE, I'LL GO... HERE!
YOU'RE CRUSHING ME!
HA HA! MY LITTLE BLOCK HEAD!!!
LOOK, SON! LIKE IN THE GOOD OLD DAYS!
DVD
DVD
DO AS I SAID, AND THEN YOU GET TO CHOOSE THE MOVIE!

YOU KNOW YOU GOT A FACE PRETTY ENOUGH TO BE WORTH $2000!

WE SHOULD GO AND SEE OLD BASIL TOO...

YEAH, BUT YOU DON'T LOOK LIKE THE ONE WHO'LL COLLECT IT...

...I'M NOT HAPPY THAT HE GOES 'ROUND FLEECING KIDS AT POKER!

"I'D BEEN COLLUDIN' WITH A RATTLESNAKE! HIS CONNIVIN' PUT ME OFF MA GUARD, AND NOW BROWN WAS FACIN' SERIOUS TROUBLE COS O' ME!"

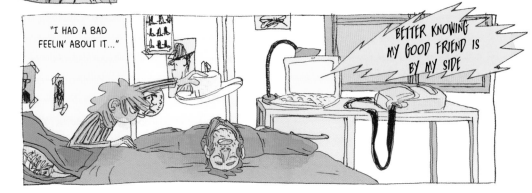

"I HAD A BAD FEELIN' ABOUT IT..."

BETTER KNOWING MY GOOD FRIEND IS BY MY SIDE

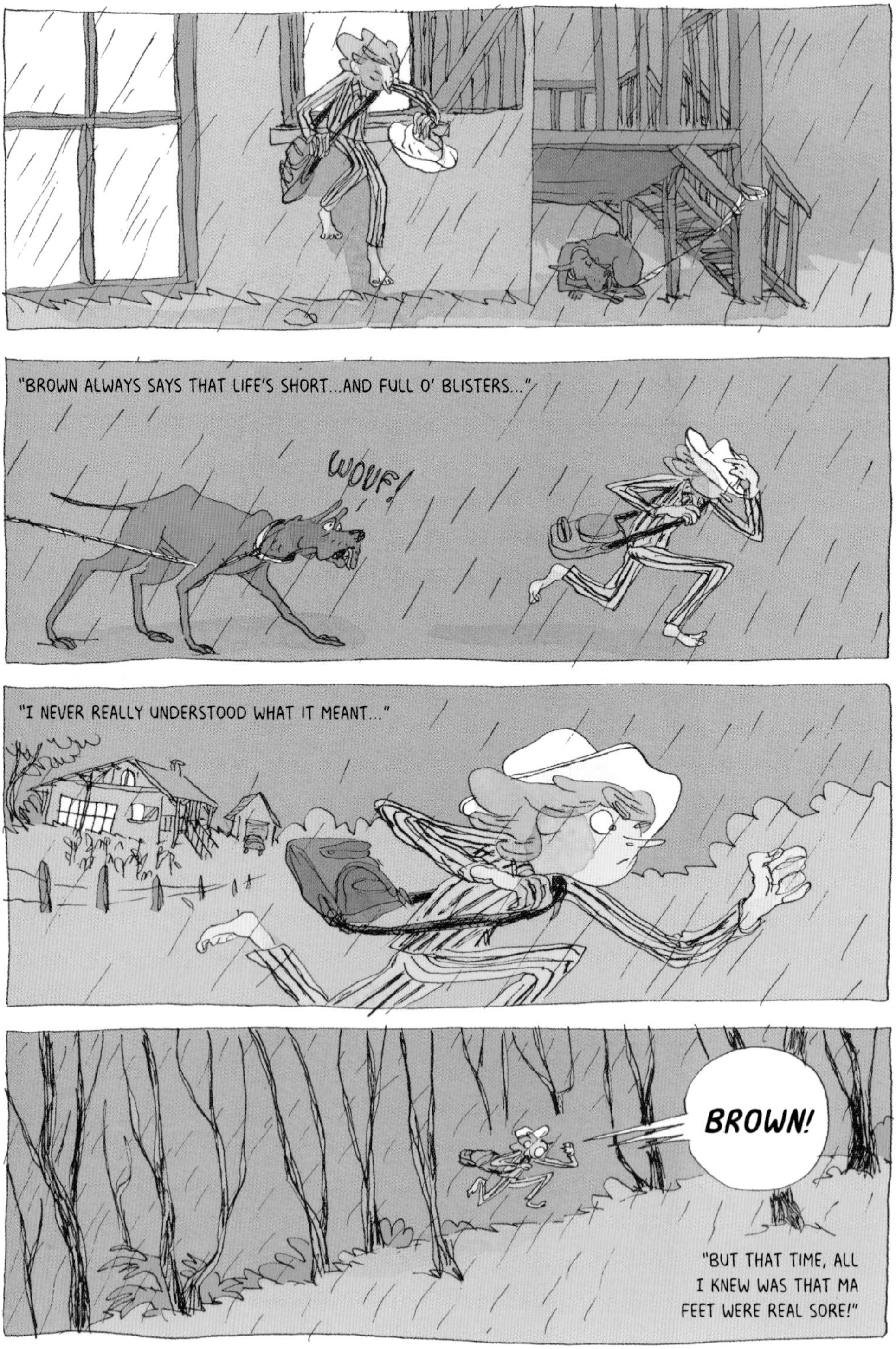
"BROWN ALWAYS SAYS THAT LIFE'S SHORT...AND FULL O' BLISTERS..."
WOUF!
"I NEVER REALLY UNDERSTOOD WHAT IT MEANT..."
BROWN!
"BUT THAT TIME, ALL I KNEW WAS THAT MA FEET WERE REAL SORE!"

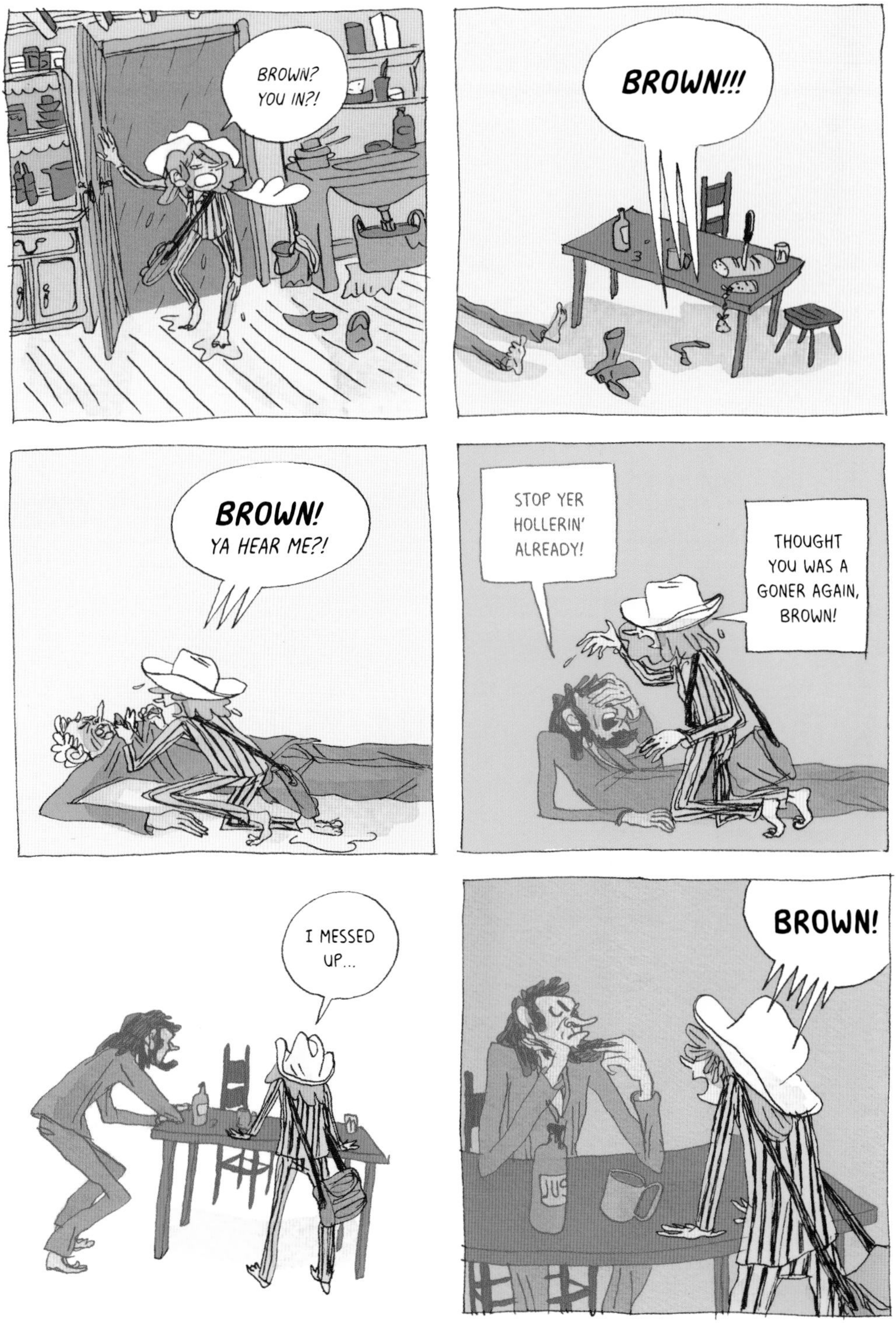
BROWN? YOU IN?!
BROWN!!!
BROWN! YA HEAR ME?!
STOP YER HOLLERIN' ALREADY!
THOUGHT YOU WAS A GONER AGAIN, BROWN!
I MESSED UP...
BROWN!

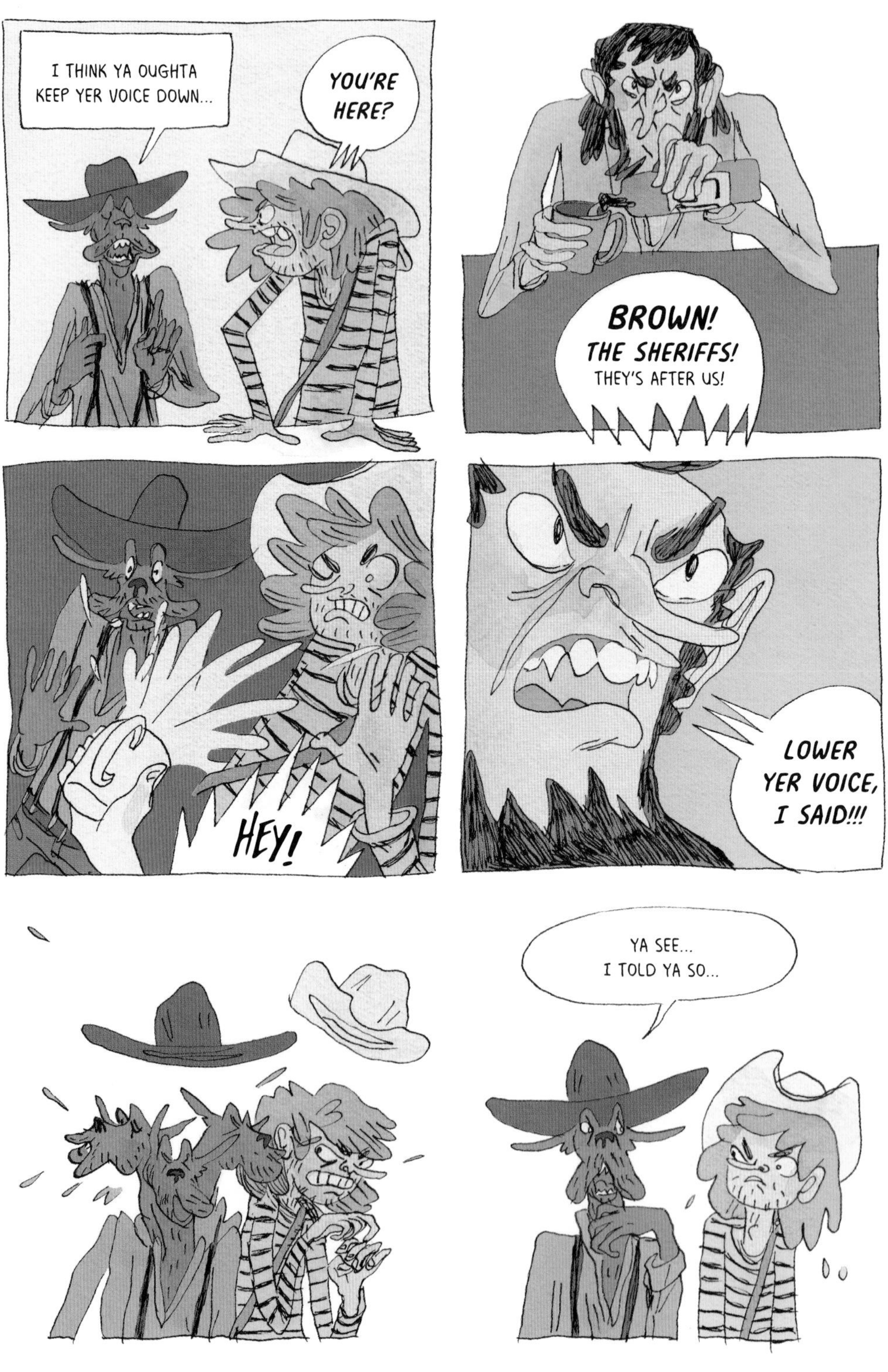
I THINK YA OUGHTA KEEP YER VOICE DOWN...
YOU'RE HERE?
BROWN! THE SHERIFFS! THEY'S AFTER US!
HEY!
LOWER YER VOICE, I SAID!!!
YA SEE... I TOLD YA SO...

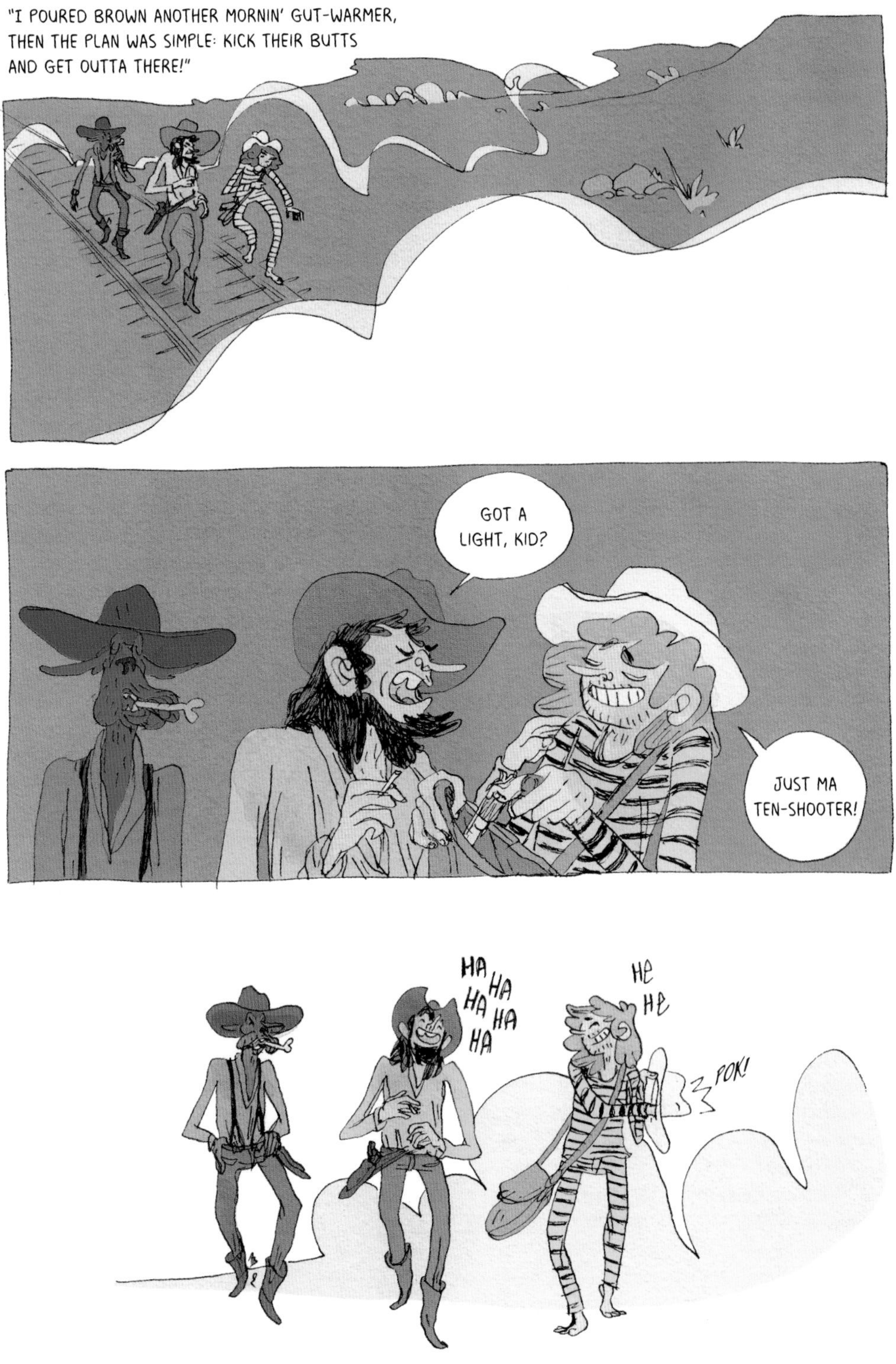
"I POURED BROWN ANOTHER MORNIN' GUT-WARMER, THEN THE PLAN WAS SIMPLE: KICK THEIR BUTTS AND GET OUTTA THERE!"
GOT A LIGHT, KID?
JUST MA TEN-SHOOTER!
HA HA HA HA HA
HE HE
POK!

"I LED THE POSSE TO THE RINGOS' HIDEOUT."

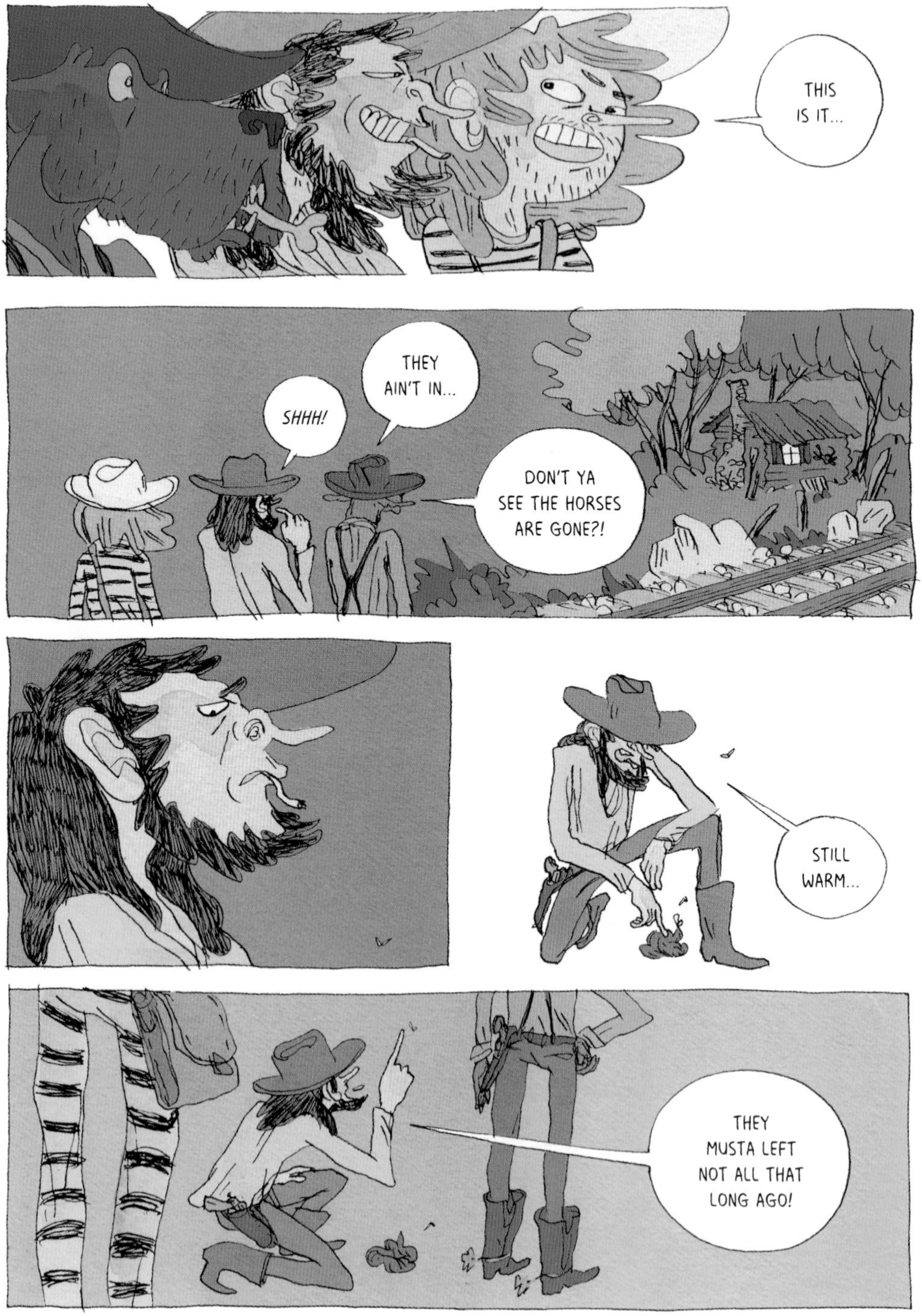
THIS IS IT...
THEY AIN'T IN...
SHHH!
DON'T YA SEE THE HORSES ARE GONE?!
STILL WARM...
THEY MUSTA LEFT NOT ALL THAT LONG AGO!

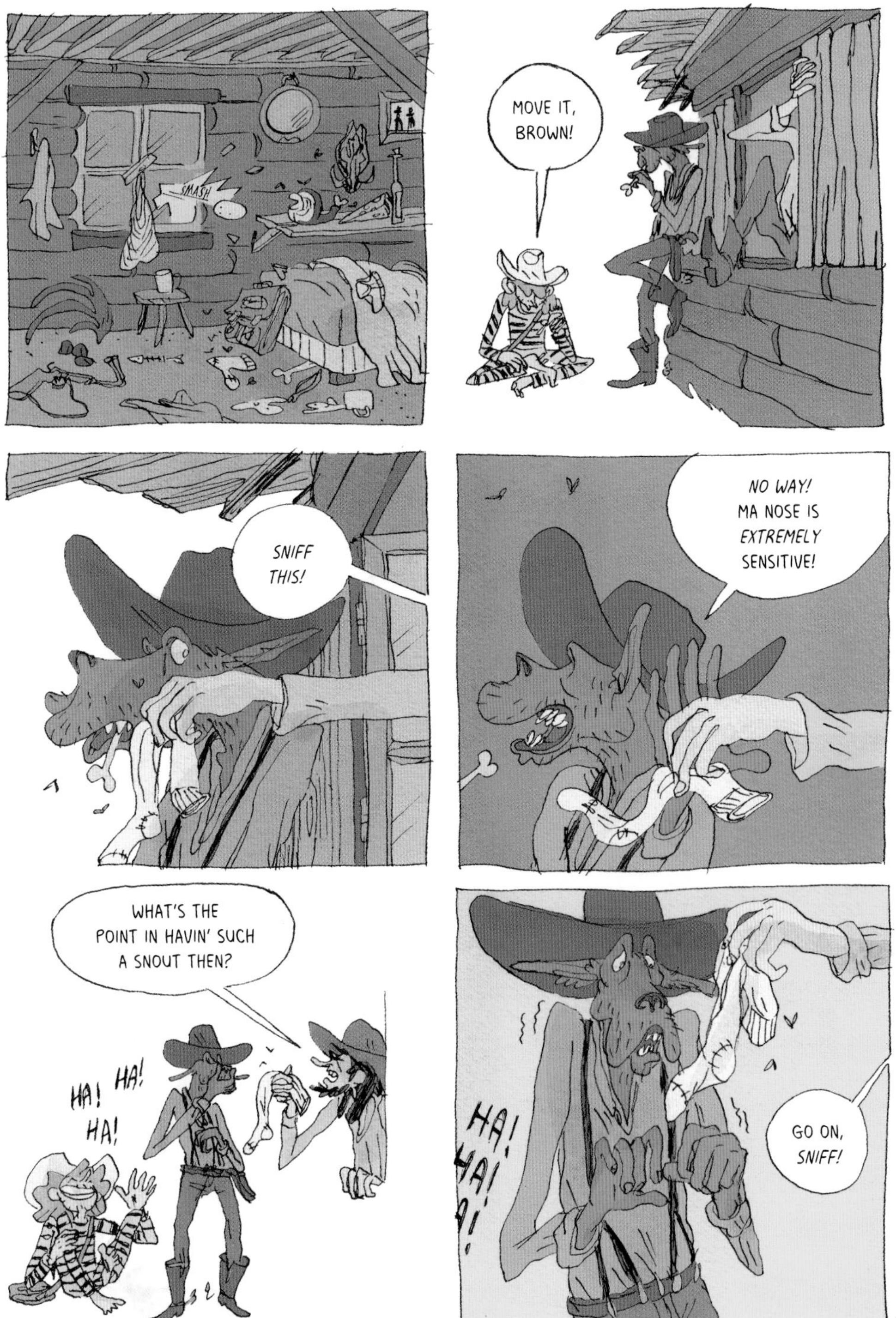
SMASH
MOVE IT, BROWN!
SNIFF THIS!
NO WAY! MA NOSE IS EXTREMELY SENSITIVE!
WHAT'S THE POINT IN HAVIN' SUCH A SNOUT THEN?
HA! HA! HA!
HA! HA!
GO ON, SNIFF!

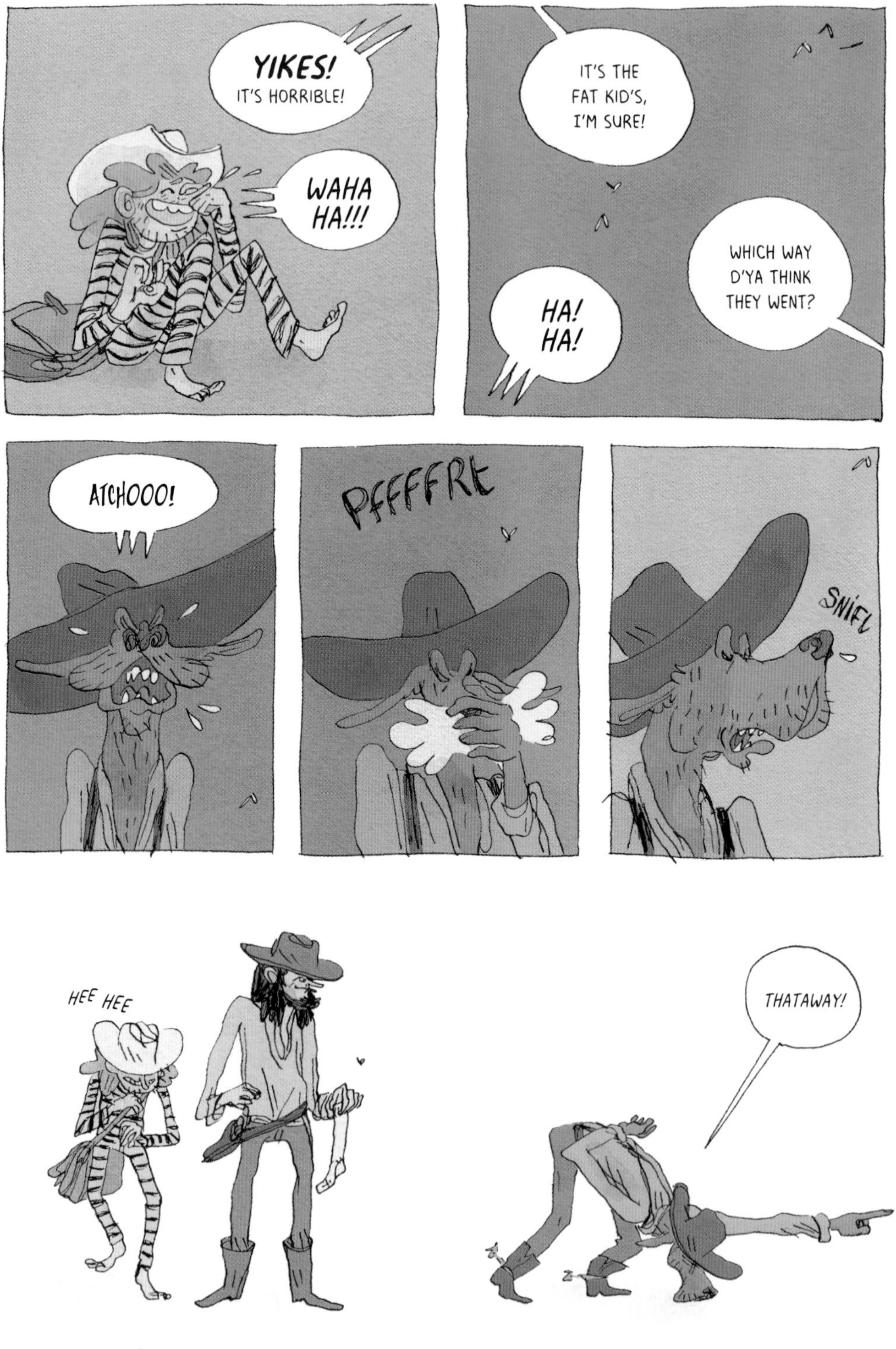
YIKES!
IT'S HORRIBLE!
WAHA HA!!!
IT'S THE FAT KID'S, I'M SURE!
HA! HA!
WHICH WAY D'YA THINK THEY WENT?
ATCHOOO!
PFFFFRT
SNIFL
HEE HEE
THATAWAY!

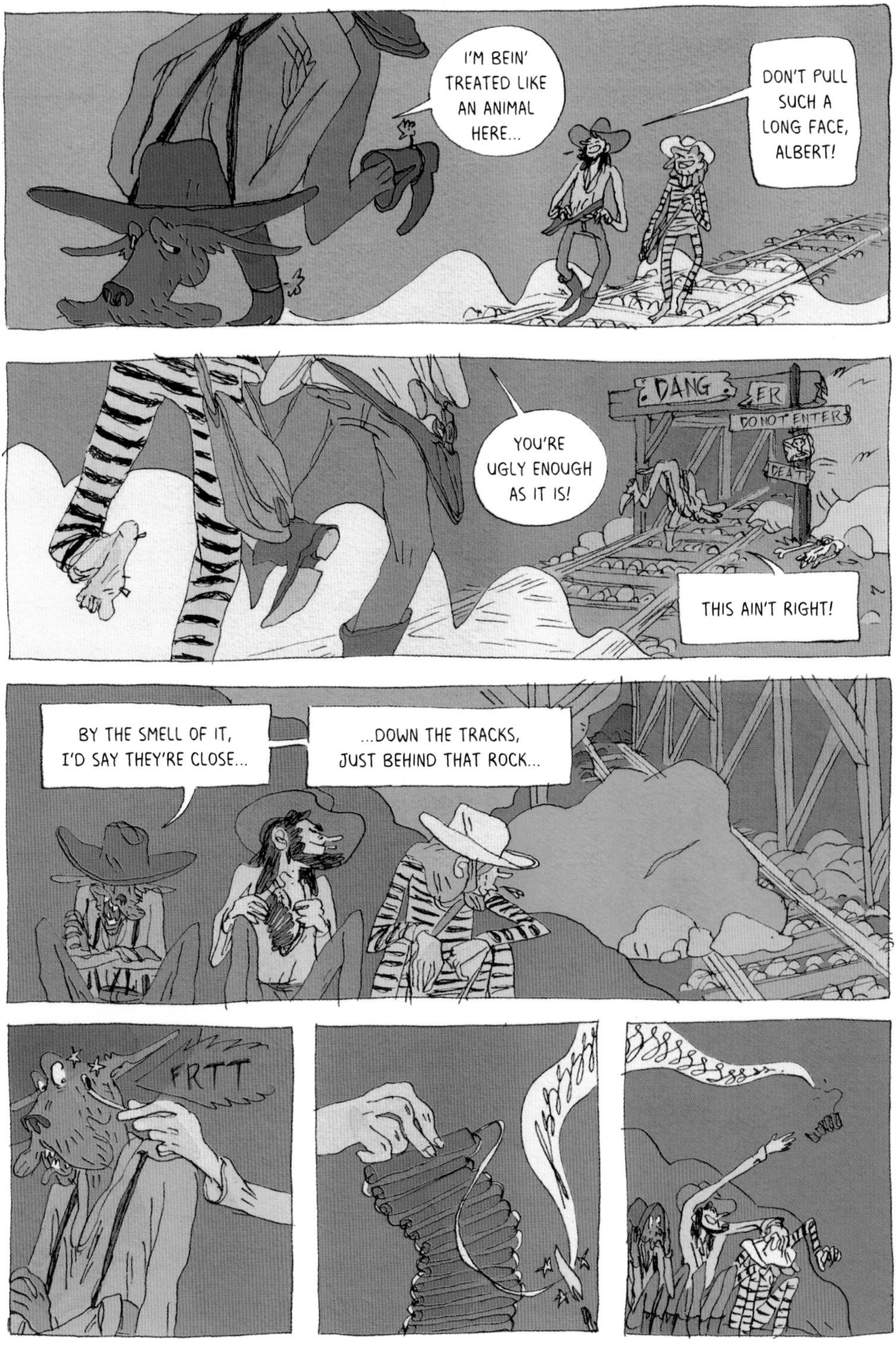
I'M BEIN' TREATED LIKE AN ANIMAL HERE...
DON'T PULL SUCH A LONG FACE, ALBERT!
DANG
ER
DO NOT ENTER
DEATH
YOU'RE UGLY ENOUGH AS IT IS!
THIS AIN'T RIGHT!
BY THE SMELL OF IT, I'D SAY THEY'RE CLOSE...
...DOWN THE TRACKS, JUST BEHIND THAT ROCK...
FRTT

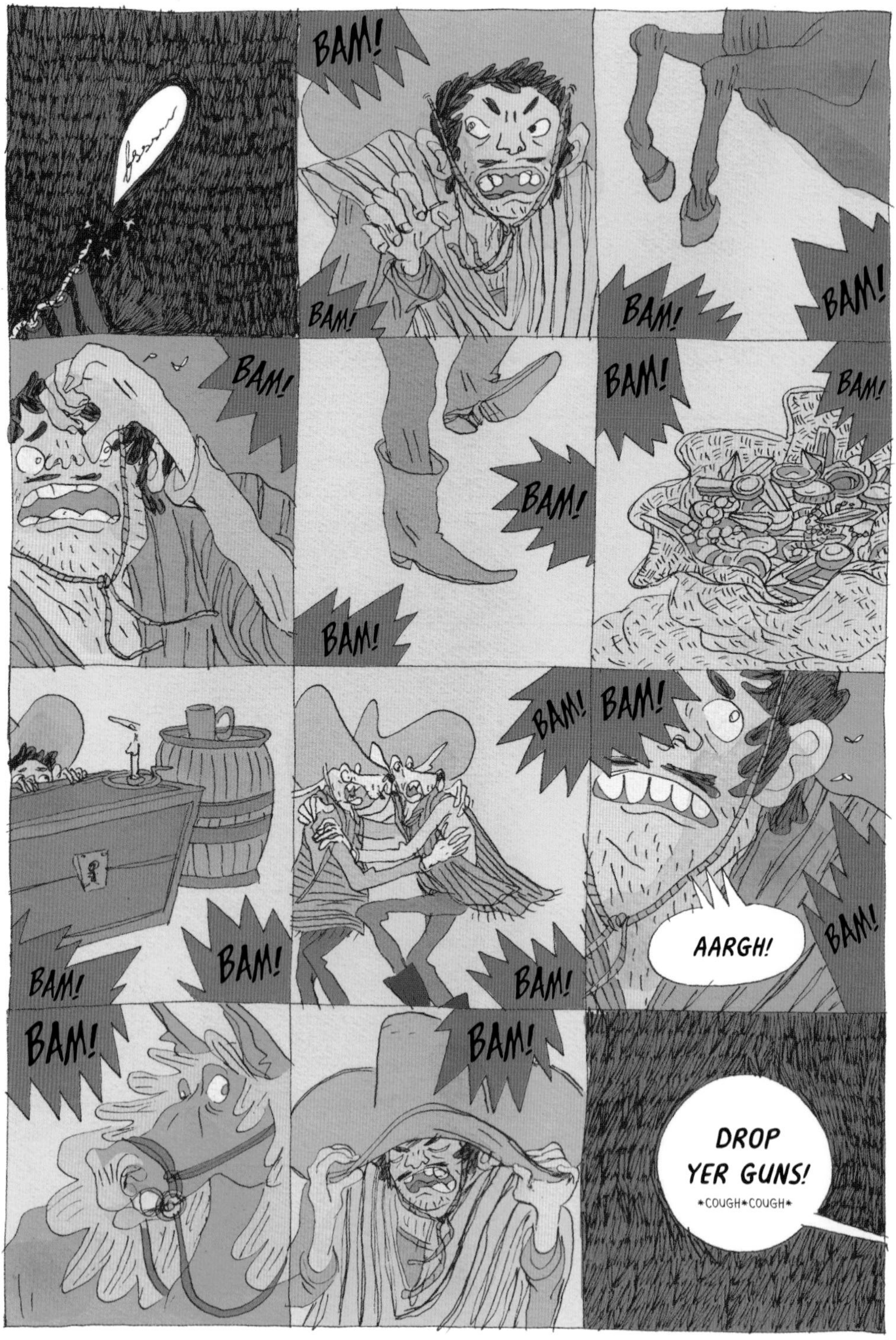
BAM!
BAM!
BAM!
BAM!
BAM!
BAM!
BAM!
BAM!
BAM!
BAM!
BAM!
BAM!
BAM!
BAM!
BAM!
AARGH!
BAM!
BAM!
BAM!
DROP YER GUNS!
*COUGH*COUGH*

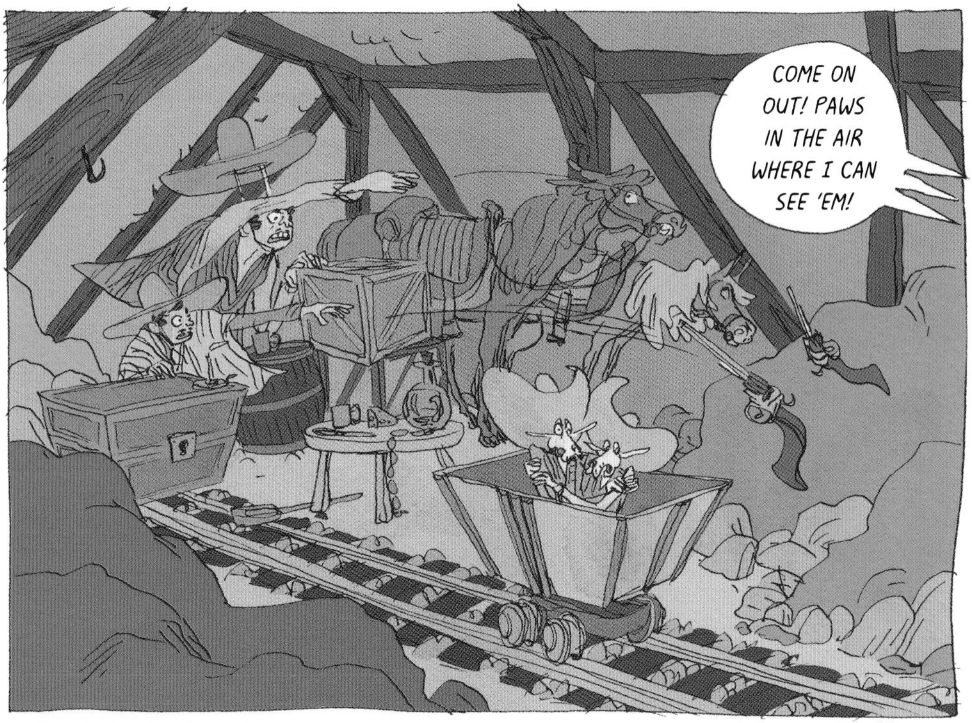
COME ON OUT! PAWS IN THE AIR WHERE I CAN SEE 'EM!

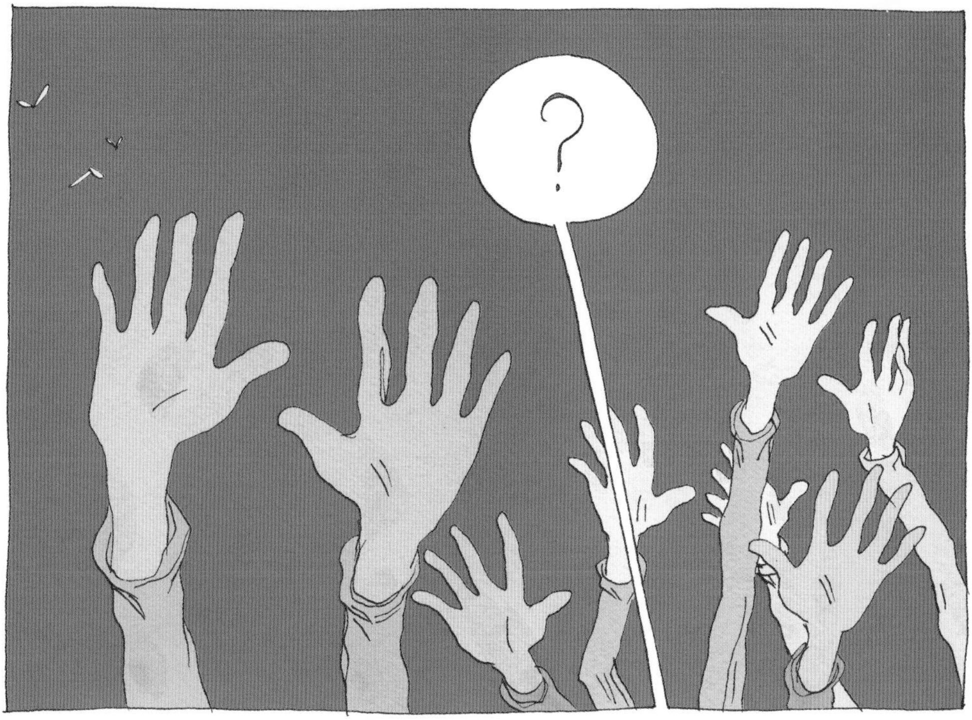
?

LOOKIE WHAT WE GOT HERE, JOHN!

AN OLD-TIMER...

A BRAT...

AND A MUTT!

YOU AGAIN, COWBOY?! YOU'RE WORSE THAN A BOIL!

YEAH, GOTTA SQUEEZE 'EM HARD TO GET RID OF 'EM!

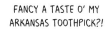

WELL, I SAY WE *AMPUTATE*... WHATCHA RECKON, COWBOY?

FANCY A TASTE O' MY ARKANSAS TOOTHPICK?!

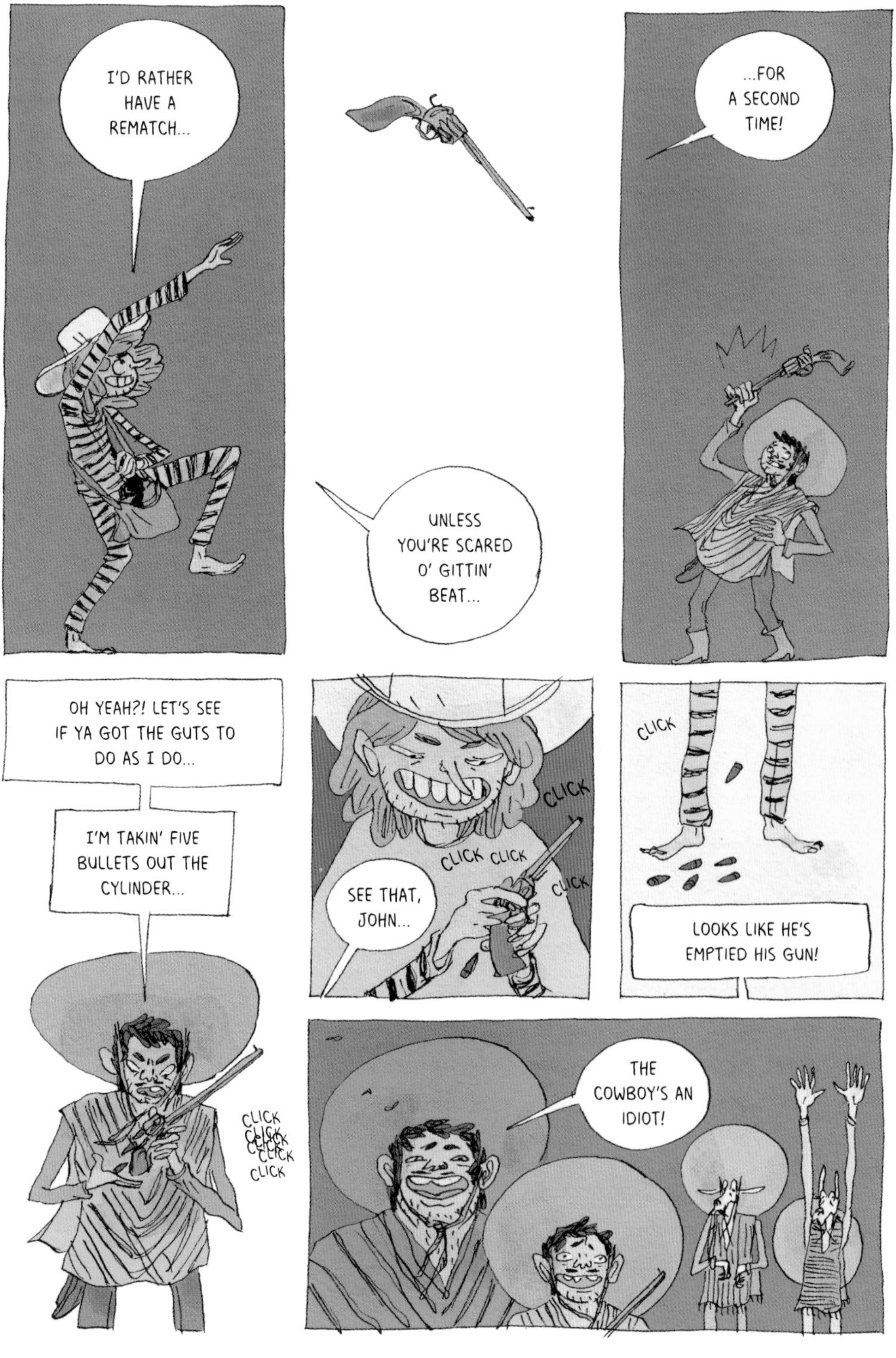
I'D RATHER HAVE A REMATCH...
UNLESS YOU'RE SCARED O' GITTIN' BEAT...
...FOR A SECOND TIME!
OH YEAH?! LET'S SEE IF YA GOT THE GUTS TO DO AS I DO...
I'M TAKIN' FIVE BULLETS OUT THE CYLINDER...
CLICK CLICK CLICK CLICK CLICK
CLICK CLICK CLICK CLICK
SEE THAT, JOHN...
CLICK
LOOKS LIKE HE'S EMPTIED HIS GUN!
THE COWBOY'S AN IDIOT!

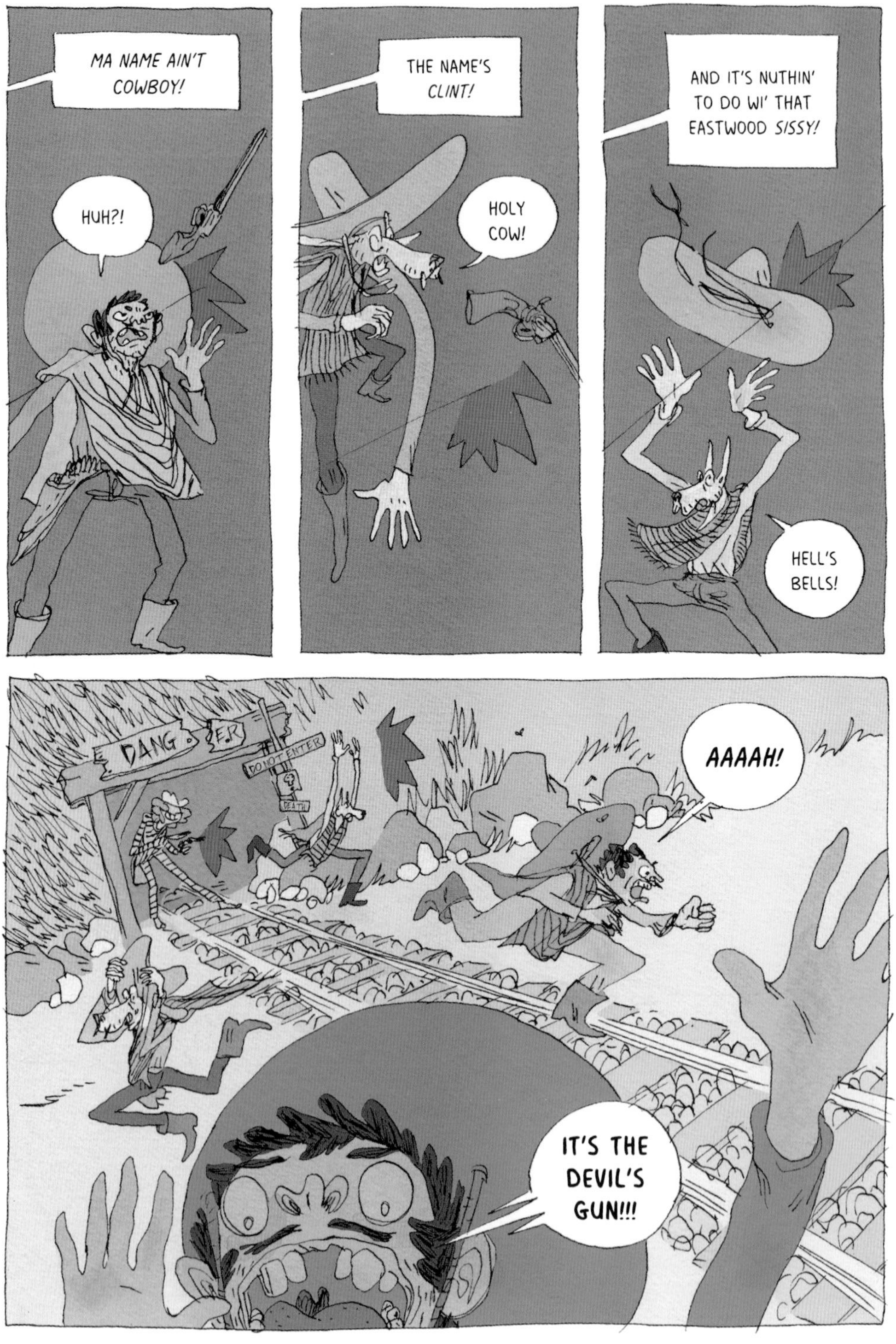
MA NAME AIN'T COWBOY!
HUH?!
THE NAME'S *CLINT!*
HOLY COW!
AND IT'S NUTHIN' TO DO WI' THAT EASTWOOD *SISSY!*
HELL'S BELLS!
DANG ER
DO NOT ENTER
AAAAH!
IT'S THE DEVIL'S GUN!!!

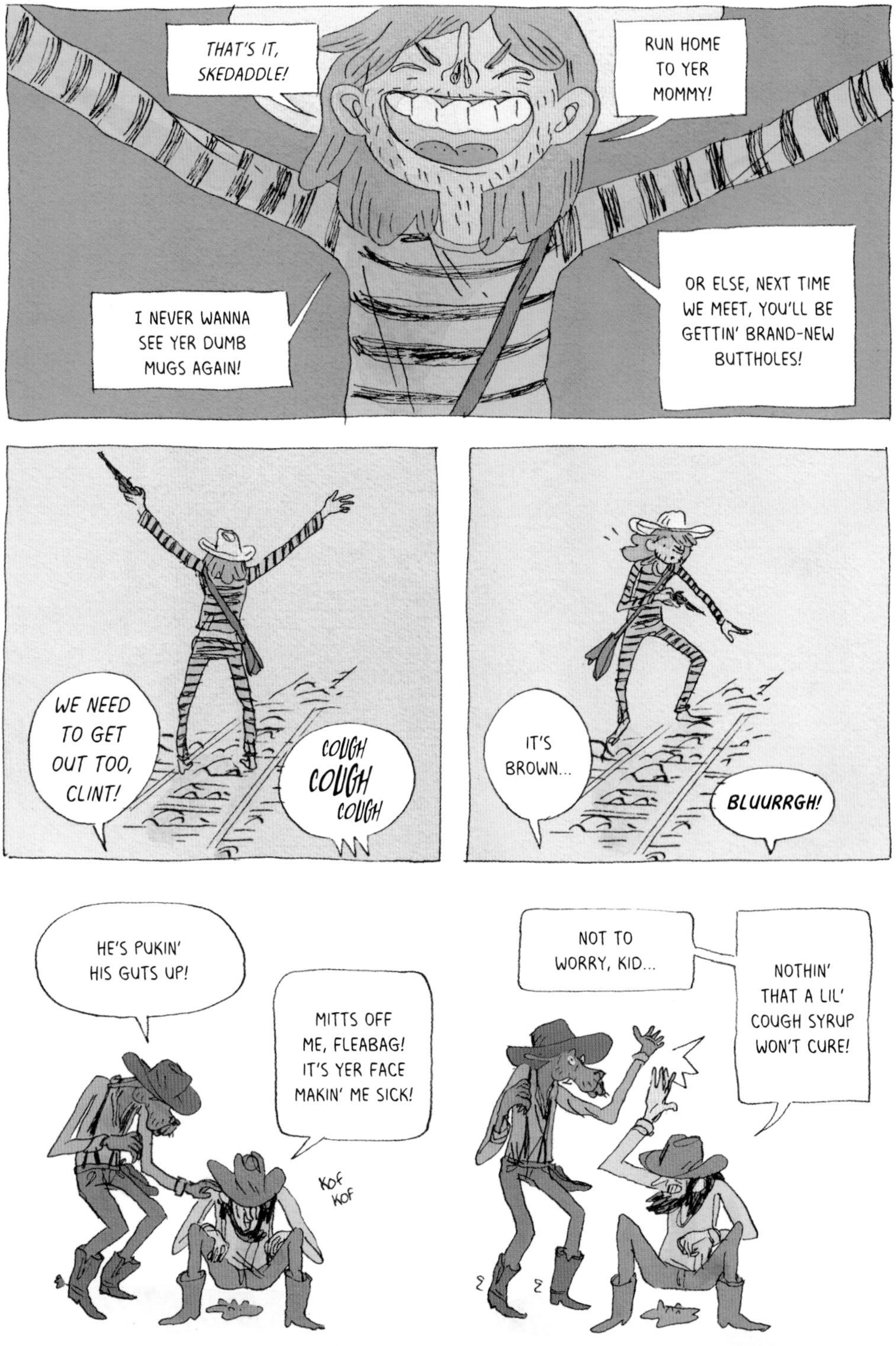
THAT'S IT, SKEDADDLE!
RUN HOME TO YER MOMMY!
I NEVER WANNA SEE YER DUMB MUGS AGAIN!
OR ELSE, NEXT TIME WE MEET, YOU'LL BE GETTIN' BRAND-NEW BUTTHOLES!
WE NEED TO GET OUT TOO, CLINT!
COUGH COUGH COUGH
IT'S BROWN...
BLUURRGH!
HE'S PUKIN' HIS GUTS UP!
MITTS OFF ME, FLEABAG! IT'S YER FACE MAKIN' ME SICK!
KOF KOF
NOT TO WORRY, KID...
NOTHIN' THAT A LIL' COUGH SYRUP WON'T CURE!

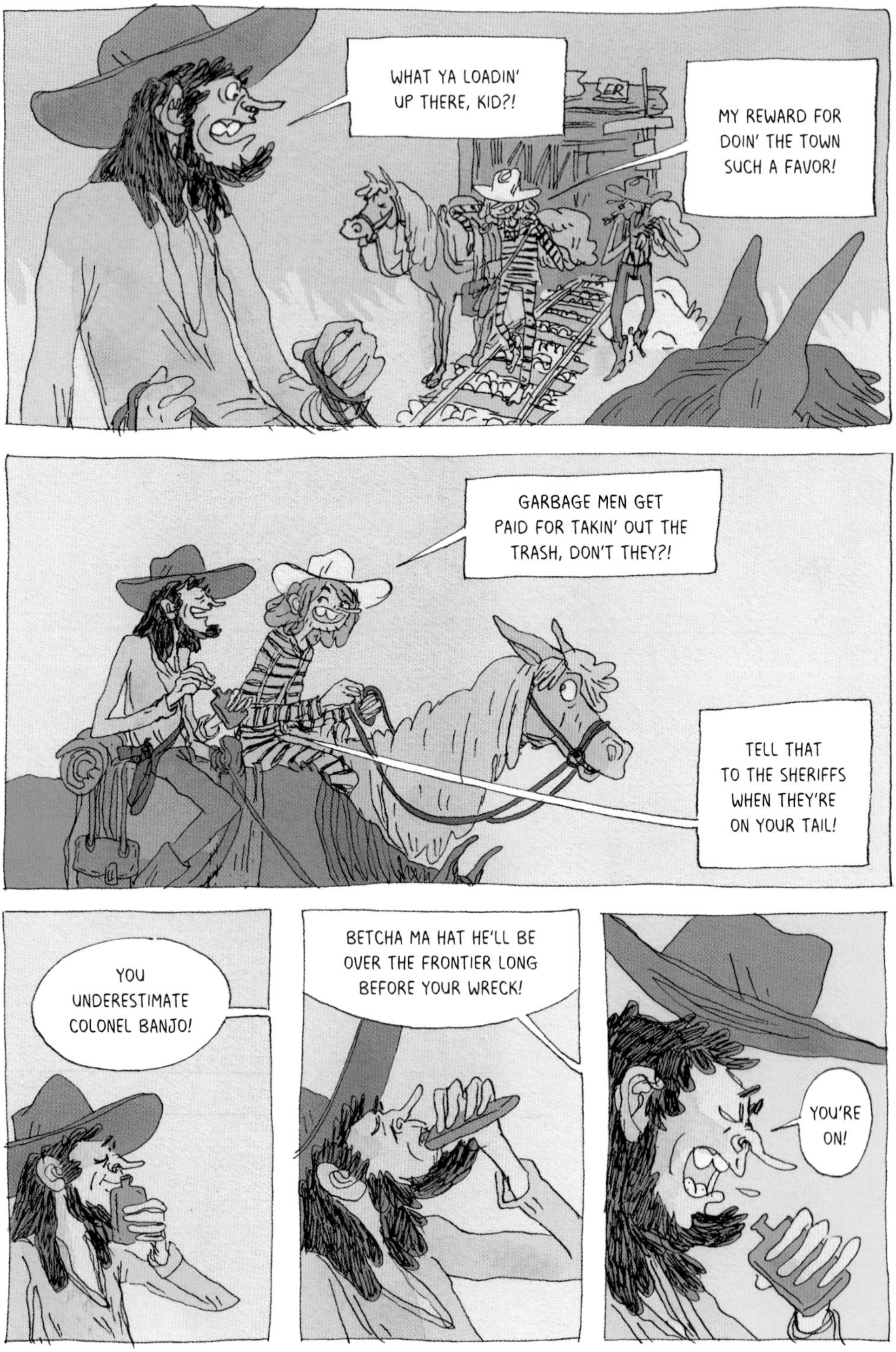
WHAT YA LOADIN' UP THERE, KID?!
MY REWARD FOR DOIN' THE TOWN SUCH A FAVOR!
GARBAGE MEN GET PAID FOR TAKIN' OUT THE TRASH, DON'T THEY?!
TELL THAT TO THE SHERIFFS WHEN THEY'RE ON YOUR TAIL!
YOU UNDERESTIMATE COLONEL BANJO!
BETCHA MA HAT HE'LL BE OVER THE FRONTIER LONG BEFORE YOUR WRECK!
YOU'RE ON!

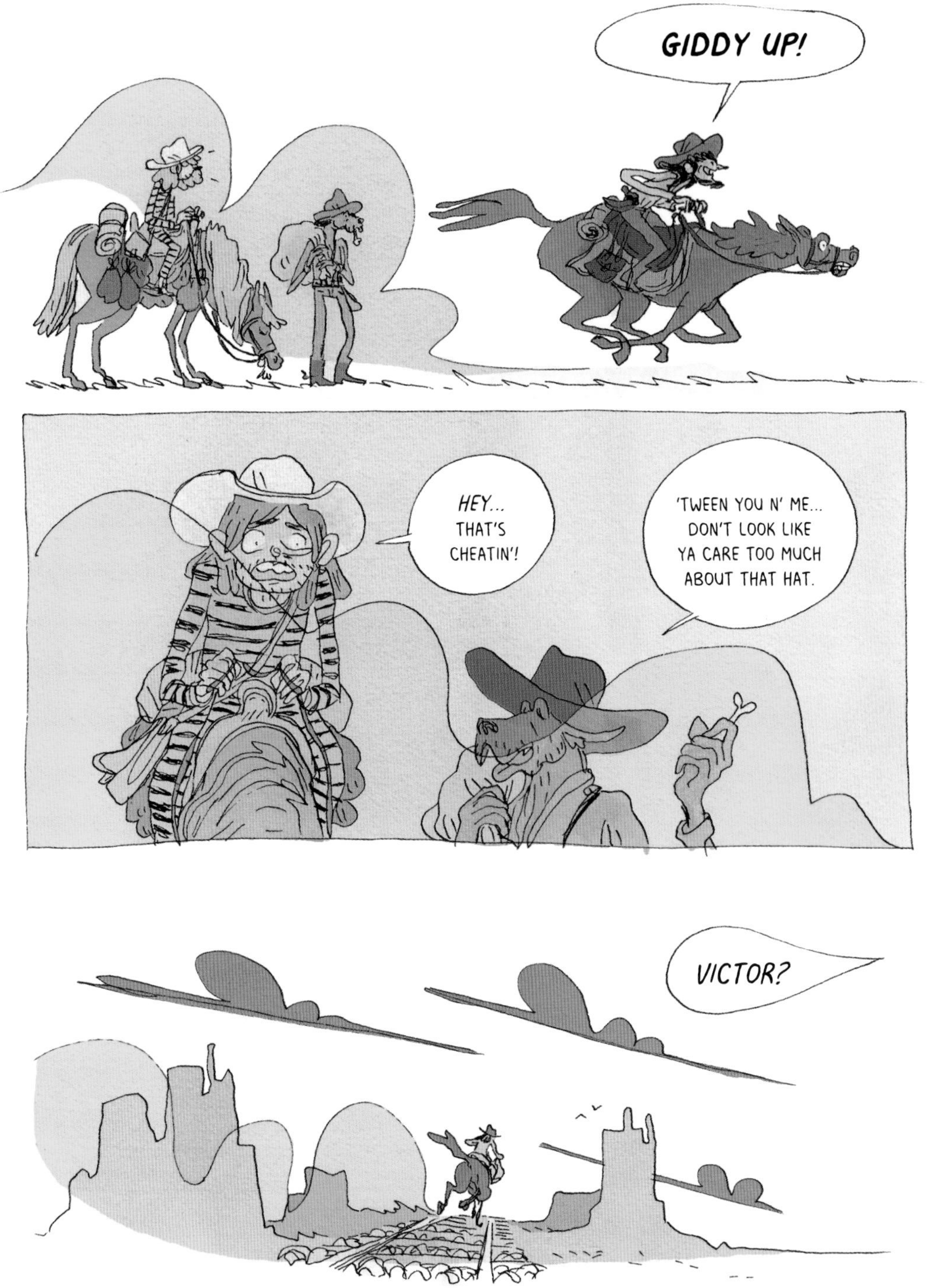
GIDDY UP!
HEY... THAT'S CHEATIN'!
'TWEEN YOU N' ME... DON'T LOOK LIKE YA CARE TOO MUCH ABOUT THAT HAT.
VICTOR?

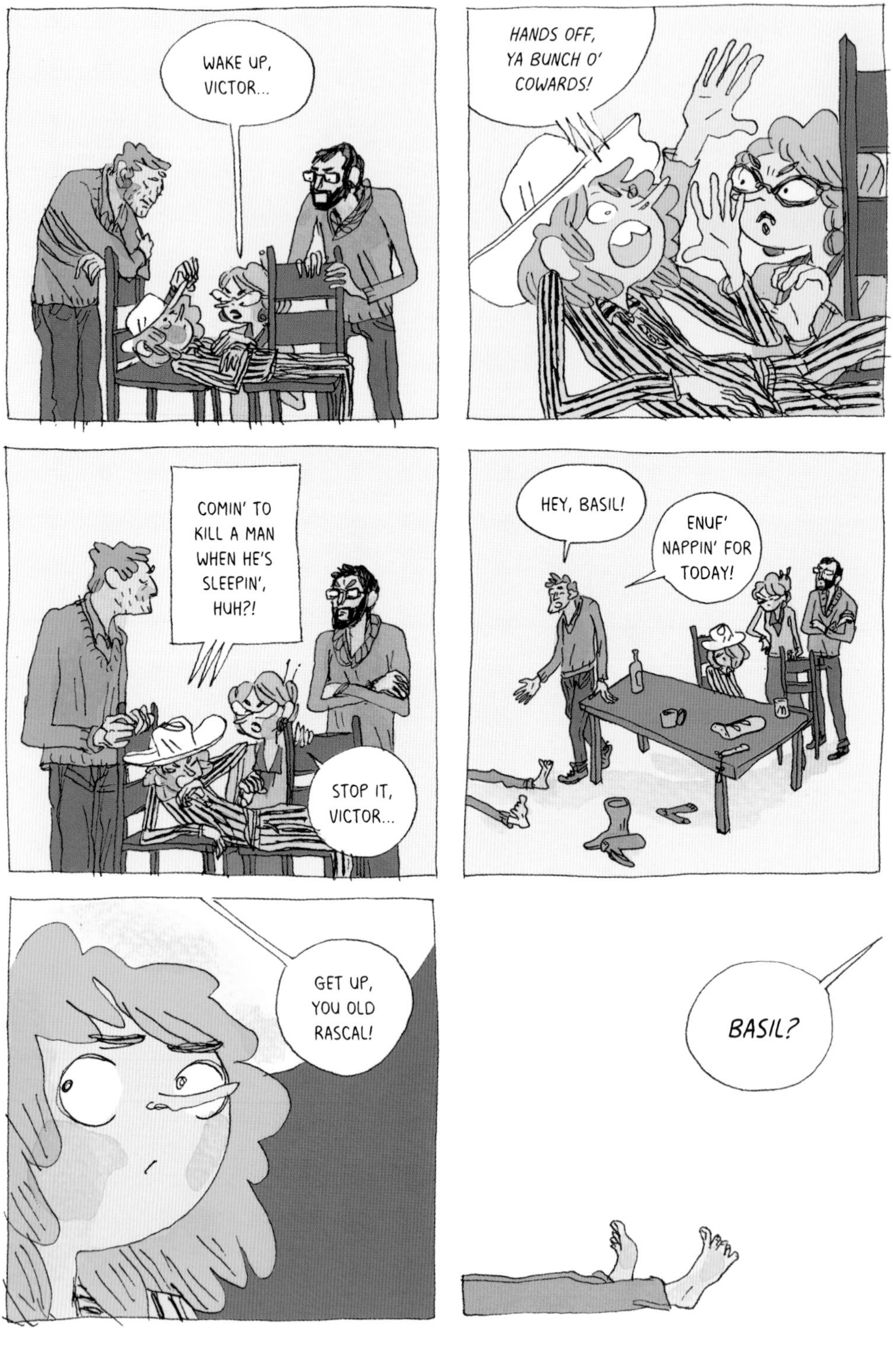
WAKE UP, VICTOR...
HANDS OFF, YA BUNCH O' COWARDS!
COMIN' TO KILL A MAN WHEN HE'S SLEEPIN', HUH?!
STOP IT, VICTOR...
HEY, BASIL!
ENUF' NAPPIN' FOR TODAY!
GET UP, YOU OLD RASCAL!
BASIL?

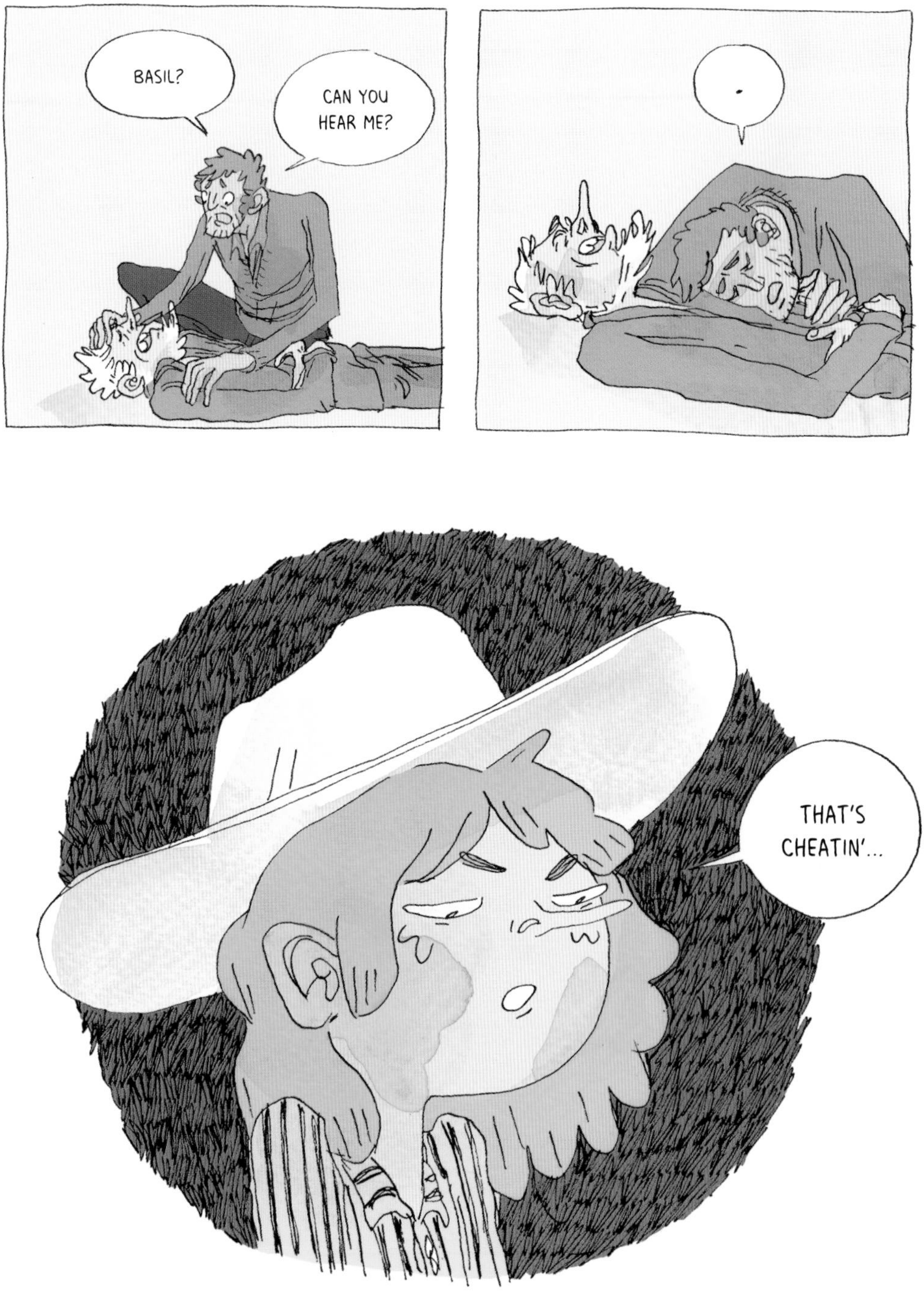
BASIL?
CAN YOU HEAR ME?
.
THAT'S CHEATIN'...

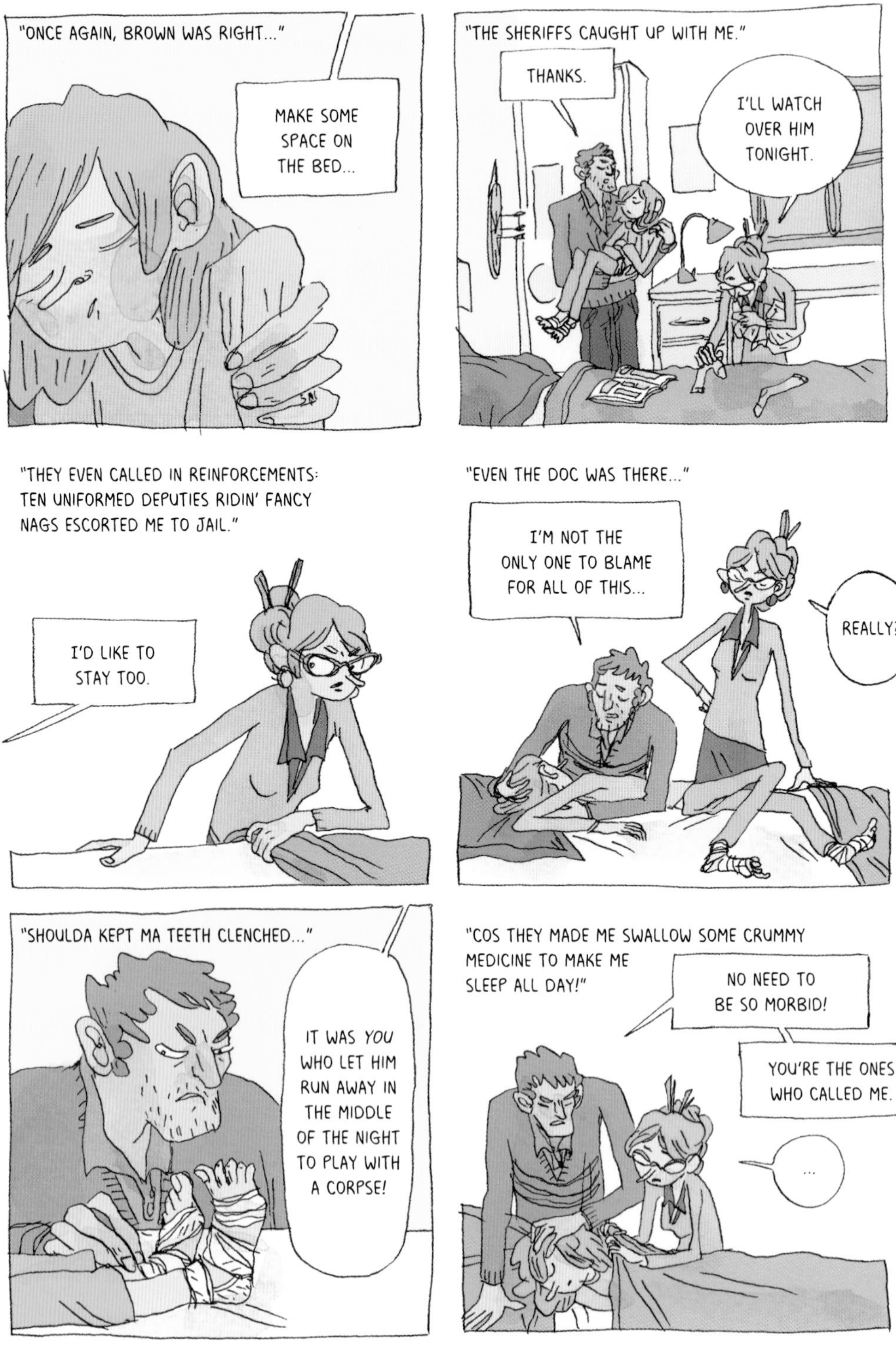
"ONCE AGAIN, BROWN WAS RIGHT..."
MAKE SOME SPACE ON THE BED...
"THE SHERIFFS CAUGHT UP WITH ME."
THANKS.
I'LL WATCH OVER HIM TONIGHT.
"THEY EVEN CALLED IN REINFORCEMENTS: TEN UNIFORMED DEPUTIES RIDIN' FANCY NAGS ESCORTED ME TO JAIL."
I'D LIKE TO STAY TOO.
"EVEN THE DOC WAS THERE..."
I'M NOT THE ONLY ONE TO BLAME FOR ALL OF THIS...
REALLY?
"SHOULDA KEPT MA TEETH CLENCHED..."
IT WAS *YOU* WHO LET HIM RUN AWAY IN THE MIDDLE OF THE NIGHT TO PLAY WITH A CORPSE!
"COS THEY MADE ME SWALLOW SOME CRUMMY MEDICINE TO MAKE ME SLEEP ALL DAY!"
NO NEED TO BE SO MORBID!
YOU'RE THE ONES WHO CALLED ME.
...

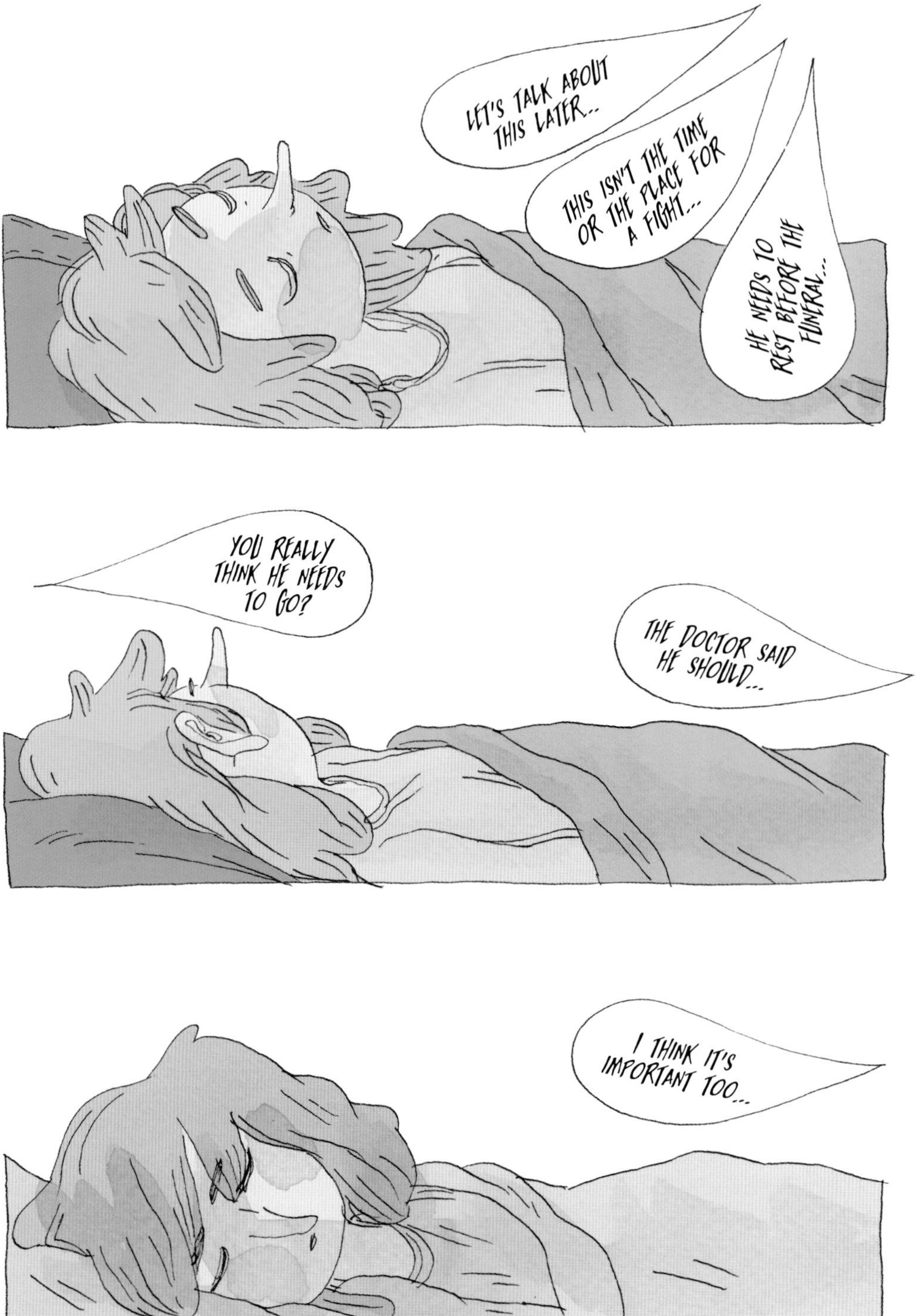
LET'S TALK ABOUT THIS LATER...
THIS ISN'T THE TIME OR THE PLACE FOR A FIGHT...
HE NEEDS TO REST BEFORE THE FUNERAL...
YOU REALLY THINK HE NEEDS TO GO?
THE DOCTOR SAID HE SHOULD...
I THINK IT'S IMPORTANT TOO...

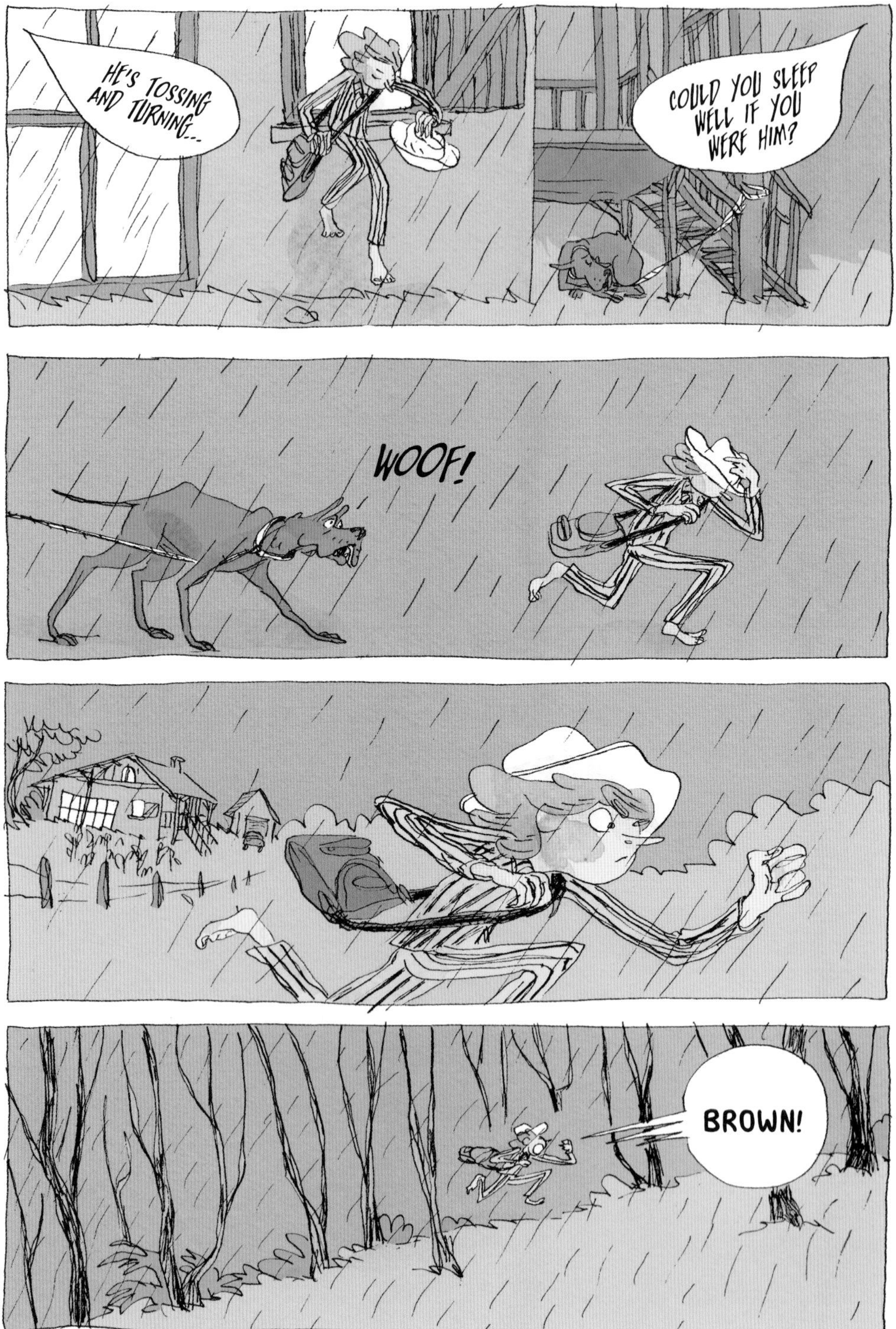
HE'S TOSSING AND TURNING...
COULD YOU SLEEP WELL IF YOU WERE HIM?
WOOF!
BROWN!

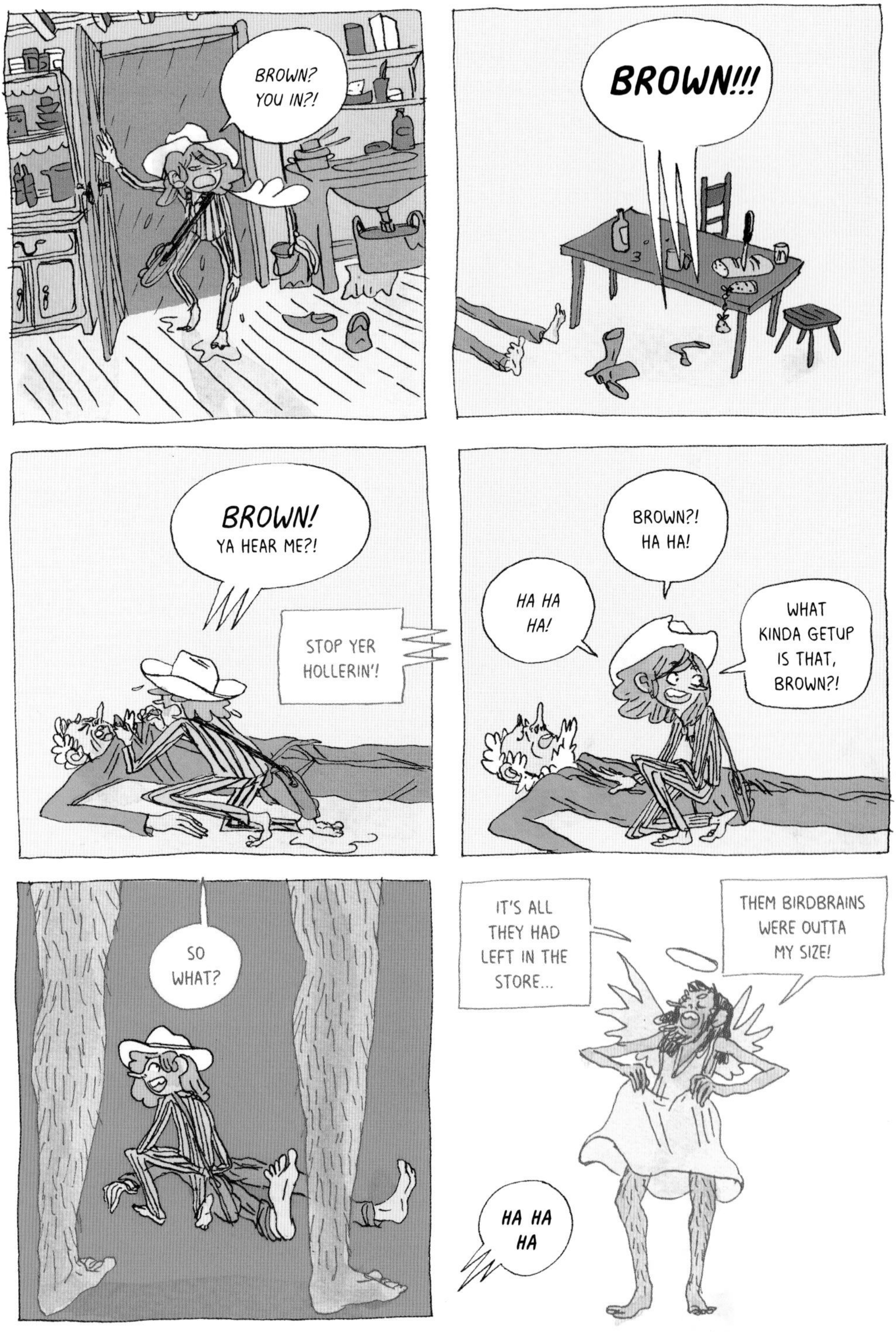
BROWN? YOU IN?!
BROWN!!!
BROWN! YA HEAR ME?!
STOP YER HOLLERIN'!
BROWN?! HA HA!
HA HA HA!
WHAT KINDA GETUP IS THAT, BROWN?!
SO WHAT?
IT'S ALL THEY HAD LEFT IN THE STORE...
THEM BIRDBRAINS WERE OUTTA MY SIZE!
HA HA HA

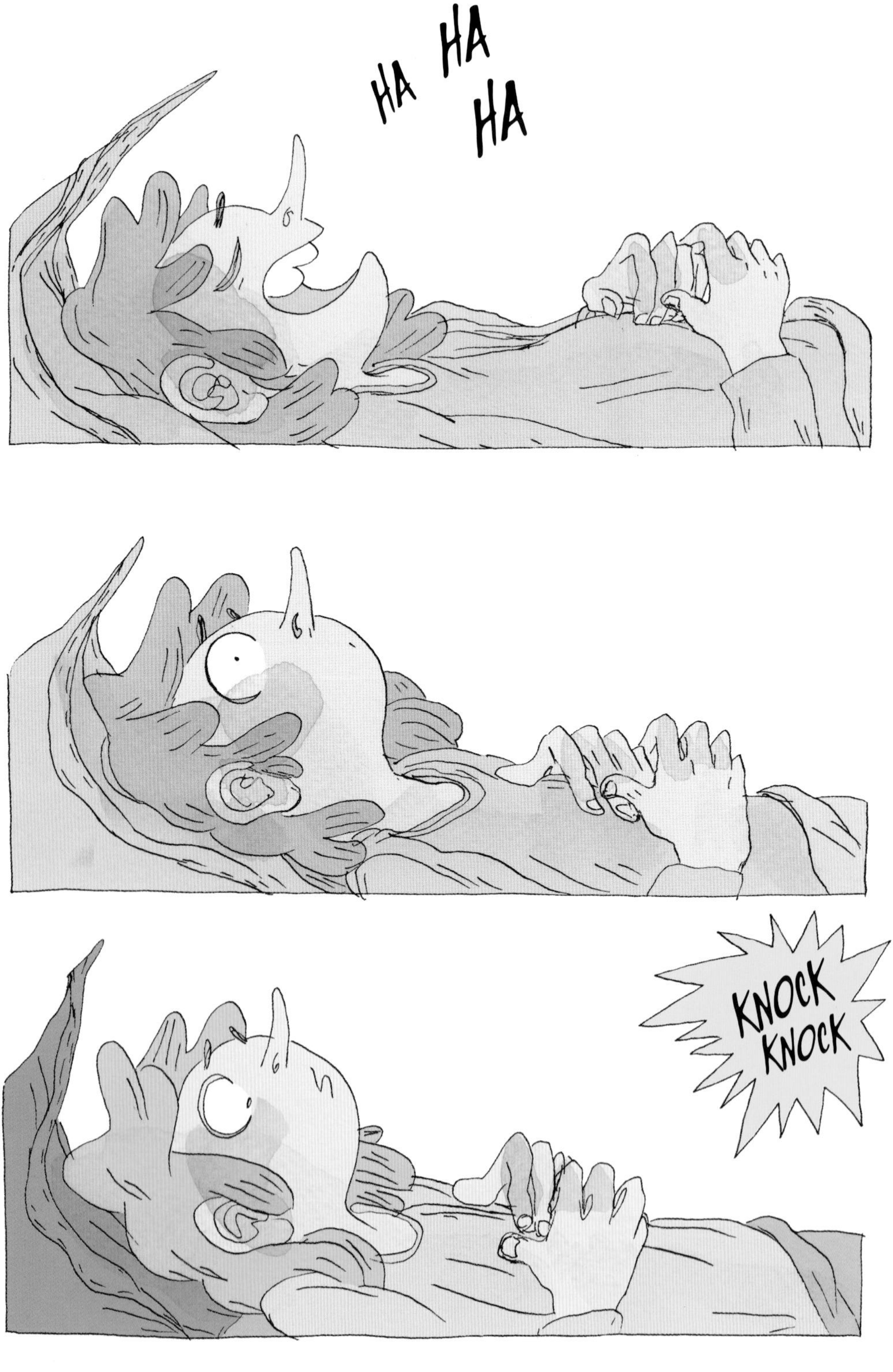
HA HA
HA
KNOCK
KNOCK

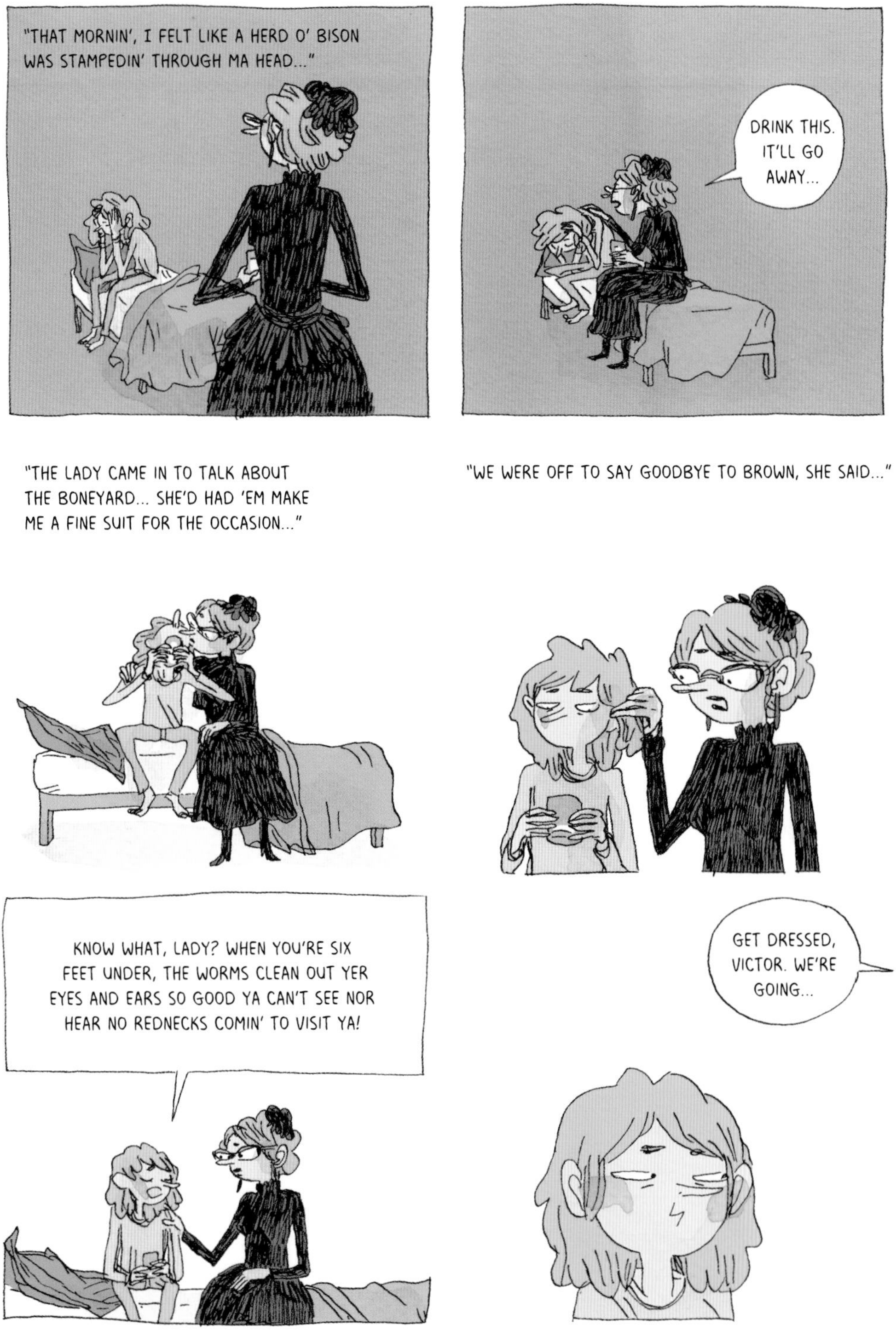
"THAT MORNIN', I FELT LIKE A HERD O' BISON WAS STAMPEDIN' THROUGH MA HEAD..."
DRINK THIS. IT'LL GO AWAY...
"THE LADY CAME IN TO TALK ABOUT THE BONEYARD... SHE'D HAD 'EM MAKE ME A FINE SUIT FOR THE OCCASION..."
"WE WERE OFF TO SAY GOODBYE TO BROWN, SHE SAID..."
KNOW WHAT, LADY? WHEN YOU'RE SIX FEET UNDER, THE WORMS CLEAN OUT YER EYES AND EARS SO GOOD YA CAN'T SEE NOR HEAR NO REDNECKS COMIN' TO VISIT YA!
GET DRESSED, VICTOR. WE'RE GOING...

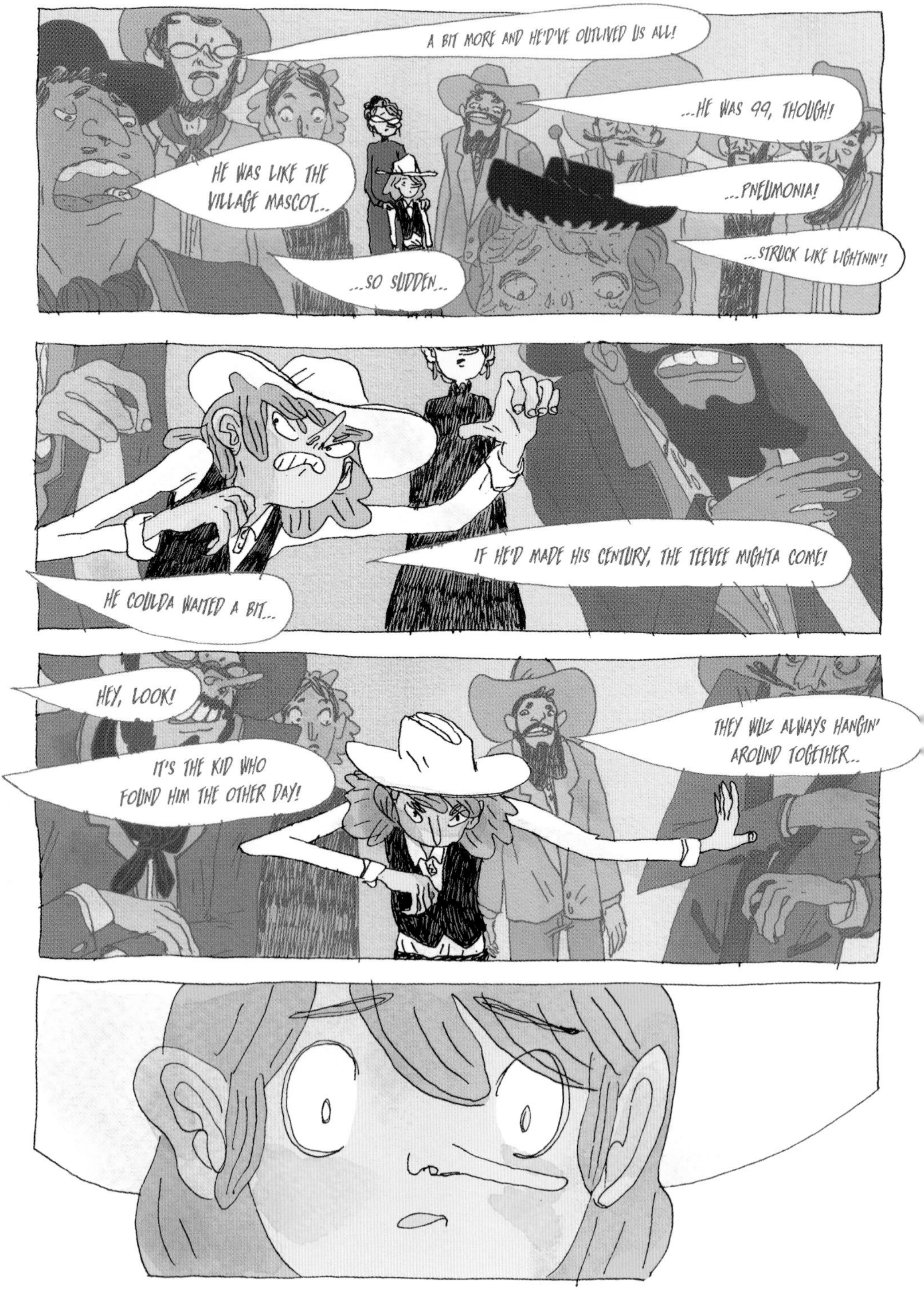
A BIT MORE AND HE'D'VE OUTLIVED US ALL!
...HE WAS 99, THOUGH!
HE WAS LIKE THE VILLAGE MASCOT...
...PNEUMONIA!
...STRUCK LIKE LIGHTNIN'!
...SO SUDDEN...
IF HE'D MADE HIS CENTURY, THE TEEVEE MIGHTA COME!
HE COULDA WAITED A BIT...
HEY, LOOK!
IT'S THE KID WHO FOUND HIM THE OTHER DAY!
THEY WUZ ALWAYS HANGIN' AROUND TOGETHER...

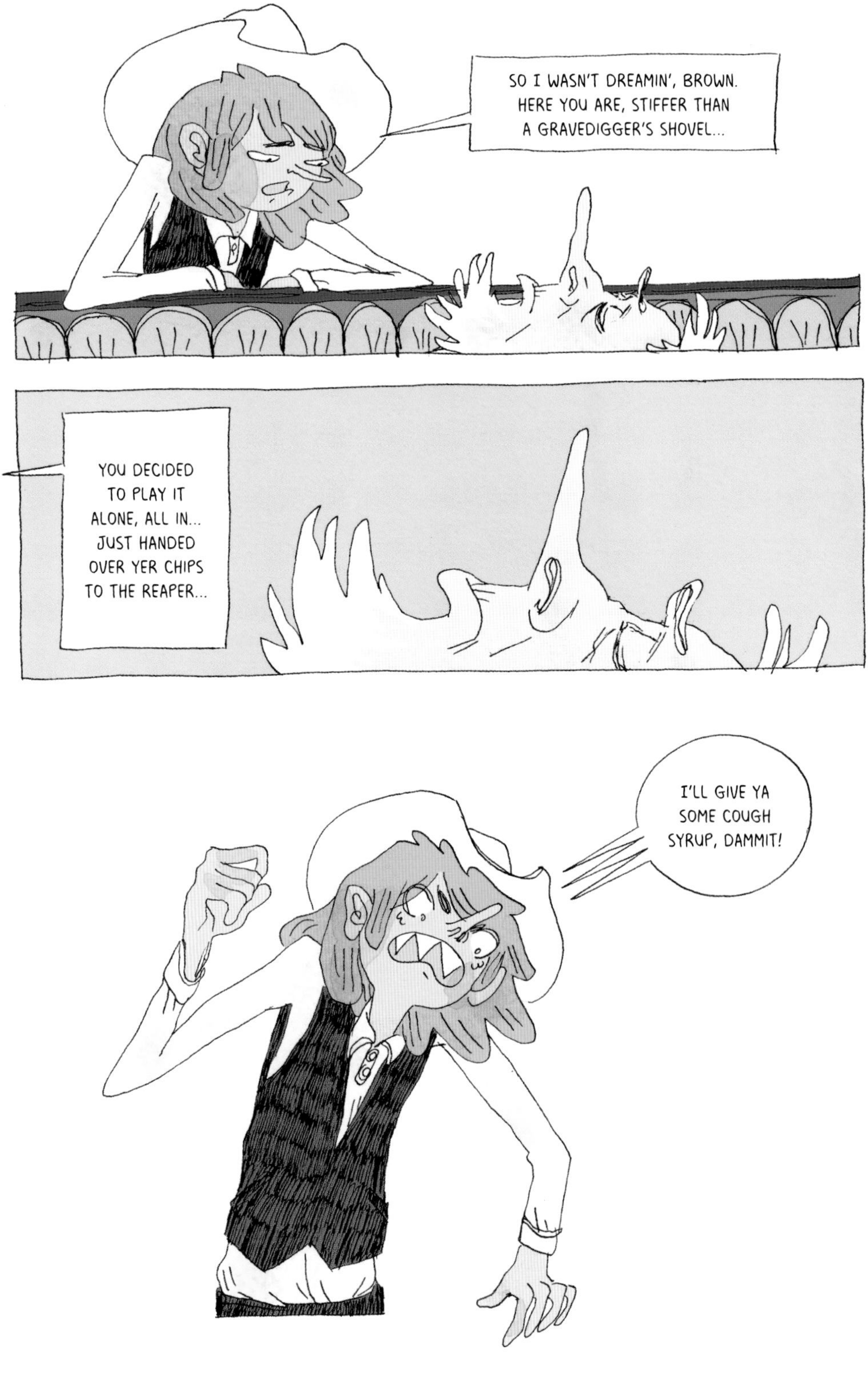
SO I WASN'T DREAMIN', BROWN. HERE YOU ARE, STIFFER THAN A GRAVEDIGGER'S SHOVEL...
YOU DECIDED TO PLAY IT ALONE, ALL IN... JUST HANDED OVER YER CHIPS TO THE REAPER...
I'LL GIVE YA SOME COUGH SYRUP, DAMMIT!

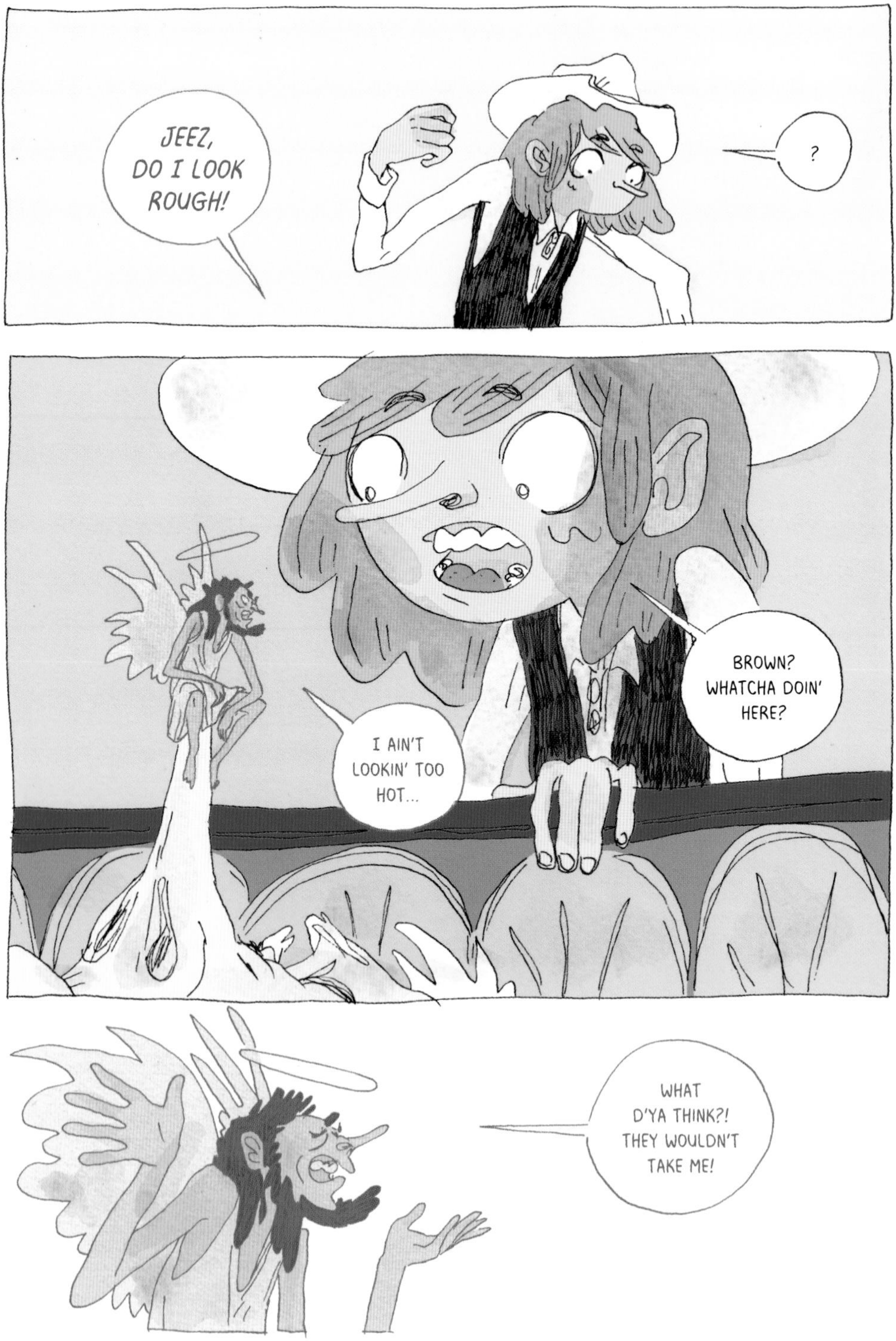
JEEZ, DO I LOOK ROUGH!
?
BROWN? WHATCHA DOIN' HERE?
I AIN'T LOOKIN' TOO HOT...
WHAT D'YA THINK?! THEY WOULDN'T TAKE ME!

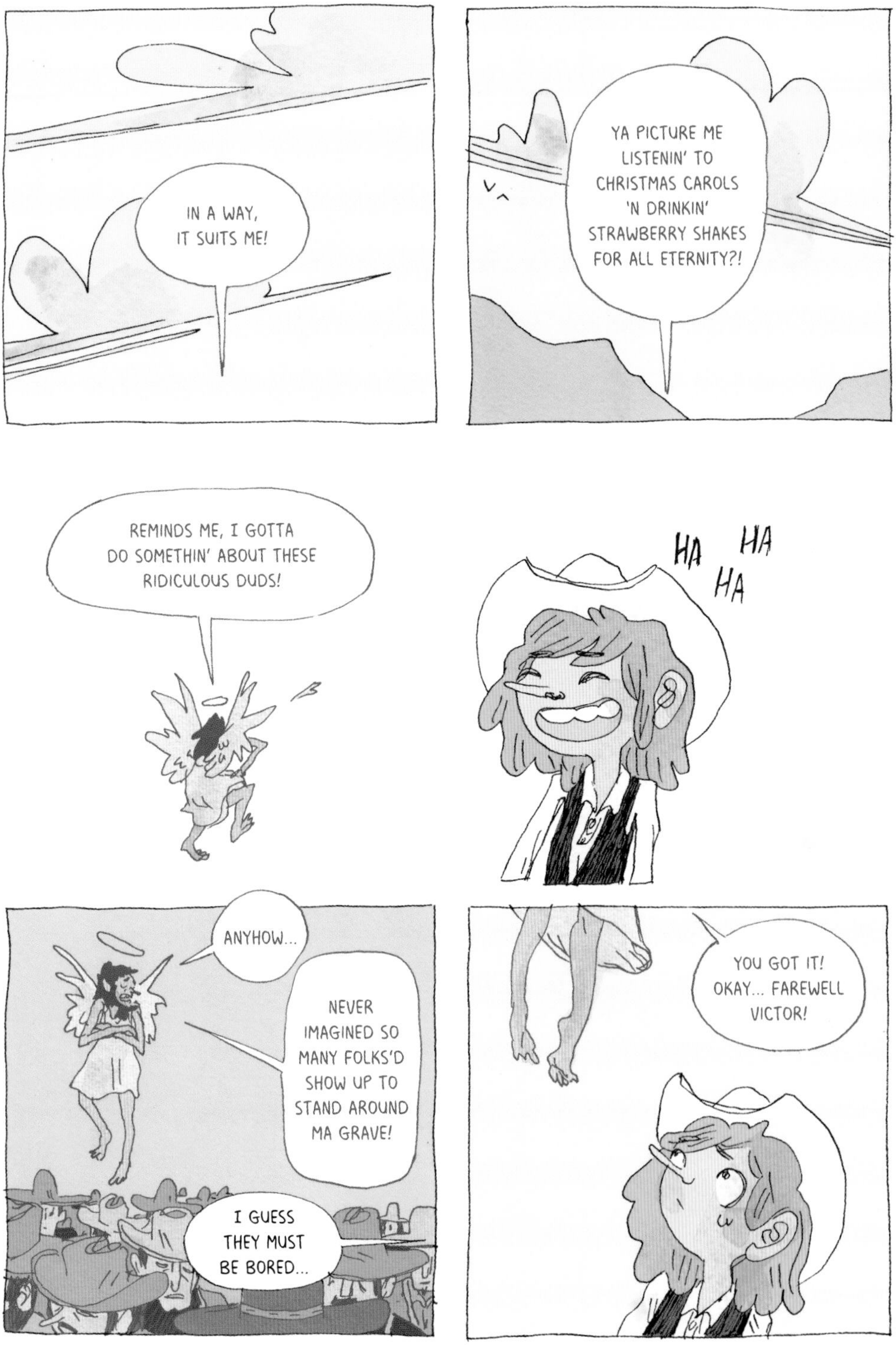
IN A WAY, IT SUITS ME!
YA PICTURE ME LISTENIN' TO CHRISTMAS CAROLS 'N DRINKIN' STRAWBERRY SHAKES FOR ALL ETERNITY?!
REMINDS ME, I GOTTA DO SOMETHIN' ABOUT THESE RIDICULOUS DUDS!
HA HA HA
ANYHOW...
NEVER IMAGINED SO MANY FOLKS'D SHOW UP TO STAND AROUND MA GRAVE!
I GUESS THEY MUST BE BORED...
YOU GOT IT! OKAY... FAREWELL VICTOR!

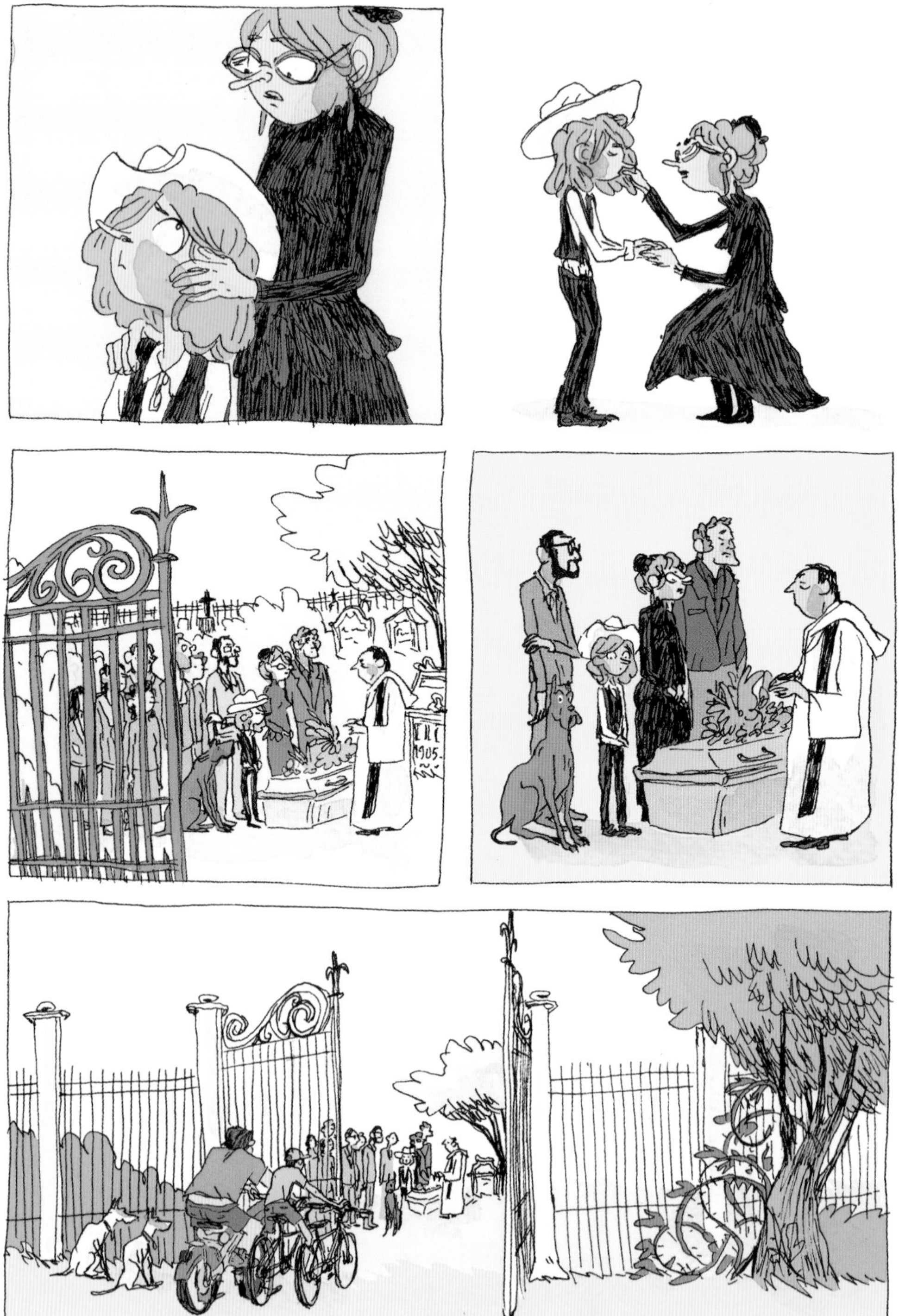

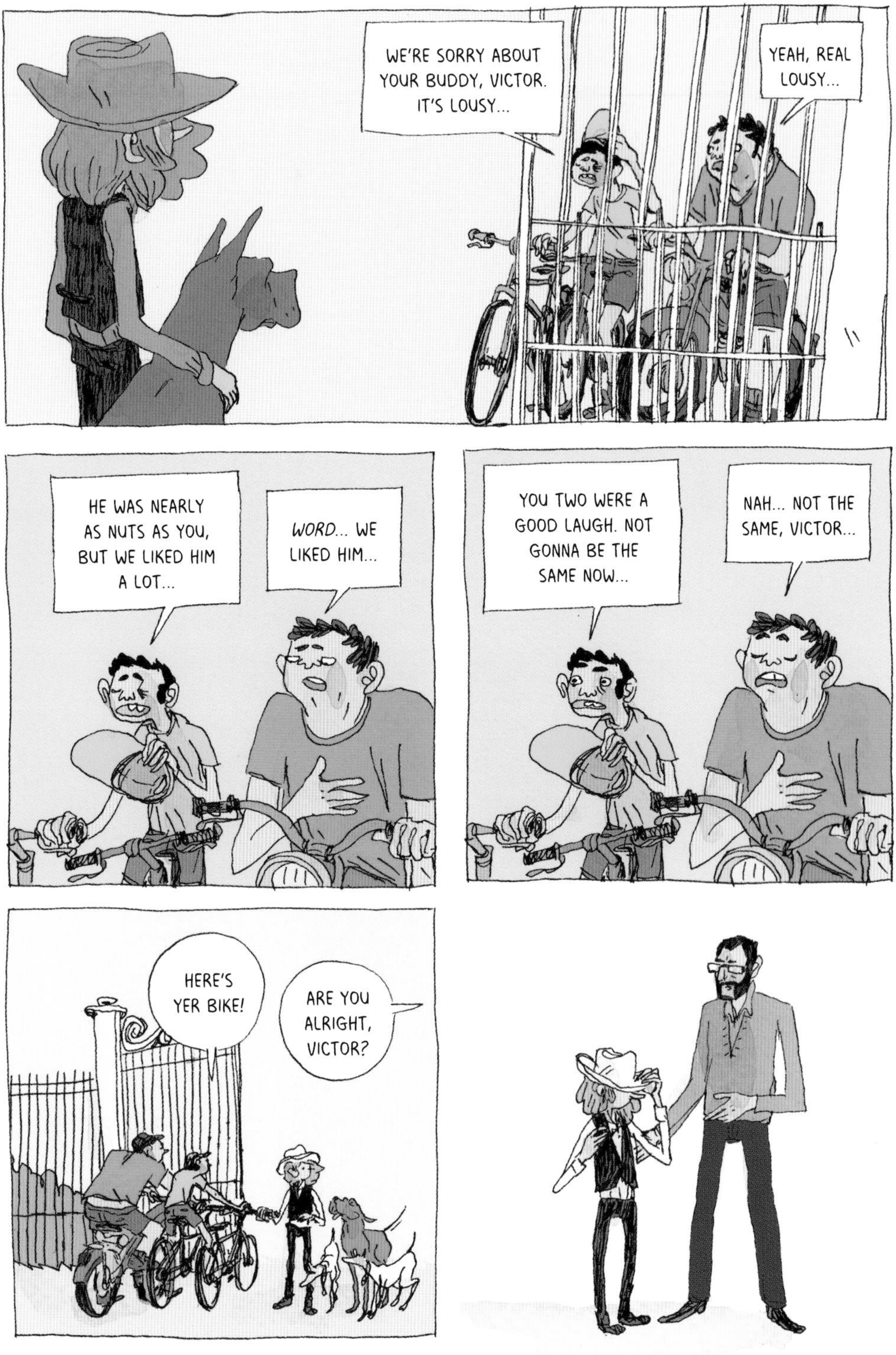
WE'RE SORRY ABOUT YOUR BUDDY, VICTOR. IT'S LOUSY...
YEAH, REAL LOUSY...
HE WAS NEARLY AS NUTS AS YOU, BUT WE LIKED HIM A LOT...
*WORD*... WE LIKED HIM...
YOU TWO WERE A GOOD LAUGH. NOT GONNA BE THE SAME NOW...
NAH... NOT THE SAME, VICTOR...
HERE'S YER BIKE!
ARE YOU ALRIGHT, VICTOR?

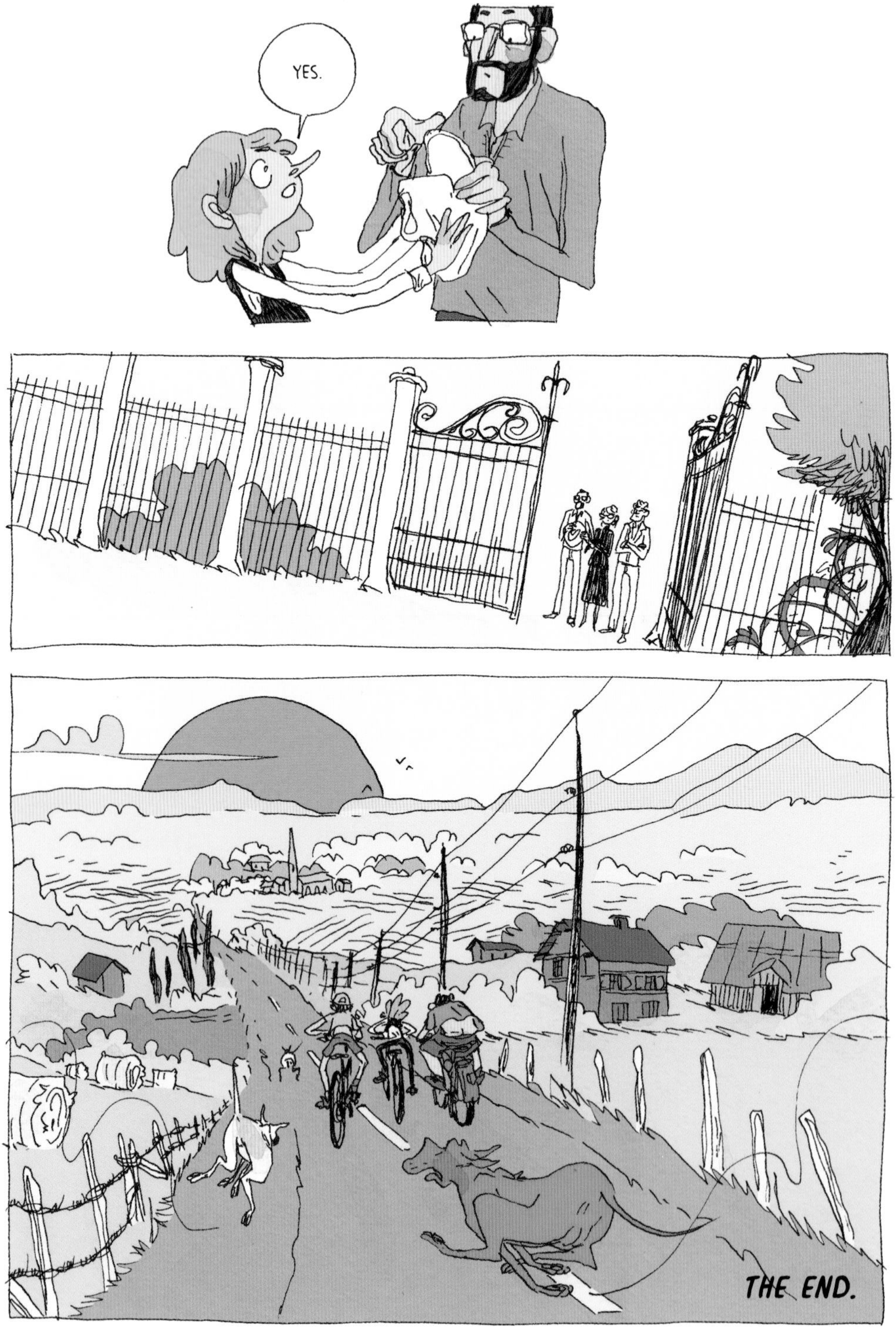
YES.
THE END.

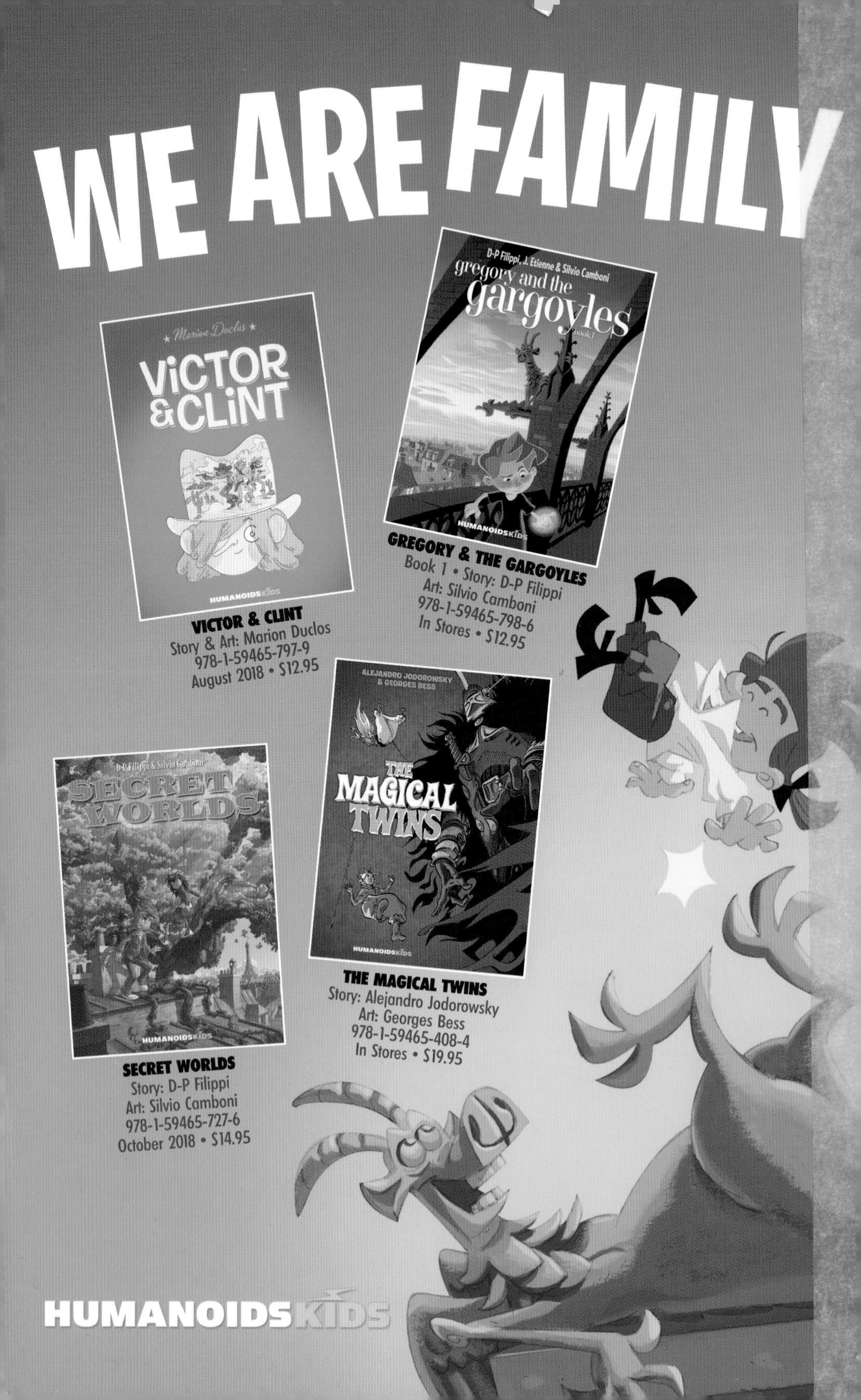
WE ARE FAMILY
VICTOR & CLINT
Story & Art: Marion Duclos
978-1-59465-797-9
August 2018 • $12.95
GREGORY & THE GARGOYLES
Book 1 • Story: D-P Filippi
Art: Silvio Camboni
978-1-59465-798-6
In Stores • $12.95
SECRET WORLDS
Story: D-P Filippi
Art: Silvio Camboni
978-1-59465-727-6
October 2018 • $14.95
THE MAGICAL TWINS
Story: Alejandro Jodorowsky
Art: Georges Bess
978-1-59465-408-4
In Stores • $19.95
HUMANOIDS KIDS